G000061154

Ascent

The Story of Poppa of Bayeux

House of Normandy
Book One

Cathie Dunn

Ocelot Press

In memory of Lady Poppa of Bayeux, courageous matriarch of the powerful House of Normandy

About the Author

Cathie Dunn writes historical fiction, mystery, and romance.

She loves historical research, often getting lost in the depths of the many history books on her shelves. She also enjoys exploring historic sites and beautiful countryside. Over the last three decades, she has travelled widely across Scotland, England, Wales, France and Germany.

After having spent many years in Scotland, Cathie now lives in the south of France with her husband, a rescue dog and an abandoned cat who appeared on her terrace one day.

Cathie is a member of the Alliance of Independent Authors and the Historical Novel Society.

Find her at www.cathiedunn.com, and on Facebook, Twitter and Instagram.

Books by Cathie Dunn

House of Normandy (historical fiction) series:
Ascent – The Story of Poppa of Bayeux
Treachery – The Story of Sprota the Breton (due out in 2022)

An Affair of the Poisons (historical fiction) series:
The Shadows of Versailles – Book One
The Alchemist's Daughter – Book Two (due out in 2022/23)

The Highland Chronicles (historical romance):
Highland Arms
A Highland Captive

Standalone titles:
Love Lost in Time – an award-winning dual-timeline mystery
Dark Deceit – a romantic murder mystery set during The Anarchy
Silent Deception – a Gothic romance novella

In progress:
The Loup de Foix Medieval Mystery series

Ascent

A Tale of Danger,
Adversity, and Love

List of Characters

Lady Poppa of Bayeux: daughter of Count Bérengar of Bayeux, handfasted to Hrólfr *in more danico*

Hrólfr: a Northman, leader of raiding parties into the Frankish territory, Jarl of the Northmen from AD 911

William: their son and heir

Geirlaug / Adela: their daughter (she took the name of Adela at her baptism in AD 911)

~~~

Gisela: illegitimate daughter of King Charles of the West Franks, Hrólfr's 'legitimate' wife

Sprota: the daughter of a minor Breton lord, William's handfasted wife *in more danico*

Richard: William and Sprota's son

Luitgarde: daughter of the Count of Vermandois, William's 'legitimate' wife

Guillaume: Count of Poitou, Adela's husband

Prologue

April, AD 890
Off the coast of Neustria, Kingdom of the West Franks

Hrólfr stood at the bow of the longship and stared at the coastline. The view ahead filled him with excitement. High cliffs were bathed in the glow of the setting sun, and the white sand in the small cove they were heading to glistened brightly. With each stroke of the oars, the karve edged closer to dry land – a land full of promise.

A land he'd ravaged before: the prosperous Frankish region of Neustria.

But this journey was not going to lead him along the River Signa again. No. On the feast the Christians called Easter, all the finery of the churches would be brought out – and his for the taking.

After a long, wet winter spent in East Anglia, and in Lundene at the court of his old friend, Guthrum, Hrólfr was rearing for a fight. There was only so much hunting and feasting he could do before boredom set in. A sad smile played on his lips at the memory of old Guthrum; his recent death was still on his mind. It had been the push he needed to return to Neustria, where there were Franks waiting to be harassed, rather than stay.

No, settling on that damp island, with King Alfred breathing down one's neck, was not for him. His was a lust for adventure, for fighting, for spoils. Alfred's power ended any thoughts of raids into Wessex Hrólfr may have harboured before. So here he was, crossing the narrow water that separated the kingdoms.

Attacking was what he was best at. And the pretty, bustling towns of Neustria, with their decorated churches and richly-adorned halls, were just the place. Smaller, and less well-defended than Paris, they promised great enjoyment.

As the coast grew nearer, he swapped places with Knud. With refreshed vigour, he pulled the oar in rhythm with the others, knowing each stroke took him closer to their chosen place; to the riches that awaited in the small town of Bayeux. During the siege of Paris four winters earlier, where he'd eventually left with purses filled with silver, a Frankish thrall had taught him to speak some of their language. It would confuse the Franks, he was certain.

Soon, he would receive his reward – an equal share of all the spoils, even thralls to sell in the slave markets. But first, it was the sweet scent of blood that would fill the air. He took a deep breath.

Finally, Knud sounded the horn – the signal to disembark.

Hrólfr was ready. His heartbeat quickened.

He brought his oar in and stood as his longship drifted into the shallows alongside a dozen others. Then he jumped into the low water, and with his men carried his ship up the stone-covered beach, out of reach of the waves.

Once the karves were secured, his band of warriors looked to him, axes and swords in hand, eyes shining. After months of inaction, they were as fired up as he was to go fighting.

Holding his axe aloft, he let out a roar. It echoed across the beach as men around him raised their weapons.

He grinned as he strode up a narrow path that led to the top of the cliffs rising from the shore. Once at the top, they saw the thatched roofs of Bayeux in the distance ahead.

Ripe for the picking.

The runes told him it was his destiny to conquer Neustria. Hrólfr only had to seize it.

PART ONE

~~~

CONQUERED

Chapter One

Easter Sunday, April 12th, AD 890
Bayeux, Neustria, Kingdom of the West Franks

Poppa wriggled her toes. They'd become numb inside her tightly laced boots during the endless sermon that followed the earlier procession across town. Keeping still for so long was simply not for her. Around her, the congregation stood in silence; people kept their gaze downcast, as if contemplating the Father Peter's words. But none of them understood a word, and she forced herself to hold back a giggle when she heard the odd snore. Now, she sighed again as Father Peter droned on in Latin. Only recently had Poppa begun her lessons in the dead language, and on the rare occasion when she recognised a word, it gave her no inkling of what the priest was talking about. Obviously, he was reading from the Holy Scriptures, and it must be something important. But if there was indeed a message in his ramblings, its meaning escaped her.

The celebration of the Easter feast – the most important event of the Christian year – was always a solemn occasion, as befitted Christ's death and resurrection. She knew that. But after the third of the nine *Kyrie Eleisons* that opened the mass, Poppa's thoughts had begun to drift. Like everyone else, she recited and intoned when prompted, but she much rather wanted to meet with her friend, Landina, by the water mill on the edge of town. The stream and the meadows were like heaven, unlike this crowded church where not even the cloying incense could not hide the stench of so many unwashed bodies.

Where were they, anyway? She cast glances to either side of her, but saw neither her friends nor their father, the miller.

11

Perhaps they were behind her. Briefly, she considered turning around, but Father's rigid stance changed her mind. Huffing, she shifted her weight to the other foot and winced at the tingling in her toes.

"Shh!" Father sent her a dark glance through lowered eyelids. He took sermons seriously, and his strong faith was the main reason she studied boring Latin with Father Peter.

Poppa knew Father was in part fulfilling Mother's dying wish by providing her with a religious education. Mother had wanted for her to join a convent. But Poppa also knew that she – as the only daughter of Count Bérengar of Bayeux – would soon become an important marriage pawn. The notion filled her with trepidation. On her fourteenth birthday, Father broached the subject for the first time, indicating there were several potential suitors for her in mind. She'd been praying Ranulf was amongst them, but his family were far below her own in station. Her hopes faltered, even though Father had promised to heed her opinion.

He indulged her, that was all. Then he would follow through with his plans. Much to her annoyance, he'd mentioned names of several men at the Frankish court. Men or boys of noble birth, all of them. Resigned, Poppa's heart had sunk.

Her childish snort at his pledge was drowned out by a loud "Alleluia!" from the gathered crowd. Swiftly, she followed Father's lead and crossed herself, else he would chide her for her straying mind.

Biting her lip, Poppa focused on Father Peter's ramblings, trying to identify words she recognised, and their meaning. It whiled away the time. Surreptitiously, she changed her weight again.

Moments later, as everyone watched the priest who had paused in his sermon, his head cocked to the side like a bird's, a sound of raised voices reached her ears. It came from outside. Shouts, which grew steadily closer. But with most of the inhabitants of Bayeux attending church, what could make such a growing noise?

Father exchanged glances with several men in the crowd.

An imperceptible nod from him, and they slowly edged closer to him. He spoke in a hushed tone, but Poppa could not hear his words.

More urgent shouting reached her ears, followed by screams that pierced the silence.

Around her, men and women glanced around nervously. Father Peter tried again to read from the Scriptures, clearly in an attempt to distract everyone. It was in vain.

"With me!" Father's voice cut through the murmurs. The men of Bayeux huddled around him.

Poppa grabbed his arm. He looked at her, giving her hand a squeeze, his expression grave. "Go to Father Peter! He will take you to safety."

Her eyes widened as he pointed towards the altar. "But—"

"Go, Poppa!" Then he turned his back on her. "Come, men of Bayeux!" he ordered and pushed his way outside. Every boy and man of fighting age – unarmed, their weapons left outside the doors, as was the custom – followed him. After they'd departed, the oak door fell shut with a thud.

Her mouth too dry to speak, Poppa stood still, unable to do as her father had bid. Time seemed to slow to a halt, as silence descended.

Then a woman to Poppa's left screamed, her voice high-pitched, her eyes wild, unfocused. Immediately, others joined her. The moment of deceptive calm was broken.

Poppa stared around in bafflement. Was her home under attack? Had the Northmen arrived again? They'd been ravaging many villages along the coast, and inland, for years, and Father often said the town must be prepared. Was that the reason why the men had rallied so swiftly?

Her heart pounded loud in her ears, and she forced herself to keep her breathing steady, just as he'd taught her.

The priest called out to restore calm, but soon, the women's wailing increased as the sound of clashing weapons came closer.

"Lock the door!" a call erupted from the back.

Father Peter wound his way through the crowd, and Poppa followed in his wake. He dangled a ring with several large keys in front of him. "Make way! Let me through, quick!" He fended off desperate hands trying to snatch the ring from his hands.

Poppa glared at the baker's wife who clung to the priest's arm. "Let him go, Irmingarde!" She pulled at her elbow. "Let him lock up."

"Who do you think you are, girl? How dare you accost me?"

"You know I'm the count's daughter. And you're holding Father Peter back from saving us."

Eventually, the rotund woman let go of the priest with a huff. "I only meant to help."

Poppa tutted when, released from Irmingarde's grip, Father Peter surged forward. Poppa followed, glaring down anyone else who tried to interfere. Aware of her status, she was not loath to use it when it suited her.

And now was the right moment.

As Father Peter approached the door, he held out the key towards the large lock, but he was knocked off balance when the door burst open. He scrambled backwards, stumbling over his long tunic.

A tall, broad shadow obscured the doorway. The steel of an axe in one hand reflected the bright sunlight. The man strode into the church, assessing the situation as his eyes roamed the interior, then alighted on the altar at the far end. A dry smile spread across his features.

The large gold cross! Poppa's heart sank. This raid was real. Would these attackers be content with gold and silver, or was more at stake?

What will they do to us? She feared for the safety of the women and girls gathered around her.

Visibly shaken, Father Peter held out his hands, dropping the keys. "This is a house of God; a place of sanctuary." He faced the intruder, and Poppa had to admit to her shame that she'd never deemed the priest to be this brave. Or foolish. "Remove yourself from this holy site forthwith!"

As the stranger stepped forward, towering over Father Peter, the priest shuffled backwards. Now the view at the enemy was clear. The stranger was brimming with confidence, clearly a leader. His long, blond hair gleamed in the rays of the sunshine filtering through the door. With his high cheekbones and a strong, straight nose, he could not be anything other than a Dane, or another Norse invader. A surprisingly well-kept beard covered the lower half of his face, but his light-blue eyes, the colour of a lake in winter – and as glacial – were compelling. They drew her to him.

Snapping out of her reverie, Poppa moved aside to avoid Father Peter bumping into her. Whimpers emerged from the women behind her as half a dozen warriors entered, their wide mouths contorted into wolfish grins.

The leader spoke in a language she did not understand, and the men laughed. Then they spread out swiftly, blocking the main doorway and the hidden side entrance, encircling the small crowd. Their eyes were raking over the girls and women.

Poppa recognised the look. Several times, she'd caught Ranulf gazing at her with that sense of…what? Desire? A shiver ran down her spine.

But theirs was not a loving desire. The stares from these fighting men were stronger than longing. They would take whatever they wanted, be that gold, silver – or women.

Was her fate sealed, together with that of all the women of Bayeux? She took a deep breath when their leader's eyes met hers.

He raised an eyebrow and issued an order, and three of the warriors pushed their way through to the altar, towards the Holy Cross.

"No!" Father Peter's voice rang loud in the silence, and he scrambled after them. "This is sacrilege." When he reached the steps, one of the warriors turned swiftly.

Poppa lifted herself to the tips of her toes to see, but others stood in front of her, blocking her view. Then a raised blade flashed in the candlelight, and Father Peter groaned.

Screams filled the church again; high-pitched, they echoed around the thick stone walls. A strong scent of iron permeated the air. The blood drained from Poppa's face as anger rose within her. One of the Norse warriors grabbed the golden cross and lifted it above his head. He shouted something in his language, and the invaders laughed again.

The light of the candle illuminated the rubies and garnets that adorned the cross.

A sense of dread settled over Poppa as she stared at them. *Like flecks of blood dripping down the holy relic...*

As the crowd shuffled to the side walls, away from the men by the altar, Poppa found herself left in the centre, alone. Now, she saw Father Peter's crumpled body on the floor. With a cry, she rushed forward, but after three steps, someone grabbed her arm, yanking her around.

She raised her head to stare at the leader who held her wrist in a tight grip. "Leave the priest, girl," he said in broken Frankish. "He's dead."

A cry hitched in her throat, as his eyes raked over her before they met her stare. His unusual height and challenging gaze exuded authority. Now, close to him, she saw his face and beard covered in dry blood, as was his tunic of green dyed wool. The blood of the good citizens of Bayeux. Father's blood, even? She shuddered.

Soon, he would let his men rape their way through the women and girls. Of that, she had no doubt. She'd heard the stories of horror and pain from up and down the coast, and far inland. If that was to be her fate, she could not change it. But she would not go down without a fight.

She stood erect, her back straight, challenging him. "How dare you threaten us in a church!"

At first, he simply blinked at her, then a grin spread across his sun-darkened features. He shouted something to his men, who burst out laughing again. He pulled her closer to him, looking her up and down.

Poppa gritted her teeth, but she did not look away, pushing her fear for Father – and for herself – to the back of her mind. Their priest was dead, and the women gathered behind her were stricken with fear. They had no one to speak on their behalf but her.

To her surprise, he suddenly released her and took a step

back. She nearly stumbled but caught herself in time.

"Who are you to tell me what to do, girl?" The sharp tone of his voice matched the contempt she saw in his eyes.

Poppa took in a sharp breath, but before she could formulate a lie, a female voice called out, "She is the daughter of Earl Bérengar."

His grin grew wider. "Oh, is she? In that case, I'm sure her father would be delighted to see her."

A chill ran down Poppa's spine as she turned around to glare at Alva, one of the baker's daughters. She'd always known the girl had feathers in her head, just like her hapless mother, Irmingarde, who stood beside her, wringing her hands.

The stupid girl just sealed Poppa's fate.

***

Later that night
The hall of Count Bérengar, Bayeux

The great hall of the count of Bayeux was cast in a play of light and shadows, as torches set in sconces along the walls tried to banish the darkness that descended outside. The room was heaving with men and women, the noise almost lifting the roof.

Grinning, Hrólfr leaned back in the comfortable chair the count had offered him to his right at the high table. Not that he'd given the man a choice.

He chuckled, then took a sip of mead. His warriors were celebrating their success. The treasure they'd amassed from the churches and homes of wealthy traders was plentiful. As promised, everything was divided equally. The large gold cross would be melted and then every man would get his share. But that was not the only item of value they'd discovered in that little church. A hoard of precious stones was discovered in an alcove, together with a casket.

Hrólfr scratched his head, baffled. The box contained something resembling a finger.

The finger of a venerable saint, no less, Count Bérengar had told him. Apparently, it was invaluable.

Well, everything had a price, and someone would pay handsomely for the gruesome find. These Christians were a funny lot, cutting up their holy men and women whilst revering them at the same time. He snorted.

"What amuses you?" The count sent him a sideways glance.

"Your customs. You call us barbaric, but you chop off bits of people you admire the most. It is…strange."

"Not at all. Saints always die a martyr's death. It is their murderers who often torture them in the most horrific way."

"Ah, of course." His own smirk showed Bérengar that he didn't believe him. "You blame someone else for their demise, I see."

"That's right, my lord." Bérengar pulled his chair closer to him.

Hrólfr detested the ingratiating manner of the man. It was fair to assume that he had the best for his townspeople in mind; well, for those who survived. But Hrólfr had expected more aversion towards him and his warriors, yet Bérengar was most accommodating.

Still, it made his stay in Bayeux more pleasant. But careful as he always was, Hrólfr he'd still ordered guards to patrol the streets. Bérengar's allies could arrive with reinforcements if word reached them.

"It's heathens, refusing the teachings of Christ, who slay our saints – they would not be saints otherwise."

Hrólfr frowned. "So they have to die for you to admire them?" He kept his expression neutral, but was secretly amused that the count was so easy to tease.

"Yes." Bérengar looked pleased with the ease with which Hrólfr had apparently understood.

Truth was that he'd heard such tales amongst the Christians in East Anglia. To him, their customs seemed more complicated than his own, and the Norse Gods were not an easy lot to appease.

"That's not good for them, is it?"

"But that is the point, Lord—"

"Hrólfr. I'm no lord, so stop calling me such."

"Of course… Rouf."

Hrólfr rolled his eyes as he emptied his cup, then gestured to a thrall to refill it. The boy rushed forward and complied.

Inhaling the sweet, potent scent of the mead, Hrólfr smiled. He could get used to this kind of life. At least for a while. Leaning back into the large seat, he stretched his long legs out before him. Half-full cup in hand, he let his gaze wander around the room.

Bérengar's hall was welcoming and warm. Its wooden walls were covered with colourful tapestries. A large fire roared in the central hearth, the smoke spiralling out the small hole in the roof above. Still, a haze had settled over the room.

The tables were still laden with cured meats, although he and his men had eaten their fill; ale, wine and mead flowed freely. It would be a long night.

All that was missing was some accommodating company to while away the dark hours – and discussing dead Christians with Count Bérengar was not it. Hrólfr's gaze fell on the count's daughter seated on her father's far side. All through the evening, her expression was as thunderous as Thor's stormy skies. He grinned. Unlike her weaselly father, the girl did not hide her true feelings. She had courage, he granted her that.

The place had likely never seen such revelling, as his men sought – and found –willing women, although the ensuing cavorting on benches and even in the shadowy corners on the rush-strewn floors might shock her. The Franks did not know how to enjoy themselves – that small fact he'd learned over the years. A miserable lot, pretending to be superior to their fellow men. Especially men like him. Forever praying to their one God for mercy.

But he'd not once heard of an occasion where their God had answered. He'd killed simpering monks whilst they waited for Him to save them. Yet He never stopped the Norse.

19

Blinking, Hrólfr shrugged himself out of his gloomy musings. Tonight was for celebrating. But when Poppa's gaze met his, he could have turned to ice under her stare. No, she would not do for the night. As pretty as she was with her long, auburn hair, full mouth, and her large, light brown eyes, taking her to his bed would not be much fun.

A lady, the daughter of a count, she would still be a virgin, ignorant of the pleasures he sought. And she was far too young for him anyway.

No. One of the other comely wenches would do. He turned away from her and looked around. Up ahead, a shapely blonde thrall was refilling cups of his warriors with ale. She weaved her way between the tables, cleverly encouraging and avoiding the warriors' wandering hands at the same time. When she noticed him watching, she bit her lower lip.

His smile encouraged her, and she approached him. "Can I refill the cup of such a fine fighting man as yourself?"

Leaning forward, he laughed out loud. "No, I prefer mead to ale. But I believe *you* may have a cup worth filling…"

"I'm Isa." Amidst cheers, she handed the pitcher to a man sitting nearby, then walked, hips swaying languidly, around the high table towards him. Playing with the laces that held her dress together at her well-rounded chest, she came to a halt beside him, ignoring Count Bérengar's half-hearted outrage. "Tell me, my strong conqueror of these lands, are you prepared to…replenish…my cup?" Her fingertips left a prickling trail along his neck, and his body began to react to her touch.

It has been too long.

A female voice hissed behind him, followed by a chair scraping on the floor. Clearly, the count's daughter was leaving. A moment later, her words confirmed his suspicion.

"I'm retiring for the night." Her voice shook as she added, "And I never want to see such disgusting behaviour in our home again. Where is your duty as a Christian lord, Father?"

Without giving Bérengar time to respond, she rushed past them, and through the thick curtains that separated the private rooms from the hall.

Hrólfr half-turned towards the count, leaving his arm possessively around the wench's hips. "Don't worry about your daughter. She'll get used to this, sooner or later." His hand moved up Isa's waist, touching the bottom of her half-exposed breasts with his fingertips as she wriggled closer to him. But unlike some of his men, he did not want to rut in front of everyone else. It was time to leave the hall for somewhere more private. "Now, Bérengar, where is your chamber?"

Four days later

Hrólfr walked through the narrow back lanes of Bayeux, pleased with the effort to re-establish some normality back into the town. He didn't wish for peddlers and traders to avoid them, so the streets had been cleared of the worst signs of fighting. Shattered debris was removed, and the cobbled ground rinsed of the spilt blood.

He'd ordered the most skilled of his men to repair houses and shops, and the forge had reopened. Like other residents providing important trades, Ragno, the Frankish blacksmith, eventually accepted Hrólfr's protection. Word had been sent out that Bayeux was open to traders.

And although he would soon take a small cohort and head eastwards along the coast towards the estuary of the River Signa, as he'd planned all along, a cluster of warriors would stay behind to defend the town against other marauders, and to ensure the locals behaved.

Pleased with progress made, he left the narrow lanes behind and entered the market square. But it was not food or trinkets on sale here today.

No. Today was about a different kind of trade. Thralls.

For the past few days, the four dozen men of young to middle age captured during the attack had been held in the church, tied up securely. Their wounds were tended to, and they'd received water and stale bread left over from the evening meals. A dead man would be no use as a thrall.

The previous night, Hrólfr ordered the release of ten men

whose wives had been begging him to show mercy. Being past their fiftieth winter, they would never survive the arduous journeys on the longships, nor would they be of much use. Instead, they'd been drafted in to help with the repairs on the destroyed buildings.

Knud lined up the Frankish captives. Their clothes and shoes lying in a pile on the dirty ground behind them, the young men of Bayeux stood in silence, naked, trying to cover their cocks with their bound hands. Well-armed guards formed a semi-circle around them.

The Franks must have known that any attempt to escape would be met with swift retribution.

Several of Hrólfr's men decided to settle, so they'd been allocated lands confiscated from the residents. But they knew they needed help to work the land.

Hrólfr had set the rules for this small slave market. Every one of his men would select two thralls at a time, with the remainder of the men being put to the oars.

He sneaked up at Knud from behind and slapped his back. His friend turned around swiftly, his dagger in hand, poised to strike. Hrólfr jumped backwards, laughing, raising his hands.

"Calm down, my friend! It's only me."

Knud grinned as he ran his finger along the flat side of his dagger, his gaze not leaving Hrólfr's. "Then you're fortunate I didn't slice you up like the roast deer I enjoyed last night. What do you think?" He gestured at the lined-up men and boys, huddled together.

"What a pitiful sight!" Hrólfr laughed. The Frankish prisoners looked sullen. Several stared at their feet, aware of their nakedness, unwilling to meet his eyes, but others glared at him. Their hatred would keep them going. That was good. An angry man worked harder to regain his freedom, eventually, although he could also turn against you if you did not pay attention. "So, who is going to have first choice?"

"Well, I think Leif should begin. He's returning to his home on Orkneyjar on the morrow and needs some strong rowers, now that half of the crew have decided to settle."

Hrólfr nodded. "That's fair. He hasn't seen his family since last summer."

"True. Although it might likely have more to do with Jarl Sigurd's successful raids into the territory of that useless King of Alba, Domnall." Knud snorted. "It brings disruption to the islands."

Leif was nothing if not ambitious to increase his personal holdings. He was close to the jarl, which boded well.

Hrólfr shrugged off the memory of the tough chief whose brother had bestowed the title of jarl on him. The vision of a pair of pale green eyes and finely-pleated long blonde hair came to him unbidden. Åsa. Jarl Sigurd's daughter by a thrall, a captured Gael. Their love had not survived Hrólfr's thirst for adventure, and he'd declined the proposed marriage alliance. The jarl had been angry, and Hrólfr never again set foot on the man's expanding territory. His life would be forfeit.

It's no good dwelling in the past.

He shrugged. Casting an eye over the ragged line of Franks, Hrólfr wasn't too hopeful. A few young males would be useful to his friend of many winters. Their muscles were still growing. Given a few weeks, they would soon adjust to the hardship of life onboard a karve. A couple of males of middle age might work well too. But the others were either too young or too big, better suited to working the fields. Choosing a slave who could not complete his tasks was pointless, only using up unnecessary space and food.

"So be it. Leif!" He called him forward. Sad to see the man had chosen to return to the windswept islands in the windswept north, he patted Leif's shoulder. "Choose two of them. Then it's the turn of the next man."

Leif nodded. A man of few words, he walked in front of the prisoners. His brows pulled together, he shrugged. "What a pitiful sight," he repeated Hrólfr's own words.

"It's all you'll get."

Passing a prisoner with receding hairline and a large belly, he prodded it with the handle of his dagger. The man's face suffused, and Leif laughed out loud. The Frank opened his mouth as if to complain, but the tip of Leif's dagger on his cheek made him close it quickly.

Like a plump stranded fish. Frankish life must be good to grow that fat. Hrólfr shook his head. "Don't fool around with the wares on offer, Leif. I have more to do than watch you torture our thralls." But the grin on his face took the sting from his words. They were used to each other's way.

"It's a shame," Leif said with a sigh. "But I don't believe this one will be suitable for the oars."

A murmur went through the line, and several Franks looked from the Northman in front of them to Hrólfr and Knud. "Oars?" "Like on a ship?" "We're to leave home?"

"Of course, like on a ship." Leif strode towards a boy of perhaps fifteen winters who stood rooted to the spot, his eyes wide. "How else would I be able to travel the seas to my homeland?" He tutted. "What's your name, lad?"

"Um, Ranulf."

"When I was your age, I dreamed of adventures. Do you have dreams, young Ranulf?"

The boy's eyes grew wider, and Hrólfr recognised his internal struggle. All boys crave adventures, keen to explore the world, but how much of an adventure would it be as a slave on a longship?

"Of course I do, but…"

Leif took a step closer, his boots almost touching the boy's toes. The warrior was half a head taller, but Ranulf's long limbs showed hints of muscles. Clearly, he was used to working. Hrólfr could see why his friend was interested in this particular prisoner.

"But?" Leif's voice was hoarse. "Discovering new lands. Learning to fight. Raiding… What's not to like?"

Ranulf swallowed. "My home is here."

Leif clapped him on the shoulder, and he jerked. "Not any longer, young man. You are coming with me."

The colour drained from Ranulf's face. "Why? Where to?"

Leif grinned. "To Orkneyjar…"

Chapter Two

Bayeux, Neustria

Hrólfr stepped forward. "Why? Because you're now a thrall, Ranulf. And a fortunate one. There are few masters as fair as Leif. Work hard, and you'll be treated well."

"But…but I'm a miller's son. I work the fields. I don't know anything about the sea or life on an island."

"Then it's time to learn." Leif looked up and down the line of men, then pointed to another Frank close by, who looked a few years older than Ranulf. The man's frame was bulkier with muscle. "You will come with me too." He turned to Hrólfr. "I have made my choices."

Knud's voice drifted over the square. "Leif has taken two thralls. Who is next? Harlond?"

"Why has he taken a miller's son? The boy would have been better suited to my new fields." Harlond's voice was petulant.

"Because those working the land are replaced more easily." Leif smirked. "I won't give him up."

Harlond strode towards Leif, his hand on the hilt of his sword. "Just because you're a friend of those two," he gestured towards Hrólfr and Knud, "doesn't give you the right to take the best men."

"There are plenty left." Leif crossed his arms and took a step towards Harlond. "Have them all, for all I care!"

Suppressing a sigh, Hrólfr stepped between them, a hand on each man's chest. "This stops right here." Taller than both men, he glared down at them, one by one. "Leif. Harlond."

Harlond's mouth formed a thin line, but he took a step back.

Leif followed suit. Then he called his new thralls over to

wait at the side, watched by a guard.

Hrólfr knew that if any half-decent workers were left, Leif would want one or two more pairs of hands. But first, it was the turn of the new settlers.

"So, Harlond. Which men are you going to pick for your fields?" He gestured towards the thralls.

Then Hrólfr and Knud stepped back as the wiry Danish warrior walked the line of prisoners.

"That was close." Knud smirked.

"It's normal. Whoever comes first will take the best. But Leif is the only one going away. Harlond and half a dozen others have decided to settle. As you know, we've carved up the fertile lands amongst them. The rest of our men will join me on the journey up the Signa River." He glanced at his friend. "Where will you be? Stay and enjoy your new role as protector of this town, or with me?"

"Can I be both?" Knud sent him a sideways glance.

Hrólfr laughed. "Of course. We'll leave several good fighting men behind, plus all those new landowners will do their bit if needed." He pointed to the small group of Northmen awaiting their turn in choosing their thralls. "Our defences must be in place before we sail. Word will get out."

"You can't stop others from trying where we've succeeded, Hrólfr."

"No, but I can bloody well make sure they're wasting their time." He nodded in confirmation as Harlond passed him with a boy of perhaps thirteen winters and a man easily twice their age.

Hrólfr gestured the next warrior-turned-settler forward.

"An alliance with a local lord might make our hold more…secure." Knud kept his gaze on the thralls, but the corners of his mouth twitched.

Hrólfr frowned. "What do you mean? Is our victory not good enough?"

"Perhaps. But to get the Franks to accept our overlordship, we must keep a sharp eye on them. It would be less of a struggle if there were an…agreement."

"Stop speaking in riddles! You sound like the Norns. They

never making any sense either."

"Ah, but the Norns predicted your victory, your success. I was just thinking of Bérengar's young daughter. A shapely girl…"

"She's but a child!" Hrólfr stared at Knud. Had his friend lost his mind? "I prefer my women a bit more mature, thank you."

Knud laughed. "She's a comely child who, one day, will grow into a beautiful woman. Think about it."

"Hmph…" The idea was preposterous. He didn't need a wife, and especially not one so young.

No. An alliance would have to be formed on a different basis. "I'm not certain it's for me, marriage."

"Well, she could become your concubine, in a few years' time. Then you can always escape when you tire of her."

Hrólfr sighed. "Leave it, Knud! I won't be drawn into an arrangement like this."

"There are rumours…"

"What kinds of rumours?" His tone was sharper than intended but, by the Gods, he was tiring of this conversation.

"That Bérengar is planning to offer her to you, so that he can stay Count of Bayeux, but with the city under your rule and protection."

Anger rose within Hrólfr. The Franks were always plotting, seeking their own advantage. Loyalty counted for nothing. But if these rumours were true, why had his informers not apprised him of them? He would have to have a word.

"If Bérengar wants something of me, he'll seek me out." And with a warning glance at Knud, he strode over to Leif.

Finally, all the thralls were chosen. They quickly dressed. Leif's group had grown to five, with two men near Leif's own age joining them.

"You're growing soft in your old lifetime, Leif. How long will these last two survive one the oars?"

His friend gave him a knowing smile. "Ah, but first glances can deceive, Hrólfr. This man here," he pointed at one of them who didn't look as if he'd ever starved in his life, "can cook. Now that my own cook has decided to stay here, we have need of another. And the other, well, he can help with the steering. He's a fisherman."

Astounded with Leif's choices, Hrólfr grinned. "You have a full ship now, Leif. Well done! I will miss you."

"No, you won't." Leif punched him hard on the upper arm, and Hrólfr rubbed his muscles. "You'll be too busy growing into a fat lord of a handsome Frankish hall."

"Ha, I don't think so! In the next two weeks, we'll be heading up the Signa again. It has been too long since I last graced the rich villages with my presence."

"Some things never change. But you can always come to Orkneyjar when you're getting bored of the Franks."

Hrólfr's smile faded. "I don't think so. Sigurd would have my balls."

"Quite likely, and rightly so." Leif snorted. "I will give Åsa your regards."

"Don't you dare!"

Leif squeezed his shoulder. "It's time I took these thralls to the boat. There's work to do before the morning. Will I see you in the hall tonight?"

Hrólfr nodded. "Of course. You can't leave us without a feast."

As Leif and one of his men herded their slaves from the market square, a cry went up.

"Ranulf! No!"

Hrólfr turned to see Poppa trying to run towards the boy, but her father held her arm in a firm grip. Frustrated, he sighed. Why did the man bring his daughter out here? It wasn't safe for a pretty young girl amongst all the men.

"Poppa, behave yourself!" Bérengar's irate words reached Hrólfr, and he walked over to them.

"No, Father. I will not. What are they doing with Ranulf?" Her voice increased a pitch, echoing across the open space. Strands of her auburn hair escaped her wimple in the struggle, framing her freckled face.

He watched her fend off her father. She had strength, both of mind and body. Uncertain whether to admire her bravery or detest it, he said bluntly, "Ranulf is going on a journey."

"He is what?" Bérengar stared at him but lowered his gaze when Hrólfr glared back. The Frankish lord knew well the fate that awaited those taken prisoner.

"Where to?" She sounded petulant now, like a normal girl her age. "And when will he come back?"

Hrólfr shrugged. "That's up to Leif."

"Who is Leif?" Anger burnt strongly in her hazel eyes.

"His owner."

"His what?" she screeched. "Ranulf!" Turning to Hrólfr, she demanded, "Let him go. This is his home."

"Not any longer." And he sent Leif a curt nod to continue on his way.

With a wave, Leif turned and walked on, Ranulf and the other thralls in tow. The boy cast a long glance at Poppa, before he was marched down the lane to the edge of town, and from there to the shore.

"No..." Poppa wailed. Her eyes filled with tears as she continued to wriggle in her father's grasp.

Ah, Hrólfr thought, young love. They would get over it.

As had he. Angrily, he brushed the unwanted memory of Åsa from his mind.

It was too long ago...

***

With tears streaming down her face, Poppa stared after Ranulf until he was out of sight. Sick with worry, she begged her father to stop them. But instead of telling the invaders to let their men go, Father gripped her shoulders tightly and shook her.

"Stop this right now, child!" His voice was hoarse, edged with impatience. And something else was lurking in his tone.

Fear?

He was afraid of Hrólfr. So much so that he was willing to sacrifice his own townsmen.

She blinked. "These are our friends, Father. Our people. Do you not care that they are treated like slaves, to be taken far from home?"

"Of course I care, but… But it is what it is, Poppa. Rouf and his men have won. We lost. This is the way of the world."

"Then I hate this world!" she spat.

When Hrólfr approached them again, leaving his second-in-command to coordinate the removal of the rest of the prisoners with their new owners, she glared at him. "How dare you…you…heathen!"

"Poppa!" Father warned her. His fingers dug deep into her arms, causing her to wince. "Know your place, young lady."

She struggled to free herself, but Father held firm.

"Where are you taking them? These are good men of Bayeux; they have never harmed anyone in their lives." With tears in her eyes, Poppa hiccuped. Little did she care if the men saw her anger.

Finally, the last group left the square. The sudden silence made everything feel like her heart – empty.

Oh, Ranulf.

"Some will stay here, working the fields," the leader interrupted her morose thoughts.

"Fields you've taken from the honest people of Bayeux."

"Poppa! I must apologise, my lord Rouf, for my daughter's unseemly behaviour. We shall return home forthwith. Come, you silly girl."

"So Ranulf will stay here after all?" She dug in her heels as her father tried to pull her away.

Hrólfr's light blue eyes glinted like splintered ice on a frozen lake. Her heart sank. "If you care for the boy, Lady Poppa, then you'd best forget about him."

She sucked in her breath. "What? Why?"

"Because young Ranulf will be rowing to the islands of Orkneyjar where Leif, his new lord, has a steading. Your friend's new life will be there from now on."

"Orkn…? The Orcades? The islands to the north of Alba?" Her throat constricted as tears welled up again. Ranulf might as well have been going to the edge of the world; he would be far beyond her reach. "Forever?"

Oh, how she hated that her voice wobbled.

The Northman raised an eyebrow as he nodded. Was he surprised? Clearly, he had not expected her to be so educated. "Yes, the same group of isles. Now put him out of your mind, girl. You won't be seeing him again in this life." Dismissing her with an arrogant tilt of his head, he turned to her father, gracing him with a sharp glare. "Remind your daughter where her loyalties should lie, *Count* Bérengar." Without another glance at her, he strode away in the direction of their hall, in the company of the man she called Hrólfr's Shadow. Canute, or something similar sounding. Where one went, the other was close by.

She'd been watching them. Not that she wanted to be near either, but it was always good to know what the enemy was plotting.

"Home, now!" Bérengar growled under his breath. He stared at the few onlookers who quickly busied themselves with their chores. His grip on her arm remained firm as he dragged her with him.

"Ow! You're hurting me, Father." Poppa almost ran to keep up with his long strides. He was seething, and she could not remember him ever having been so irate.

"If you were a boy, you would receive a beating to remember for the rest of your life, young lady. As it is, you will be confined to your chamber unless you are required in the hall." He stopped so suddenly that she bumped into him, making him even more angry, if that was possible.

Poppa met his gaze evenly. She had nothing more to lose.

The skin around his eyes seemed even more creased, but not from laughter. Deep grooves had appeared on his forehead. In a matter of days, he'd aged by at least ten years. Of course, he would not find the Northmen's arrival easy to deal with, but at least he was still Count of Bayeux. And he was still in his own, very comfortable hall.

Unlike Ranulf and the others who'd been sent away, as slaves, rowing the dangerous seas to an uncertain fate.

Under his unflinching stare, Poppa lowered her gaze, tears blurring her sight.

"Under no circumstances will you go outside again."

"But you took me with you—"

"By the Rood, daughter! Your head is full of the Devil's words. I fear all that reading you learned does you no good. Now come, and not another word of disagreement, or I will forget myself."

A deep sense of loss washed over her. She'd lost the boy she'd secretly dreamed of marrying, even though she'd known all along that such dreams were futile. She was a count's daughter, and as such, aware of her station.

But now, her old way of life was gone, banished by the arrival of these northern Pagans. Everyone's future held nothing but uncertainty.

She knew her father was ambitious, but weak. When she'd listened to Father Peter's tales about the emperors of the Romans, they were strong-willed and able-bodied, invoking loyalty and fear alike. Father, although adept at sword-fight, was no hardened warrior like Hrólfr and is followers were. The brave men of Bayeux had been slaughtered or taken as slaves. They were merchants and bakers and butchers and millers, not fighting men.

Thoughts tumbled through her mind as they approached the hall. The town should have been better prepared. It was no secret that Northmen roamed the shores, attacking at whim. They'd done it for many years. So why had Bayeux been so unprepared?

Poppa's musings came to a halt when Father pulled her inside. In the dim light, she saw the heathen leader lounging in Father's big, beautifully carved chair. Its seat and back padded with soft furs, and the man looked much at ease. His legs were stretched out in front of him, and he held a drinking horn in hand which Pepin, only a few years younger than her, was quick to fill.

A shiver ran down her spine.

When Hrólfr spotted her, she glared at him as fury surged through her. The man made himself at home too fast. Father had even given up his bedchamber at the back of the hall to the Northman. It was adjoining hers, and ever since Hrólfr

32

had taken it over, she had to cover her ears. The man was loud!

Father had moved his belongings into the small chamber opposite hers that used to be her mother's, and she often wondered if he heard the noises too.

Clearly, it was something else Bérengar tolerated, regardless of the feelings of his household.

Now, Hrólfr had the gall to claim Father's chair at the centre of their high table on the dais. His Shadow, Canute, sat to his left. That way, she saw, his sword arm was free, should he need it.

She acknowledged that Hrólfr was not stupid. He was cunning, and she only hoped he'd be bored soon and, on his way to pester some other poor Franks elsewhere.

Their eyes met and his mouth twitched, then he raised his drinking horn to her. He must have realised she was scrutinising him.

Huffing, her face burning, she pulled her arm from Father's grasp, which had loosened after they entered. Quickly, she ran past the dais to her tiny chamber at the back. She leaned against the partition, breathing rapidly. Outside the thick curtain that had fallen back into place behind her, footsteps halted.

The partition between the rooms was flimsy, barely providing an impression of sequestration, and the curtains did not completely muffle all sounds. At night-time, they were held in place by leather thongs tucked around a wooden peg on either side. That was all the privacy she would have.

Not for the Count of Bayeux the luxury of stone walls, despite Father's high ambitions. At this moment, Poppa would give anything for a solid oak door with a lock, to shut out the world forever.

Instead, she felt a movement against the curtain.

"Poppa, can I come in?" Father's voice sounded irritated.

What did he want now? Was he not glad to be rid of her?

She held back the thick fabric and let him enter, then she stood in the middle of her chamber, the back of her legs touching the wooden frame of her narrow bed. With her arms crossed in front of her, she looked down her nose at him. "What?"

"We must talk."

"I thought we've done that all afternoon."

Bérengar ruffled his thinning hair. A little devil in her ear whispered, 'He should really keep it cropped short.' She snorted.

"What's so funny, girl?" He stepped towards her, and she shrunk away, but the bed stopped her movement. She nearly stumbled. "What Devil beset you, daughter? You've been nothing but trouble these last few days."

Poppa nearly laughed out loud but stopped herself when she saw the seriousness in his eyes. Had he read her mind? "Nothing has beset me, Father. I merely disagree with our conquerors' disgraceful behaviour."

"They are not conquerors. They are our—"

"What are they? Friends? Well, they certainly know how to treat their friends well – by condemning them to their ships!"

The slap came so fast Poppa could not move in time to avoid it. Her cheek burned, and she gently put a hand over it. Tears brimmed at the corners of her eyes.

Father came so close, they stood toe to toe. He looked down his aquiline nose with blazing eyes. Rubbing the hand he'd hit her with, he hissed, "From now on you will be an obedient daughter, Poppa. You will answer only when addressed, and you will treat our visitors with the respect we owe them." His voice was deceptively calm.

She opened her mouth, but he put an index finger across her lips.

"I have not permitted you to speak. You will personally serve Lord Rouf, as befits the role of the lady of this house and daughter of a count. You will also learn to accept your place as a woman. No more roaming the fields with those never-do-goods, the miller's children. Ranulf is gone." He sighed. "You had your sights on him, but you must always be aware of your station. He would never have made an acceptable husband for you."

34

"And…Landina?" Poppa blinked. She realised she had not seen her dear friend. In her fear for Ranulf, she'd almost forgotten his sister. After the miller was slain during the attack, she'd been taken in by the Irmingarde's family. But as an unmarried young girl in a town firmly in the grasp of unruly Northmen, her virtue was still in danger. Men were quick to slide a hand under a girl's dress. Poppa had witnessed this over the past few nights in the hall.

Not that anyone tried it with her. A sense of relief swept through her, followed quickly by guilt. She did not even know how her friend fared. Her only thoughts had been for herself, mourning the life that they'd shared.

Father must have had an inkling of what went on in her mind, as he stepped back and walked the length of the small space. "She's working for the baker now."

"But they have two daughters of their own already, and three boys. They hardly need another mouth to feed." An idea formed in her head, and she put on her most endearing smile, as much as it vexed her. "Can Landina not live here, with me, as my companion?"

"Here?" Father's eyes slid across her sanctuary.

"Yes, there's space enough for a pallet," she pointed on the floor beside the bed. "Or we can share my bed." Poppa was not sure, but she could not let Father see her doubts. She stepped closer to him and placed a hand on his chest. It struck her as odd that he wore his best tunic every day, as if to impress the conquerors. "She would keep me company."

His eyes widened, and she knew he understood. Having a companion meant less mischief. After a long moment, Father nodded. "So be it. I will speak with the baker."

"Thank you." She took his hand. "We will both feel safer now."

"Yes, yes, of course. Now, I have a…" His voice trailed off as he cocked his head and stared through her as if of uncertain mind.

"What, Father?" A new sense of unease hit her.

Father shrugged his shoulders, as if ridding himself of unwanted thoughts. "'Tis nothing, daughter. Stay in here until

35

I call you to our meal. Wear your best gown and have a maid brush your hair and re-arrange your wimple. We may have a reason to celebrate tonight."

Celebrate? After half the town had been enslaved? But Poppa held her counsel and merely nodded.

With a wry smile on his thin lips, he headed for the curtain. As his hand reached out to pull it aside, he sighed, then faced her once more. "Until later, Poppa. And don't disappoint me!"

As the curtain fell back into place, she swiftly hooked it in on both sides. Confusion tore through her. *'A reason to celebrate…'* What was that about? Father had not mentioned any positive tidings, mainly because there had been none.

And why should it matter how she looked? Unless…

Her skin began to crawl. What was Father up to?

Chapter Three

Bayeux, Neustria

Darkness had fallen when Hrólfr returned to Bérengar's hall, Leif and Knud in tow. The'd been inspecting the boats and issuing instructions to a group of men guarding them, and the thralls, who would be leaving with Leif at sunrise on the morrow.

Hrólfr was sad to see his friend go, but there was still Knud, and Sigurd, and all the other men who were keen to join him on a journey along the river.

Four days had passed since their successful attack on Bayeux, and, already, he was bored with the routine. Now that those who preferred to settle had chosen their plots, he knew the town would be well-defended if needed.

"You look so serious tonight, Hrólfr. What ails you?" Leif sent him a sideways glance.

Hrólfr shrugged. "Nothing in particular. It has just been a long day." He could hardly tell the seasoned warrior he'd had second thoughts about one of the thralls; and all to banish the sadness in Poppa's large doe eyes. But it was not his decision to make. Each man was entitled to their share, and young Ranulf now belonged to Leif.

The skálds often spoke of separated lovers. The girl would be fine, once Bérengar had chosen a husband for her. Whoever the lucky man would be, he had a task on his hand when the feisty girl grew into womanhood. Hrólfr gave a wry smile.

Knud punched his arm. "You're not getting soft in your old age, are you?" He mimicked a man bent over, as if walking on a stick, patting his lower back. "Ow, ow…"

With a swift move, Hrólfr wound an arm around Knud's

neck and held him loosely. "I can still kill you should I desire to…"

His friend chuckled, tilting his head left and right. Hrólfr released his grip.

"You wouldn't do it. You can't live without me."

Leif burst out laughing and patted each man's backs. "I always thought they must have separated you two in your cots!" Then he stepped ahead of them and held the door to the hall open. "Enter, my lords," he said with a mock bow. "Now, where's that ale you promised us, Hrólfr?"

Still chuckling, Hrólfr beckoned Pepin over, who emerged from the shadows.

"Lord?" The boy kept his head half-bent.

"Is everything prepared for the feast?"

"Yes." Pepin nodded. "I shall tell the cook you've returned, then I'll be with you right away, lord." And without waiting for his response, Pepin escaped through a side door in the direction of the kitchen building behind the hall.

"He's keen to please," Knud observed.

Hrólfr nodded. "He knows how to survive." Then he extracted his drinking horn from his belt and headed for the dais. There was no sign of Bérengar or Poppa. At the other trestle tables, the men not tasked with the watch tonight were already deep in their cups. He slapped a couple of shoulders on his way, and a cheer went through the rows.

"This is for you, Leif. Everyone will miss you," he said, then he settled in Bérengar's chair, stretching his legs.

Leif and Knud took the seats on either side of him and removed their drinking horns from their belts.

"No, this is not for me. They're happy you found a place with a fountain of ale. Those pitchers are never empty."

"That is likely because my father the count has demanded your supply must not dry up." The lady Poppa's sharp voice behind him made him turn his head, and he watched her walk slowly in front of their table.

He blinked at the sight of her. The girl held a plain jug of ale in her hands, but that was not what caught his attention. She wore a finely woven gown made of blue silk, criss-crossed with silver thread. The close fit accentuated her comely figure, with feminine curves already in place for one so young still. Wide sleeves, their edges embroidered with an interlaced silver border, reached almost to the floor. A vertical split down her skirt allowed glimpses of a black linen shift beneath. Having discarded the plain wimple she'd worn earlier, strands of auburn hair escaped from a thick braid trailing down her back now peeked out beneath a thin veil, as if intended. They framed her face and shone like burnished bronze in the light of the tallow candles. A filigree circlet held the delicate veil in place. Her neck was adorned with a large silver cross pendant inlaid with amber.

A hush went over the room, and the hair on the back of Hrólfr's neck stood on end. A careful glance around confirmed his suspicions. Every man in the room was gawping.

Was the girl aware of how tempting she looked? Poppa was barely fourteen winters old, yet dressed like a…

A what?

Watching her, he sensed her discontent; a fragile uncertainty in her expression was the only sign she gave. Most men would not notice it, but he did.

This was not Poppa's doing, but her father's. What exactly was Bérengar playing at?

Beside him, Knud let his gaze wander up and down Poppa's body. Hrólfr elbowed him in the side, and his friend huffed in response but averted his eyes.

He rose and inclined his head. "Lady Poppa. You seem to have silenced the room with your mere presence."

The smile she gave did not quite reach her eyes as they darted from him to the gathered men beyond. "Don't let me stop you in your…cavorting, my *lord*. I'm merely here to serve you ale." She held out the jug and filled his drinking horn, then Leif's and Knud's. "It is my father's wish."

Ah. So he was right. He smirked at the way she clearly hated to call him lord. By the Gods, he hated the title too. He was no lord; merely a leader of men. A warrior, not a snivelling turncoat like her father, a born and bred lord.

"Speaking of which...where is Bérengar tonight? Will he not join us?"

Having completed the task, she took a step back. "I do not know where he is. I thought he was here, with you." Her eyes searched the room, then met his, and he almost winced at the storm in them.

A true count's daughter, her attitude full of disapproval and disgust. Hrólfr pitied the man who would take her to wife.

"Then I hope at least you will stay with us. After all, this is your hall." At his nod, Knud moved one seat to the other side and offered her the vacated chair.

Inclining her head, she sat down, put the jug on the table and folded her hands in her lap. "Thank you. But please don't expect me to make polite conversations with you."

Knud choked on his ale and burst into a coughing fit. Leif chuckled.

Hrólfr sat down again and took a sip. The cool liquid soothed his frantic thoughts.

"I suspect you will have to guard that sharp tongue of yours when Bérengar returns from wherever he is."

She lowered her gaze, her mouth drawn into a thin line.

He preferred her haughty, showing her spirit. But it was as he'd suspected. Her father had scolded her in public earlier today, and he was certain she would not forget it. And just where was his host?

At this moment, Pepin entered from the side door, followed by several thralls bearing trays of food. Gone was the tension in the room as men began to chat again. Food was the perfect distraction from the sight of a beautiful young woman.

At least, he hoped so. Casting a sideways glance at her, he knew he had to take responsibility for her. No one would dare touch the girl as long as she remained under his protection. That decided, he smiled as a thrall placed a tray with particularly succulent chunks of goose in front of him. The scent of rosemary, oregano and coriander teased his nostrils, and he helped himself to a large piece.

"Can I cut a slice for you?" he asked Poppa.

Her stomach rumbled in response, and she nodded. "Yes, please." The expression on her face – closed, enduring – belied her words. Poppa did not want to be here.

He swore under his breath as he handed her a juicy morsel which she gently pulled with trembling hands from his eating knife.

He sent her an encouraging nod, then turned away, as not to show her his annoyance. It was not directed at her, after all. Yes, she was blunt, and said what she thought. But despite himself, it was a character trait he appreciated. It was a far cry from her worm of a father, at whom he directed his growing anger.

What was the count playing at, having her serve them without his protective presence? If it were not for the high level of discipline Hrólfr demanded of his warriors, she would easily fall victim to any man's lusts. They pillaged monasteries and murdered men, but the one thing he did not allow his followers to indulge in was rape.

The few who, in the past, ignored his orders had swiftly felt his wrath – at his orders, they had been unmanned and left in the forest, bleeding and without a weapon. He hoped they would roam the earth forever, alive or dead, in perpetual pain.

Hrólfr took a bite of the fatty meat, whilst he scanned the room. Still no sign of Bérengar. His fury festered.

He must have a word with the man when he crossed his path.

***

Poppa forced herself to smile as Hrólfr gave her another large slice of goose. She'd realised she'd not eaten since breaking her fast early that morning, the worry about her friends too strong.

Every one of the men who'd been taken away she knew. They'd sold their wares at market or from their workshops, and many used to spend their evenings in the hall with her and Father, especially on feast days.

With the men gone, what happened to the wives and children now?

In her heart, she knew the answer. They would be kept as slaves. Women forced to become servants or even whores to their new masters.

Her thoughts returned to Ranulf. How would he find rowing? It was hard work. Weak men rarely survived the hardship on board. But he was strong. He'd cope. But could he adjust to a new life in the cold north? He was a Frank, used to living according to the seasons here in Neustria; not cut out to live on an island, exposed to the elements, so far away from home, in the coarse company of raiders.

No. An idea formed in her head. Perhaps if she sneaked out to where the prisoners were held, she might be able to free him? They could run away together, travel south, perhaps, out of reach of the Frankish king or the Northmen.

A new sense of hope surged through her. *I must try it.*

But how would she escape her duties? Beside her, Hrólfr was in deep conversation with Leif, Ranulf's master. As long as the men remained in the hall, she had a chance. Of course, there would be a guard with the boats and slaves, so she must move silently. The solid presence of her own knife, sheathed and tied to her belt, reassured her. She needed it in case Ranulf was bound.

The thought made her stomach queasy. Or did that come from the fat of the goose-meat?

Suddenly, she was no longer hungry.

From a nearby table, a man waved to Hrólfr's Shadow, Canute. No, Knud. That was his name. In her mind, she tried the different pronunciation. K-n-u-d. Poppa had sworn to learn the invaders' language, so she could overhear them. Already, she mastered many names, and a smattering of words.

Not that she'd dare tell anyone. It was her secret.

She startled when Knud addressed her.

"Excuse me, Lady Poppa, but you'll have to do without my presence as I'm wanted elsewhere." With a curt nod to her, not hiding his customary smirk which told her his apology was not meant seriously, he rose and joined his companions. It suited her well. One less to worry about where she was going…

More ale was served, and the noise in the hall grew louder. The strong scent wafted towards her, and she picked up her own cup, not wishing to have it refilled. Tonight, she needed a clear head.

When Hrólfr touched her arm, she jumped, almost spilling her ale. For once, his pale blue eyes were not icy, as so often. "Is everything in order, Lady Poppa?"

"Yes, of course." She straightened, pulling herself together. "I'm merely feeling a little tired."

He nodded. "I understand. It has been an eventful day for you."

Poppa knew exactly what he meant. The slave market. Had he realised how it affected her? Did he now try to…to what? Tell her all was well, after all?

She was about to counter when their gazes locked. The man was genuinely concerned.

Why has Father not shown such consideration?

"I know our customs are different from yours; it's plain to see. But you will get used to them. You won't be affected the way others are, so I can assure you nothing much will change for you."

"But my friends…" Furiously, she blinked back a stray tear.

"Your friends are a different story. You are the daughter of a count, a lady of importance. They are—"

"Of no consequence, yes." Her voice dripped with sarcasm, but she did not care. If he wanted to berate her again, so be it. But to her surprise he was merely watching her. Discomfited, she muttered, "What?"

The Northman leaned back, and a faint smile played on his lips. "Indeed, 'of no consequence'. I'm afraid you're right. It is the way of the world."

"Your world."

"Ah, but not only ours. Even you must have heard about

43

how the Franks treat anyone worshipping different gods. The skalds tell not only of the bravery of our warriors, but also of unspeakable massacres. Your men can be as cruel to those they conquer as my fellow warriors from the north. Surely, your priest would have told you, wouldn't he?" He raised an eyebrow in question as he looked at her over the rim of his drinking horn. Then he took a long draught.

Poppa blinked. Of course, tidings of battles and skirmishes often reached them. Were her own people truly as cruel as these wild Northmen?

He put the horn down in its stand and turned to face her. "Look. You may not like the way we do things, but I set strict rules. We may not spare prisoners, but during the attack on Bayeux no women were…ravished. Some may have been locked up, but if I hear any complaints about misbehaviour towards the women of your town, I will act."

"But what about the wives of those men you sent away? The mothers and daughters and sisters?"

Rape was a fate that awaited many women in these uncertain times. Did Hrólfr really have the power to stop his men from helping themselves?

He shrugged. "They may decide to ally themselves to the new owners of their lands. Several dozen men will remain here in Bayeux. They keep watch and are ready to defend their property, but more than anything, they want to settle; start a new life. Some women may prefer to join family members elsewhere, but others may decide that sharing the life of a miller or a blacksmith is not so bad. It is their choice."

"Thank you." She played with the embroidered rim of the sleeves. Oh, how she hated this gown. She felt like the men of Bayeux this afternoon – nude, gawped at. Although no one had actually touched her.

Feigning a yawn, Poppa gave a weary smile. "If you agree, I wish to retire now. There is no sign of Father, so I assume I must ask you, in his stead, for permission."

"Of course, Lady Poppa. I will have a word with your father when I see him next. He sends you out here to serve us, but without keeping you under his protection. You will be safe in your chamber, fear not."

Guilt nudged at her conscience at his friendly words. The stories she'd heard of other Northmen painted a very different image. No doubt, she would feel his ire when he discovered she'd freed Ranulf.

With a whispered, "Good night," Poppa rose and went to her chamber at the back of the hall.

Hooking the curtain in place on both sides, she breathed in deeply. Tonight was to be the beginning of a new life for her and Ranulf. She opened her clothes chest and dug out an old hose and tunic. They would be a tight fit, as she'd grown much since.

Wriggling into them, she cursed her breasts. The fabric covered them tightly. Oh, why could she not remain a child forever? The hose proved an easier fit, only a little shorter now her legs were longer. Finally, she slipped into the fur-lined winter boots.

Poppa looked down at herself and sniggered. Father would be mortified.

With a belt securely fastened around her waist, she stared at the deer bone handle of her knife for a moment. Then she filled a leather bag with coins and the few pieces of jewellery she owned. Father kept a chest in his room with her mother's rings and pendants made with precious stones, but it was always locked. There was no point wasting time. Her own few rings and bracelets, decorated with sparkling red garnets and amber, would not fetch that much, but it was a start. Finally, she shoved a simple linen gown into the bag and slung the strap over her shoulder.

She sent a longing glance at her gowns hanging from hooks on the wall, and a lump formed in her throat. Her life as it had been ended here.

"So be it," she whispered.

The dark-brown cloak she wrapped around her hid her hair and face. Poppa was convinced she would pass for a member of the household, or a servant, if spotted.

Extinguishing the candle, she left it on the small table

beside the bed then unhooked the curtain. The noise in the hall had grown further, and as she glanced towards the large room, she saw men standing in groups, chatting and drinking. The ale and mead did their work. Everyone was distracted.

Without another glance back, she strode purposefully to the back door. As she slid into the fresh air, she took a deep, shaky breath.

There was no going back.

Chapter Four

Bayeux, Neustria

The low, overhanging roof of the store house provided the shadow Poppa needed to plot her route to the shore. A muddy path led to the coast and then down to the beach where the boats lay moored. At least, she did not have to stumble through boggy terrain.

But the bright moonlight – whilst useful to keep her bearings – also spelt danger. Without doubt, Hrólfr left guards not only with the boats, but likely around the edge of town, too.

I must tread carefully.

Flitting, hunched over, from building to building, she stayed close to the walls. Here, all was quiet. The chill of the night air crept beneath her cloak, and she pulled it tighter around her shoulder and re-attached the clasp. The full moon had brought back the cold.

Ranulf would need a cloak, too! Last time she saw him, he was clad in his linen tunic, the fabric covered in blood. Poppa closed her eyes and hissed through clenched teeth. This was not going well.

They would have to steal clothes somewhere. Perhaps from his home? No, some Northman would be staying there. She huffed, the steam rising from her lips.

I'd better hurry.

The moonlight illuminated one side of the houses, so Poppa stayed in the shade. A short while later, she neared the open field, where the path towards the sea veered off. To her dismay, the track, flanked by grass on both sides, was flooded with light. Here were no buildings to hide behind, and she was certain guards were lurking somewhere.

Voices rose nearby, and she slid deeper beneath the overhanging roof at the back of the last house. She was so close; not ready to give up now.

Laughter reached her, and soon two Northmen passed mere yards from her hiding place. The watch, clearly doing a round. The men stopped at the path, scanning the area around them, axes in hand. The metal glinted in the moonlight. Of them glanced in her direction, but then turned away.

Poppa was grateful for her dark cloak. Slowly, she released her held breath.

Moments later, the guards walked back into town, and their voices soon faded. She kept wait until her feet tingled from standing still. Eventually, she peeked around the corner. The street was deserted. Shutters were closed, and she only heard muffled sounds from inside the houses. No one would venture out voluntarily on a chilly night like this.

Except me.

Without hesitation, she walked as silently as she could on the grass beside the path towards the sea. The clear air would carry any sounds, so she should be careful, even with the guards out of sight.

After several hundred yards, she turned around, but the field was empty. She'd not been spotted. Relief washed through her, and she took a few deep breaths.

Stars shimmered in the clear sky, and the moon bathed the meadow and the first reeds in a warm glow. Just another few hundred yards, and she would be approaching the coastline.

That would prove the trickiest part.

"Get there first," she whispered to herself. Then she set off again.

When she reached the edge of the cliffs, she stopped at the point where the trail veered off, weaving its way down towards the sea. Crouching, she shuffled to the edge and peered over it.

Off the shore, a dozen longships lay moored, their carved prows dipping gently up and down with the undulating movement of the sea. On the beach, two large fires burnt brightly, and at least a half a dozen Northmen sat clustered around each, their voices drifting up in the breeze.

Christ's Blood, they were all still awake! Closing her eyes briefly, Poppa berated herself. Of course they would be. They were watching the ships. But surely, some of them would go to sleep, leaving a small number of men to do the actual guarding. But it was too early. She would have to find a hiding place and wait.

I hope Father won't be looking for me.

Where did they keep the slaves? Her eyes adjusted to the light, she searched the wide beach and finally spotted a cluster of shadows huddled together on the sand. Anger rose within her. Were the poor men of Bayeux not given covers? They'd be of no use to their new masters if they fell ill. She huffed.

But at least Ranulf must be amongst them. The bad tidings were that the two campfires lay between the path and the group. She may be able to smuggle one man past whoever stayed awake, but not all of them.

Her heart sank. If she approached Ranulf, others might wake. And could she really leave the rest of them behind?

It seemed she had no choice. But first, she was in for a long wait. Poppa retreated from the edge and looked around. Grass and reeds covered the rocky ground.

As she turned, a light in the distance caught her eye. At that moment, the sky began to cloud over. That light was not a star. It was moving.

A torch. No, at least two, or even more.

"Leif must be returning already," she muttered, annoyed. Could he not get drunk in the hall and fall asleep there?

Clearly not. The flickering lights came closer.

She had to get away from the path, well out of sight. Swiftly, she scrambled along the top of the cliff, staying clear of the edge. Poppa had no intention of falling to her death.

Eventually, she spotted a larger rock and crouched behind it. Here, she was safely out of reach of the torchlight.

Now voices reached her, cheerful, joking. The sound of laughter drifted over the countryside. Relieved that the clouds had moved over the moon, plunging her hiding place in full darkness, she dared peek.

As expected, Leif and several of his men made their way to the cliff edge. Torn between swearing at his untimely arrival and rejoicing that neither Hrólfr nor Father were with them, she watched as the Northman stood at the top of the path, shouting something in their strange tongue. A raucous reply came from the beach.

Forming a line, the men made their way down. Soon, their voices mingled with those of the guards below. There would be no sleep for any of them soon.

Poppa sighed.

With no moonlight, traipsing around near the edge of the cliffs was too dangerous. The rock also served as protection; in case they sent a guard up. She leaned her back against the stone. The hard, uneven ground beneath her dug into her bottom. It would be a long wait.

Closing her eyes, she deeply breathed in the fresh sea air.
Just for a moment…

Poppa woke with a start. Disoriented, she banged her head against the rock.

"Ow!" Quickly, her hand covered her mouth when she realised where she was. The moon stood high in the sky; the clouds having disappeared. No voices reached her ears.

Wondering how long she'd been asleep, she rose and stretched. Gingerly, she felt the spot where her head had hit the stone. A small lump was already forming. Gritting her teeth, she waited until her eyes adjusted to the light. Then she slowly walked back to the top of the path where she crouched down to peek over the edge.

Now, only one fire remained lit. Three men sat by it, talking so quietly, she could not hear them. Dying embers showed where the other fire had been. Several shapes nestled around it, not moving. The remainder of the beach lay in darkness.

Ahead, on one ship, a lit torch showed someone aboard. It must be Leif. Was he still awake, preparing for his long journey? He'd seemed the responsible type.

He is still a slave trader!

Despite the bright moonlight, Poppa had to try and descend the path down to the beach. If darkness returned, any attempt would be foolish. She would likely fall and break her neck.

So if I stay close to the ground, they might not spot me.

A glance behind her gave reassurance that no more men came from town. Bent forward, she began to weave her way down carefully, but the steep drop made it difficult. Several times, she slid on stones, sending them rolling over the edge and cascading onto the sand. Pressed against the shrubs, she watched as the guards glanced around. The second time it happened, one of the men rose and walked to the bottom of the path, looking up.

Poppa leaned deep into the rocks. Her breathing stopped when the guard walked up a few yards. Fortunately, she was still too far up. When he shrugged and returned to his companions, she let out a slow breath. For what seemed like an eternity, she dared not move.

Then the moon slid behind a cloud and the world went dark.

Shuffling her way down the path on her bottom, Poppa reached the beach. But as she stepped on the sand, the Northmen's voices carried clearly to her. She hid in the shadow of the rocks and slid towards where the men of Bayeux lay asleep. Here, out of sight of the fire's light, she was able to search for Ranulf without being seen. Once the moon, which had reappeared, was obscured again!

The silence grated on her nerves. Even the guards were quiet.

Craning her neck, she tried to distinguish the sleeping men from her hiding place, but it was hopeless. How could she wake Ranulf without rousing everyone else? Once the men started to mumble, the guards would hear them.

No, it was too much of a risk.

After what felt like an eternity, a large cloud covered the moon. Poppa did not lose any time.

In several large strides, she rushed across the soft sand that

51

swallowed up her footsteps. Crouching on all fours, she passed the sleeping men one by one.

Where was Ranulf? Fear gripped her heart.

What if he was held on the ship? Biting her lip, she silently admonished herself. One step at a time.

She neared the end of the row when she spotted him, the second last. He looked so peaceful. Poppa reached out her hand and gently touched his cheek. In his sleep, he tried to swat it away with a grunt, like an obtrusive fly.

"Ranulf," she whispered, poking him harder.

He raised his head, then stared at her. "Poppa?"

"Shh!" A finger held to her lips, she pointed at the guards with her other hand.

His head swivelled from the Northmen to her and back. Then he nodded and slid a little across the sand towards her but stopped before he reached her. "What are you doing here?" His voice, so low, was hoarse.

Was he not pleased to see her?

"I've come to rescue you."

His eyes widened. "You have what?" Rolling on his front, he faced her. "Are you mad?"

Poppa let out a long breath. "Of course I'm not. Come, we must leave before they hear us."

"I can't."

"What? Why not?"

He pointed at his hands and feet. "We're all tied together."

With dismay, Poppa realised he was right. His hands were bound in front of him. A thicker rope connected him to the men on either side. Ranulf's feet were hidden beneath a grimy blanket.

She knelt by his head. An anxious glance towards the fire confirmed that the guards had not spotted her. They remained close to the fire.

"I can free you," she whispered and withdrew her knife from its sheath.

Eyes wide, never leaving her face, Ranulf stretched out his hands.

Slowly, she cut through the bindings, not wishing to nick

his skin. But the rope, thin as it was, was sturdy, and she huffed with the effort.

"You're doing well, Poppa. The guards haven't moved. But hurry." Ranulf's warm voice was barely a whisper.

She nodded, concentrating on the sawing. Finally, his hands were freed. She gave him the knife, and he leant forward to untie his feet. But those ropes seemed even tighter, and he quietly cursed under his breath as he slid the knife back and forth. When the rope moved, the prisoners began to stir in their sleep.

Please, God, don't let them wake.

But it was too late. The man on Ranulf's left, a merchant if she remembered correctly, raised his head. Then he sat up, staring at them. "What are you doing?" he blurted out.

"Shh!" Poppa raised her finger to her lips, her heart sinking.

Already, the man on Ranulf's other side rubbed his eyes. When he recognised her, he frowned. "Lady Poppa."

This was not going to plan.

"I'm done, Poppa. Come!" Knife in hand, Ranulf moved away from the others.

But could she leave the men who were watching her? Would they even let them escape, knowing their own fate was sealed?

The merchant crawled towards her. "Give me that knife!" His voice was too loud in the silence, and a cry went up from the guards.

A sense of dread shot through Poppa.

Chapter Five

The coast near Bayeux, Neustria

"Quick, Poppa. We must run!"

Staring in terror at the sight of the advancing warriors, her limbs felt like rocks. When the snarling Northmen drew their swords, her body began to shake. Their warning shouts cut alerted the others.

"Christ's Bones, Poppa! If you don't come, I'll go alone." Ranulf swore under his breath. "So be it." Still carrying her knife, he hurried past her but halted when the guards moved to cut him off. Turning on his heel, he ran the other way.

Unable to move, tears filled her eyes when he scrambled towards a steeper rabbit path up the cliffs. It was unsafe. Her heart pounded loud in her chest.

The merchant swore. Following his gaze, she saw other warriors gather their weapons.

A cry went up. "Halt!"

But Ranulf kept scurrying along the beach. Moments later, he reached the narrow track.

Two guards rushed past her, their faces contorted in anger, but the third grabbed her by the arm and twisted it against her back, nearly dislocating her shoulder.

"Ow! Let me go, you oaf!" Poppa tried to kick his shin, but he was too experienced to fall for it, holding her close. "Ranulf, run!"

Cold metal was pressed against her exposed neck. She gasped. A trickle of blood escaped the nick the sharp blade cut on her skin. She dared not breathe.

"Hey, Ranulf!" The man holding her shouted in broken Frankish. "If you value this bitch's life, you get your scrawny arse over here."

"You wouldn't harm the daughter of Count Bérengar." Ranulf's voice sounded strained as it carried down to them.

"Ha, are you sure? I could always have some fun while she bleeds to death. Your choice."

Several warriors followed the first two who also started the ascent. A dozen of them, the metal of their axes gleaming in the moonlight, formed a ring around the slaves.

Poppa glared at the merchant, but his eyes were downcast. If it had not been for him, Ranulf would have been safe by now. Tears welled in her eyes.

"You wouldn't dare," Ranulf retorted. "She's of value. Your leader would have your head."

The man laughed and tightened his grip on her arm. A shot of pain surged through her, and she yelped.

"Well, I wouldn't have to kill her right away, that's true. I could just break a bone here and there…" He pulled her arm higher up her back, and she screamed. "Do you think she'll enjoy that? Bone by bone."

The moonlight illuminated Ranulf standing on a ledge jutting out from the cliff face, watching them. His shoulders slumped.

Poppa's hope crashed to the ground. *Don't give up!* But she did not find the voice to say it out loud.

The sound of oars dipping in the water reached them. A groan escaped her. More Northmen were coming over from the ships.

Everything had been in vain. Only now, they were angered – and might take their fury out on Ranulf. And perhaps on her.

Her throat went dry.

"Don't listen to them, Ranulf," she croaked. "They won't hurt me."

But her friend hesitated, allowing the warriors to get closer to him.

"Come down here now, you son of a bitch! Do you really think you can escape us?" Leif called out. He stopped beside her. Pointing to the clifftop, he added, "Some of my men are already waiting for you. Look up."

Unable to move, she said, "Why can't you let him stay? He's still so young."

Leif grinned, then crossed his arms in front of him. "And that's the very reason." Turning to her captor, he said, "Let her go. The boy will see sense, or he'll learn to fly when we catch up with him."

Poppa drew in a sharp breath. "You would not dare!" She rubbed her sore elbow, then carefully wriggled her shoulder, relieved to move it. Tears rolled down her face when Ranulf was caught and forced down the steep slope. He landed on the sand on his hands and feet, and the guards dragged him along the beach until they threw him before Leif.

"Ranulf!" She lunged at his heaving body, but her captor caught her wrist and pulled her back.

"He carried this." One guard held up a knife.

"It's mine," Poppa hissed. "Give it to me."

Leif took it and regarded it. "It is a fine piece. I may keep it."

"No! It was my late mother's."

The old warrior stared at her. "You should've thought of that before you came out here, trying to save your lover."

Heat shot into her cheeks. "He's not my lover; he is a friend. That's not something you'd understand."

"Oh, but I do." Leif chuckled. "That's why I know how important it is to have friends."

"What should we do with him?" asked one guard, his foot firmly pressed on Ranulf's back, keeping him prone on the sand.

"Hmm." Leif's gaze swept from Ranulf to Poppa and back. "I think it's time this young woman here learns a what it means to deceive us."

"What?" Ranulf cried, then spat out a mouthful of sand.

Poppa panicked, blinking back the blackness that threatened to overwhelm her. "What do you mean?"

A cold green gaze met hers. "You tried to free a thrall who is rightfully mine. That requires punishment."

Poppa straightened her back. She would not be intimidated by him. "You have no right to take him away from home. Nor any of these men." She pointed at the group from Bayeux who now all sat up, watching in fearful silence.

"Be quiet, woman! And be glad I'm not going to punish you, although, by Thor's might, you deserve it." Leif glared at her, then turned to his guards. "Bind his hands behind him, then give him a good beating." He paused and held up a hand as his men grinned. "Not too badly, mind, as he needs to work the oars in the morning. I don't want to waste food on him if he gets sick."

To the sound of snorts and moans, the men set to task.

"No!" Ranulf wriggled but his hands were pulled roughly behind his back and tied up securely. "Leave me alone!" But four Northmen already dragged him to the water's edge, then pushed him down.

Poppa stared in shock. "What—"

"You come with me." Leif pulled her towards the path. "Hrólfr won't be pleased with your behaviour, nor will your father." He issued orders for an escort of two warriors; one guiding them up the cliff with a torch, the other at the rear.

She climbed between Leif and the last man, trying not to stop and look. Ranulf's cries followed her all the way up – a tortuous climb in semi-darkness. She hitched up her gown to get better foothold, ignoring Leif's raised eyebrows at her tunic and hose peeking out from beneath. Her focus on the rocks, she could not allow herself to be distracted. Still, it was difficult to see with tears streaming down her face.

It's all my fault.

How had she expected to trick these ruthless conquerors? They'd certainly seen it all before. As she let the misery flow through her, she realised Ranulf's fate was sealed. Never would she see him again; roam the fields together in the summer sun; laugh at his silly jests.

He's not jesting now.

She prayed to God that his punishment was not too severe if Leif wanted him to row in a few hours. But it brought her no consolation.

At the top of the cliff, Leif paused to let her regain her breath. The Northmen were unfazed by the strenuous climb.

Poppa brushed off the dust from her hose, unhitched her dress, then wrapped her cloak firmly around her.

"You've wasted much of my time tonight, Lady Poppa. Let's get you home quickly."

"And Ranulf?" she whispered.

"You don't give up, do you?" Leif scoffed. "If you weren't Count Bérengar's daughter, I'd be of a mind to take you with us. We always have use of feisty women."

***

Hrólfr leaned forward, elbows on the trestle table, cradling his drinking horn. Following Leif's departure, many had begun to leave the hall. His friend was popular, and the split in the camp made everyone morose.

Not even the skáld could lift the mood. Hrólfr waved him away. The young man nodded, then wrapped his lyre into a cloth before placing it into a large leather bag. For a moment, Hrólfr wondered if the skáld preferred to go to Orkneyjar, but he'd stayed without a word following his brisk farewell from Leif.

Knud, who had been sitting with some of his own men, joined Hrólfr on the dais. Grabbing a pitcher, he refilled their drinking horns. "It's not like you to be so broody, my friend."

Hrólfr shrugged. "I'm not broody. I'm watching."

"Anyone in particular?" Knud's gaze slid across the room. "No."

"I was right." His companion of many winters grinned. "You are truly cheerful tonight."

He sighed and sat back, stretching his legs under the table. "If you must know, I'm concerned about Bérengar's disappearance. I haven't seen him since the afternoon. He's plotting something."

"The count? One of the men said they saw him with the new Churchman. The replacement for the one we killed."

Hrólfr's mind was whirling. What could the scheming count have to discuss with a priest? Then a thought occurred to him.

Of course! Was that the reason Poppa had to wear her best gown tonight? To appeal to him? "Well, well. I have my suspicions, Knud, that the backboneless oaf is plotting my demise."

"Your demise?" Knud's eyebrows rose sharply. "He means to have you killed…by a monk?"

Hrólfr laughed. "No. They're too squeamish, these followers of the one God. They can't handle blood." His body shook with mirth until he recovered his composure. "It's something else these men do. Like…a ceremony."

Knud snorted. "You mean he wants you to wed his daughter?" Then he grew serious. "Hm. It would make sense, though. I say it again."

"She's too young, Knud. Barely fourteen winters, to my twenty-eight."

"The girl seems mature for her age."

"She had to, given her mother died when she was young. It's her duty to look after the hall."

"The perfect wife, then." Knud grinned. "A comely figure, adept at running a household, pretty to look at."

"Don't get carried away," Hrólfr said sharply, then shrugged. "Regardless of all that, I still find her too young. Also, I don't want to be tied down. We're leaving for Rouen soon. I want to subdue Rouen and settle there. A wife requires too much attention. Especially one as opinionated as Poppa…"

Knud took a draught of his ale, then cocked his head. "But you have to admit, a union makes sense. She is your way into Frankish society. An important step to consolidate our influence here in Neustria."

He nodded, reluctantly coming round to Knud's idea. "It doesn't make it any more appealing, though. I'm used to my freedom."

"And who says you can't have it? You can leave her in Bayeux until we've set up our base at Rouen. By then she'll be old enough to follow."

"Still…" Thoughts were warring with each other. Hrólfr knew a marriage would be advantageous, but he was used to living his own life, without commitment and responsibility other than to his men. A wife, and perhaps children, were something entirely different. "We shall see. Perhaps he's looking for penance – something else these Franks seem keen on doing all the time."

Knud grinned. "True. So it's as well that our fate is woven by the Norns. That way, we don't have to worry about the guilt these Christ followers are so keen to carry."

Hrólfr agreed. He touched the Thor's hammer amulet at his neck. It was made of whalebone and tied with a leather thong. Åsa had made it for him after he'd lost his late mother's pendant. "Yes. I'm content to live without all that guilt. And—"

A commotion at the entrance made them both look up.

"Ha!" Knud chuckled. "There he is, Bérengar."

Hrólfr glared. "Hmm. And he looks mightily pleased with himself." His heart sank when the count waved to him, as he made his way to the dais.

His drinking horn in hand, Knud rose and patted Hrólfr's shoulder. A smirk played on his lips. "I'll leave you to it."

He sighed, then watched as the count took a cup of wine from Pepin. Then he came over and settled in the chair vacated by Knud. "Bérengar. Your absence was noted tonight." There was no point wasting time with what the Frank called polite conversation.

"Lord Rouf." Bérengar took a few sips, then put his cup down. He smiled.

The hairs on Hrólfr's neck rose. Everything about the count was false, his smile most of all. He almost felt sorry for Poppa, having such a worm for a father. He met the older man's gaze evenly but said nothing.

"Where is my daughter?" The count looked behind him where Pepin and another thrall stood waiting. "I cannot see her."

"She has retired for the night."

"Ah, perhaps 'tis as well. I, um, wanted to speak with you, my lord. In private." Bérengar's voice was barely a whisper.

Hrólfr let his gaze roam the hall. There were only the few

of them seated on the dais. Most of the warriors were settled at their tables, talking quietly in small groups. The rest had already left to retire to their quarters. "I dare say this is as private as you can get, Bérengar. What is it you wish to discuss?"

"I have been thinking, Lord Rouf."

Hrólfr sent him a dark glance. He hated to be called 'lord', and even more combined with this mispronunciation of his name. Was it deliberate? He knew not. Again, he remained quiet.

Bérengar shuffled in his seat, then ran a hand through his sparse hair. "I...well, with you now commanding Bayeux and the coastline here, I thought we could, well, come to an agreement."

"Why would I need an agreement with you if I – as you pointed out so correctly – am in command of the town?"

"'Tis one that benefits you...and me, yes. Me too. You see, I was talking to Father Godefroi...who has taken over our church duties."

Hrólfr smirked. "Where did you find him so quickly?" Leif's band had raided a small monastery several miles inland the day before, and he wondered if the conveniently appointed priest was a monk who'd fled prior to Leif's arrival.

· "That is of no concern to you." Bérengar bristled, then added, "my lord."

"I told you not to call me lord, Bérengar. Unlike you, I don't hold such titles in much esteem."

"But you are our new overlord – apart from the king, of course. The king still rules over us all."

He laughed. "Does he? I've yet to receive word of him coming to your aid."

Bérengar's face turned puce.

Still chuckling, Hrólfr leaned forward. "I'm aware that you sent messengers, requesting help. Don't expect any! That weasel of a king won't come to your aid. He has enough problems of his own."

The count averted his eyes, then lifted his cup with a

shaky hand and took a sip.

Content to have rattled the worm, Hrólfr relaxed again, slinging his arm over the back of his chair, half-turning towards the man. "I'm still at a loss as to what kind of agreement you were going to propose, Bérengar. Spit it out!"

The count swallowed, then took a deep breath.

"As I said... I have spoken with Father Godefroi, and he agrees. To keep the peace in Bayeux, I'm willing to strike a bargain with you. That would ensure you our goodwill and give us our quiet life back."

Hrólfr sighed loudly. "Don't make me ask you again, or you'll find your new priest strung up by his feet and tied to the rafters, for my men to play with as they see fit." He glared at Bérengar, getting bored of the matter.

"I'm offering my daughter to you." The words escaped in a tumble. "Poppa."

So Knud had been right. A political union. Although Hrólfr had his doubts about Bérengar's goodwill. The scheming count would break any word if he could, regardless of his daughter's fate.

Hrólfr's experience of men like Bérengar taught him always to expect surprises. Like a knife in the back. He grimaced.

"Let me understand your thoughts. You want me to wed your daughter, so that your life here continues as before."

"Yes, and to confirm your status as our conqu— um, overlord. My fellow Franks will have no choice but to accept you."

"They don't anyway." Hrólfr grinned. "I can act as I wish already, and there's nothing you can do about it."

Bérengar squirmed in his seat, then sent him a sly glance. "Is my daughter not to your liking?"

The man could outwit Loki! "That is not the question, Bérengar." Hrólfr growled. "The lady Poppa is pretty, but also very young. She's half my age, if I'm right."

"Many girls marry that young, and I know that she is a woman in every sense of the word." Bérengar gave a conspiratory nod. "Ready for childbearing, too."

The implication was too much. "I like women to be of a certain age, not with one foot in their cradle, Bérengar!"

"Then you could still wed her now but leave her here in Bayeux until she is of an age that's acceptable to you, Lord Rouf, whilst you go…exploring the coast."

Hrólfr's anger welled up. The man was selling his daughter like a cow. No, worse. Like a piece of meat. He wondered what the lady herself thought of that. 'Twas a shame she'd gone to bed.

On second thought, Knud had made a valid point. A marriage to a Frankish count's daughter would validate his reason to stay and pursue his strategy in Neustria. His plan was to seize Rouen and set up his base there. The town was at a strategic location, unlike tiny Bayeux. The girl could follow when he considered her old enough.

He took several deep breaths until his initial fury had subsided. "And how would you like me to do that? No marriage is accepted until husband and wife have clearly shared a bed, and I refuse to do so with one so young."

"That would be a minor issue. Our priest has said that, in our church, with holy blessing, you—"

"Wait a moment!" Hrólfr held up a hand. "What blessing? Any monk who comes near me will be a dead monk."

The count sat up, his eyes widening. "There cannot be a wedding without a blessing by Holy Mother Church."

Hrólfr removed an imaginary speck of dirt from his sleeve, a smile playing on his lips. "Then, I'm afraid, I'll have to reject your offer."

Bérengar paled. He emptied his cup and put it down with a shaky hand.

Was the man afraid? Why was he so nervous?

The count looked at him. "How else would you get married? You're a Pagan."

"By handfasting; a promise on oath that binds husband and wife together."

"But in that case, Poppa would not be properly wed. No, I…" Bérengar mumbled something to himself that Hrólfr could not catch. Then he fell silent.

Regarding the matter closed, Hrólfr rose. "If that is all, I shall bid you goodnight. I must check on the guards." He stretched, his bones cracking after the long evening in the chair.

"No, wait!" Bérengar's voice sounded desperate. "Please." He stood, too, but took a step back when Hrólfr pulled himself up to his full height.

The weasel was afraid of him. Good. He grinned. "What?"

"I agree. A handfasting ceremony, but on the steps of the Church…if that would be acceptable you."

"I don't care where, as long as it's not *inside* any church."

What was he doing? He did not need a wife! There was still time to back out of the situation.

"Then we have an agreement, Lord Rouf?"

The trap sprung closed. Hrólfr swore under his breath, but he could not deny the political advantage of having a Frankish wife, even if it was under his own rules.

"Yes, we do, Bérengar. When do you want to tell her the good tidings?" The corner of his mouth quirked.

"Why, straight away, I thought." The count turned towards the back of the hall, but Hrólfr grabbed his upper arm.

"No word to anyone but Poppa tonight, Bérengar. Not even to your monk."

"Priest."

"Whatever you call him, I don't care. We shall make the announcement on the morrow and hold the handfasting the day after. Everyone will then gather that night for a feast, before I leave."

"Of course…you shall have your feast."

"And Poppa hers."

"And Poppa, yes. I will tell her now."

"Then I bid you good night, Bérengar. And good luck!"

He chuckled as he stepped off the dais and walked towards the door. The girl's screams would probably be heard across the sleeping town. She would not take the prospect kindly.

As he was about to step outside, he heard his name called. With a sigh, he turned. The man really was becoming annoying.

Hrólfr could not wait to be away from Bayeux. "What is it now?"

Bérengar rushed towards him and grabbed his arm. "She's gone."

"What do you mean, gone?" He frowned.

Poppa had bid him goodnight and disappeared through the screen into the private rooms.

"She's not in her chamber."

"Perhaps she followed a call of nature." He shrugged, his hand on the door.

"No, she can't have done." The count's voice rose in panic. "Her boots and cloak are missing."

"Then go search for her, Bérengar. Would she not wear them to the pits? It's cold out there. I'm not wed to her yet, so she is still your problem, not mine." Hrólfr pushed open the door, but even as he spoke the words, he knew he would not rest until the girl was found.

Had she been abducted?

He stepped outside and drew in the chilly air. All was calm.

Bérengar was on his heel, arms flailing.

Hrólfr rolled his eyes. "Don't you want to send someone to check the pits before we end running around for nothing?"

The count poked his head back inside and called for a thrall to go, then looked around as if she was to appear from out of nowhere.

"What happened, Hrólfr?" Knud reached his side, a look of concern on his face. "Is something amiss?"

"Yes, the lady Poppa has disappeared."

"But we would've seen her…"

"She could have used the door at the back."

"True."

"What?" He stared at Knud.

"Well, earlier tonight one of the men mentioned a figure leaving through the back door. He thought it was someone from the household." Knud ruffled his hair.

Hrólfr nodded. "That could have been her."

"My daughter would not go out at night, unaccompanied."

"Are you sure?"

The thrall returned, a frown on his face. "My lord, there is no sign of the lady Poppa near the pits."

Bérengar sent the young man to search their quarters again, then stared at Hrólfr. "If she did not leave of her own accord, she must have been taken. One of your men—"

Hrólfr rounded on him. "My men have strict instructions to leave your daughter – and all the women of Bayeux – in peace. I don't want you going round accusing any of them." He was seething. But he also could not shake of a sense of concern. Had something befallen her? "We must search the town. Knud, get the…"

Lost for words, he stared at two figures approaching the hall, followed by another two.

Leif and…Poppa, and two warriors.

"Let go of my daughter, you beast!" Bérengar rushed forward and pulled his daughter away from Leif.

The Northman was in fits of laughter. "With pleasure. She's nothing but trouble, this one."

"What have you done to her?" The count glared at the men, then looked the girl up and down. "Has he hurt you, Poppa?" His fingers grabbed her chin, and she wriggled from his grasp.

"*You* are hurting me, Father. And no, he has not." Her head held high, she folded her arms.

"Then what is this?" Bérengar waved her company.

Leif grew serious. "*This* is your troublesome daughter attempting to free one of our thralls."

"What? She would never do such a thing. No, you must be mistaken."

Hrólfr ignored the confused count, instead watching Poppa closely. Her expression had changed from arrogance to… fear? "Who did you want to save, Poppa?" he asked quietly.

She merely sent him a sharp glance but stayed silent. Her mouth formed a thin line, but her eyes were damp. The girl had been crying.

"Leif?"

"The same lad she was so enraged about this afternoon."

"Ranulf?" Bérengar hissed. "You embarrass me by going after the miller's son?"

The slap the count gave her sent her reeling, and Leif caught her before she fell backwards, allowing her to regain her balance. She held a hand on her cheek. "Ranulf is my friend, and I love him."

Hrólfr shook his head as laughter welled up inside him. "So you took it upon yourself to release him? And then what? Where would you have gone?"

Poppa glared at him. "South. Far away from you and your murderous men."

"Poppa, be quiet!"

Bérengar lifted his arm to strike her again, but this time Hrólfr expected the move. He grabbed the man's wrist and held him in place.

"Stop hitting your daughter, Bérengar. Can't you see she's been through a lot tonight already?"

"She certainly has." Leif tutted. "The stupid girl could have broken her neck on the cliffs. I could have fed her to my men, or to the waves." His voice held no anger.

"Thank you for bringing her back, Leif. Her father was fraught with worry for her."

The count stared at him.

"It's alright, Hrólfr. We've all been the lady Poppa's age; we've all taken risks. Fortunately for me, her attempt failed. I still have my rower."

"But you had Ranulf beaten!" Tears streamed down Poppa's face.

"I'm afraid it's what he deserved for running away, lady. He'd have left you with us if we hadn't threatened you."

"You would not have dared to hurt me." Her glance was challenging Leif, and Hrólfr suppressed a laugh. Distraught or not, this young woman had courage.

Leif met her gaze, then bowed. "You are right. I wouldn't have done anything to harm you. But then, Ranulf didn't know that…" He turned to Hrólfr. "Now I must bid you farewell. This little adventure has delayed my preparations for our departure."

They clasped arms as Hrólfr nodded. "Safe travels, my friend."

After Leif and his warriors were gone, Poppa stared at her feet.

"What do you think you were doing, daughter? Running away with the miller's son!"

"Don't be so harsh on her, Bérengar. She is back here, safe, and Ranulf will head to Orkneyjar in the morning. They will never see each other again." He was surprised he felt sorry for her, but she showed more loyalty towards her friends than her father had done. "Now you best retire, Lady Poppa. You've had an eventful evening."

"Thank you, Hrólfr." To his surprise, she sent him a grateful glance. He liked the way she tried to say his name correctly.

"Not so fast, Poppa." Bérengar grabbed her arm. "I was searching for you to share some important tidings when we noticed you were gone."

Hrólfr winced, seeing her startled look. "Bérengar, I don't think it's wise now, under the circumstances." They'd had enough upheaval for one night.

"I disagree. In fact, there is no better time." The count raised his chin, looking down his narrow nose at her. "You see, dear daughter, you have a great life ahead of you."

"Do I? How?" She frowned, and Hrólfr thought she was right to be wary.

"You will be wed the day after tomorrow."

Hrólfr wished himself anywhere but here at this moment. Behind him, Knud gasped.

"What? To whom?" To no one's surprise, her voice shook.

Bérengar stepped back with a wide smile. "Well, you may wish goodnight to your husband-to-be, Poppa. You shall be Hrólfr's wife. Are you not fortunate?"

The gleam in the man's eyes made Hrólfr want to punch him. He clenched his fists, then unclenched them. Nothing good would come of it.

Full of ambition, Bérengar clearly wanted an alliance with him, even though he was a Pagan in the Christian's eyes.

But as Knud had said, such an alliance made sense. It gave him a sense of Frankish respectability.

Yes, as much as it galled him, this marriage served his purpose too.

"I'll be what? Wed to this…this… No, never! I'd rather die!" Without another word, Poppa ran into the hall, slamming the door shut behind her.

"Well done, Bérengar!" His voice dripped with sarcasm. Hrólfr glared at the count. Why did the bastard have to make his daughter's night even more miserable than what it already was?

"Knud, come with me. We must check on the guards." Hrólfr had to walk away from the odious man before he did something he might regret.

Chapter Six

The next morning
Bayeux, Neustria

"Poppa?" A female voice drifted through the curtain, followed by a gentle knock on the partition. "Are you awake?"

Poppa blinked, confused for a moment. Then the memories of last night returned. She yawned, as she watched the curtain twitch.

Having unhooked the tie from the outside, Landina slid into the small room and secured it again. "You are!" Despite tears glistening in her dark eyes, she smiled widely as she rushed over to Poppa's bed and clasped her hand. "Thank you for trying to save Ranulf." Her brown hair made her face appear paler than it likely was, but the pallor in her friend's face could easily seem worse in the dim light of her chamber.

Poppa's own eyes welled up, and she rubbed them with the back of her hand. She did not want to cry in front of her friend whose brother she could not help. "Don't thank me, Landina. I failed."

"You didn't fail, Poppa. You tried your best. The whole town is in awe of your courage. I am." Landina swallowed hard. Lowering her gaze to the floor, she added, "I never even thought about it. I...I didn't think I would succeed."

Poppa huffed, then sat up, extracting her hand from her friend's clasp. "I thought I could, but the other men woke and wanted me to free them too." Now she let her tears roll. It did not matter if Landina saw them. "If we'd been quieter, we may have escaped. But when they caught Ranulf, they..." she hiccupped, "...they beat him. And it was all my fault."

Landina sat on the edge of the bed and wrapped her into

her arms. "Hush, Poppa. None of this is your fault. If anyone's to blame, it's the Northmen who attack our peaceful lands. These marauders take what they want and leave only death and misery behind."

The venom in Landina's voice made Poppa feel uncomfortable. Had her friend not heard the other tidings?

"Thank you." She extracted herself, changing the subject. It was better not to dwell too long on last night's events. "So much has happened, and we were not prepared. Father was remiss in fortifying the town." Laying the blame at his feet helped her a little. She sighed. "How did you fare? I have not seen you since…"

Since the day before the attack.

Landina stood and adjusted her gown. Then she paced the small room, her fingers interlinking. "Easter morning, Father found several sacks of grain slashed, so we had to help him gather it together. Then we heard the screams. He told me to stay with the other women and…got his sword from under his bed and…and left to see what was going on. Ranulf went with him."

"Were you safe?" Poppa sent Landina a nervous glance. Whilst she – as a count's daughter – had been under protection, she had no inkling how other women fared, apart from the rumours she'd heard. Apparently, no women were harmed; something she could scarcely believe.

Landina nodded. "Yes. To our horror, we were all ushered together into the small church near the mill. You can imagine the panic." She sighed. "Then their leader arrived and told us that our fathers and brothers and husbands were either killed or taken as slaves. They'd laid out the dead behind the barn and we were allowed, in small groups, to go and identify them. Father's body was there." A sad smile played on her lips, but she kept her composure. "I saw no injury to his face, and he looked so peaceful. Then they dumped them all into one large pit." She glowered and rubbed her arms.

"Oh, Landina, I am so sorry. Father did not let me leave the hall until yesterday when we walked in on their slave market." She shuddered. "That's where I saw Ranulf."

Her friend sat again, taking her hands. "You did a very brave thing, trying to save him. I'd have rejoiced had you and Ranulf fled. But, alas, it was God's will that my brother travel to the north with the heathens. He must have plans for him."

"Hmm." Poppa had her own opinion about a God who permitted such treatment of honest folk, and it was not as accepting as her friend's. Nor did she consider Ranulf wanting to spread the word of the one true God.

"He will return one day." Landina nodded, too vigorously.

Poppa kept her doubts to herself. Although Ranulf was young and strong, the journey was arduous, and his life as a slave likely full of backbreaking work, little food and poor shelter. She'd seen some households in Bayeux treat their servants little better than dogs, but until now, it had not really concerned her. But after the last few days, she'd learnt a lot about the realities of life; and none of them were positive.

Perhaps she never wanted to know how those less fortunate fared. Her home was warm, dry, clean; she held the keys to the hall and the larder. Well, she did until Hrólfr told her to relinquish them to Pepin.

Her friend chatted on. "The leader allowed several of the men to stay, such as the smith. I guess their skills are useful. Many homes have been given to the attackers, who apparently want to settle here, and several newly widowed women decided to share their hearths with them. Can you imagine?" Anger sparked in Landina's eyes. "I have refused the man who took over the mill. That's why I accepted refuge with Irmingarde's family, until your father sent Pepin to fetch me this morning. My bundle is just outside your chamber, but I'm not sure what I'm meant to be doing."

"You are to stay with me, Landina. I wanted to ensure your safety, so I suggested to Father that you be brought here. You can either share my bed, or we'll place a pallet and furs beside it for you. Come, bring your things in."

Belying her cheerful tone, doubts had already begun to creep into Poppa's head. Her friend seemed unstable, not certain how to deal with the situation. How would she react to Poppa marrying a Pagan? Clearly, word about that had not reached her.

Landina brought her bundle from outside and placed it beside the clothes chest. "What would you have me do first, Poppa?"

The sudden sharpness in Landina's voice made Poppa look up. Had she been right in doubting her decision? Would her friend not be content here, safe? Together?

"If you could help me dress and brush my hair, I'd be grateful. But first, I must tell you something I was sure you'd have heard." She paused as her childhood friend stared at her blandly. She seemed detached, distant. But Poppa had no choice, or Landina would hear the tidings when they joined the others in the hall. She let out a deep breath. "I am to be wed on the morrow, Landina."

The girl's eyes widened. "Truly? But who could you wed, with most of our men dead or taken?" She wrung her hands in the air. "It's not like you, as a count's daughter, could simply marry anyone. It would have to be a noble man, a man of honour. There are none left in Bayeux…" Her brow furrowed as she stared beyond Poppa at something invisible on the wall.

Poppa gave a wry smile. "You speak the truth. Father only told me last night after Leif brought me back." She briefly closed her eyes before she met Landina's enquiring gaze. "I'm to be the wife of that Northman – Rouf – or Hrólfr as they call him."

"What? That…heathen? But he's not a noble lord. No one knows anything about him. How can your father do that to you?"

"Because he can." Poppa snorted. "I'm but a pawn in Father's game; always have been. I think he considers Hrólfr will stay in Neustria for a long time. And the man will need something to bargain with when he meets the king."

"So you're to be his bargaining tool."

"Yes." Poppa swallowed hard but could not rid herself of the bitter taste in her mouth. Father had sold her to the enemy.

Subdued, she allowed her friend to make her look presentable. Then, in continuing silence Landina plaited her hair and tied it back with green ribbons before she covered it with the wimple.

Poppa's thoughts turned darker. If only she could escape with Landina. But on leaving her chamber, she found a guard standing outside in the dark corridor that led to the hall. He blocked the back door.

Her heart sank further. She would be tied to a man twice her age, a man who could do with her what he wanted, and when. Her fate was sealed.

Could this really be God's will? Just whose God was he?

***

A day later
Bayeux, Neustria

Hrólfr was taking large gulps of ale, but it tasted bitter in his throat. Nor did the gruel he'd been served to break his fast improve his mood this morning. Not even the added berries helped today.

The hall was deserted – unlike last night, when Bérengar made the announcement of their upcoming ceremony. Hrólfr had felt Poppa simmering in suppressed anger as she stood beside him, her head held high, hands balled into fists which she tried to hide in the folds of her flowing tunic of blue silk. Should he consider himself fortunate to have such a beautiful bride? Or would their marriage feel like a golden cage?

Unaware of her effect on the men gathered, she could not completely hide her unhappiness. The girl had grown up in recent days.

But he could barely contain his own fury when he discovered that Bérengar had not warned Poppa about the handfasting ceremony.

'Do you want me to live in sin, Father?'

Her words hovered in his head all night. Of course, handfasting outside a church was against her religion. These

74

days only a blessing by a priests meant a ceremony became valid.

Not that he should care whether she approved or not, but he would share his life with her, and he wished the odious man had told his daughter the truth before she was embarrassed in front of not only Hrólfr's warriors, but also the remaining Franks left in the village.

Part of him wanted to take her away with him when he left, but the journey was hazardous. He had to establish his settlement first, ensuring no dangers lurked, before he brought a wife to Rouen. There was also still the issue of her age. And whilst many men of his own age and older had no qualms about taking a girl of fourteen winters to their bed, he found the thought unappealing.

Hrólfr preferred his women grown-up – and willing. Poppa was neither.

Yes, the alliance to a Frankish count was to his advantage, and he would exploit it to the limits, especially with that treacherous king, Eudes, the former Count of Neustria, on the throne. Hrólfr blamed the man for their failure at the siege of Paris, and he knew he had to combine his warriors' superior might with a level of diplomacy if he wanted to establish bases along the River Signa. But it still felt wrong to take a young girl like Poppa to his bed, despite her enticing looks.

Or was it merely the idea of having a wife at all that brought out his doubts? So far, he'd fared well on his own, with no responsibility other than for his men.

Truth was, Hrólfr was not ready to settle, to consider a wife and children as part of his life. A smile played on his lips. Perhaps their difference in age was not so bad after all?

She would wait here in Bayeux, as he'd agreed with Bérengar. Who said he had to return soon? A few winters away would be enough to allow her to grow into a woman. And it would ensure he retained his freedom in the meantime.

"What makes you grin into your morning ale, my friend?" Knud walked up to the dais, then filled a cup from Hrólfr's pitcher.

Sweat beaded his skin, and he downed the liquid in large gulps.

"How was the training?" Hrólfr asked, ignoring Knud's question.

Knud settled himself in Poppa's chair and stretched his legs in front of him. "It went well." He pulled up a sleeve and showed off his arm, grinning. "I have gained a few more bumps."

Hrólfr sniggered at the spots where the skin was already changing colour to a faint blue. "Did you not wear your arm guard?"

"Yes, of course I did. But some of the young bloods are keen for more serious action."

He had noticed some of his men becoming impatient, after a week's stay in this quiet town. "We will set off on the morrow, as planned. Tell them to get ready."

"And your new bride?" A smirk on his lips, Knud punched him lightly on the upper arm. "See, I was right."

"So you were, brother. And as I told you before, the girl's too young for my taste. She'll stay here, I've agreed with Bérengar."

Knud nodded. "A wise move, Hrólfr. The last thing our men needed on the journey was the company of a spoilt brat."

Poppa chose this moment to appear from behind the screen that separated the private chambers from the hall, and Hrólfr wondered how much of their conversation she'd witnessed. He rose.

"Lady Poppa."

Her mouth formed a thin line. Her skin was pale, and dark shadows beneath her eyes proof of a bad night's sleep. Hrólfr was sorry for her, although why should he? He'd not felt guilty when he left Åsa behind in Orkneyjar. How long ago had that been? Twelve, fourteen winters? And the blonde beauty had barely been much more of age than Poppa was now.

But then he'd not been much older. He brushed aside the unwelcome memory.

"Would you like to break your fast with me, Poppa? With everyone busy out of doors, it may be our only chance to speak in private."

He sent Knud a quick glance, and his friend stood, emptying his cup. "I have a weapon or two to clean..." Without another word, he strode through the side door, letting it fall shut behind him.

For a moment, Hrólfr thought Poppa would reject him, but then she nodded and took her seat. He poured her a cup of ale and refilled his drinking horn.

From the shadows, Pepin appeared. "Would you like me to bring you some gruel, Lady Poppa? We have fresh berries to go with it." To her curt nod, he hurried out the same door Knud had just taken.

Hrólfr had forgotten his presence, and he wondered if the thrall had overheard their conversation. It did not matter. Soon, everyone in Bayeux would be aware of what was going to happen.

"How did you sleep?" he asked gently.

She sipped her ale, then put the cup down. Her hand shook slightly. "Very well, thank you." She sent him a challenging glance with wide, dark-rimmed eyes, and he knew she was lying.

But he had no intention to dent her pride any further. "I'm happy to hear. It will be a long day, with the feasting tonight."

Poppa merely nodded, then smiled at Pepin when he brought her a steaming bowl of gruel. A pile of red and blue berries sat piled up in the centre.

"Be careful; it's hot." Then the boy withdrew, giving them space.

"Take good care of that boy, Poppa." He gestured towards the youth. "He is a good friend to have if you need one in my absence."

She brought a spoonful of gruel to her lips and blew on it gently. "I shall, Hrólfr."

Hrólfr looked away. He liked the way she pronounced his name. Unlike her father, who did not even try to get it right, he found her softly rolled 'r' endearing. Letting her eat, he pushed his own bowl away, half-empty. There was much to do before the short ceremony at midday, but he was content to stay here with her for the moment, keeping her company. His thoughts wandered as she slowly ate some the fruit, before she paused.

"What do you expect from me?"

Her voice barely above a hiss, he startled.

Her cheeks flamed, and she quickly blinked, keeping her gaze lowered. He placed his forefinger under her chin and tilted up her head, so their eyes met. In hers, he saw concern, fear, even.

"I want you to look after yourself while I'm away. I will be gone some time. Your life here won't change very much, so you may wish to continue your learning."

Her eyes widened, shining green rather than pale brown in the flickering light of a tallow candle nearby. His mouth twitched. Clearly, she assumed he disapproved. "If I may?"

"Of course." He let go of her chin and for some inexplicable reason mourned the loss of touch. It had felt right. Yet she was fragile, and he did not want to force her to anything she was not prepared to do. "It can't do any harm, having an intelligent, well-learned wife."

"Thank you." Poppa beamed, then a shadow crossed her face. "Although your men killed Father Peter, and Father Godefroi has already voiced his disapproval of my reading from the Bible. He said women should know their place... whatever that means."

"Ha!" Hrólfr snorted. "He seems to have an issue with women."

She laughed out loud. "You could say so, yes." Reading seemed important to her.

"I will speak with your father and insist that you take up reading again should you so wish. There must be someone else who would be happy to teach you."

"I would like that very much."

"Apart from your learning, I would like you to oversee this hall again, so you'll learn how to run a household. You are already doing much more than a mere daughter does."

Poppa nodded.

"And I would like you not to be afraid. We are very different, but…" He hesitated, uncertain of how to speak his mind without insulting her. Then he decided that bluntness was the best way forward. "Well, you may be surprised, but I won't insist on the wedding night."

A frown appeared between her delicate eyebrows, and he swiftly took her hand.

"You are still very young, Poppa. As we've decided moments ago, there is much left for you to learn. And I shall be away for a long time, perhaps even a year or two. The last thing I'd want now is for you to become with child, then feel abandoned. I…I'd rather we wait until the time is right." His voice was hoarse, and his heart beat loudly in his ears. "Would you not agree?" With his calloused thumb, he gently stroked the inside of her hand, the soft skin in such contrast to his own.

For a long moment, she remained silent. Then she sighed and squeezed his hand. "Thank you. I never…expected this."

"What? The wedding or…?"

"Both." She blushed.

At midday, Hrólfr stood beside Poppa in front of the archway that led into the church. It was as far as he would go. After their earlier talk, Poppa seemed more at ease in his company.

Now, she looked pretty in a dark green linen gown, the hems embroidered with red silk thread. The colours brought out the green in her eyes, and the auburn hues of her braided hair, decorated with colourful ribbons, that rippled down her back beneath the delicate veil kept in place by a silver circlet.

If she was this beautiful now, what would she be like when he returned?

Suddenly, Hrólfr considered himself fortunate.

Inside the doorframe, the priest stood straight. Hands placed together in the way the followers of Christ prayed, he was mumbling words in Latin, the ancient Roman tongue.

Hrólfr turned his back on him, not wishing the haggard man's miserable mien to spoil the moment. He sent his wife-to-be an encouraging smile which she returned.

The priest's involvement was minimal, at best. Hrólfr was to say the important words, and Poppa would repeat them. That way, both had voiced their commitment in front of witnesses.

Knud was tasked with tying their hands together with long silk ribbons he'd found in a dead merchant's house. Poppa did not know where they had hailed from, and Hrólfr had no intention of telling her.

Like earlier in the hall, he took Poppa's hands in his, only this time, he clasped them firmly. "Ready?"

She took a deep breath, then gave a quick nod.

"Knud?"

His friend patted him on the shoulder, winked at Poppa, then went about wrapping the bindings around their hands. He mumbled words in their own language that a wisewoman would say, and only Hrólfr knew their meaning. One day, he would translate them for Poppa.

Once the soft fabric held their entwined hands together, Knud stepped back, until he came to a halt beside Bérengar. The two men could not be any more different. The count, looking down his long nose at them, wore a costly tunic trimmed with fox fur. In the light of the warm spring sunshine, Hrólfr suppressed a snort. The man was too full of his own importance.

But he was a useful ally, who was soon tied to him by marriage.

Inside the church, the priest's voice rose in chant, the whiny sound grating in his ears. Hrólfr sent the offender a baleful glance, and the chanting turned to a whisper.

Then he locked eyes with the girl in front of him, and the world around them faded away. Over the last two days, he had thought long and hard about which words to use. He did not wish to offend Poppa or her beliefs, but he was not prepared to sacrifice his own, and he felt comforted by the weight of the Thor's Hammer pendant beneath his finest tunic of embroidered blue linen; the black stone a solid presence that gave him confidence.

"Poppa, please repeat after me."

"I shall." She sent him a small smile.

Hrólfr was glad he'd had the chance to speak with her earlier. It had helped to soothe her frayed nerves. Poppa's breathing was calm, and her hands lay warm in his.

"We have gathered today…"

"We have gathered today…" Poppa's voice was barely above a whisper, but the gaze that held his remained steady.

"Beneath Frigg's watchful eye…"

Godefroi's hiss threatened to ruin the moment, and a frown appeared between Poppa's brows. Then she spoke, "Beneath Frigg's watchful eye…"

Relief coursed through him, though he silently beseeched the goddess of marriage and motherhood to shut the priest up. As much as it irked him if the man kept disrupting the ceremony, he wanted no bloodshed today.

"To celebrate our marriage to one another.

I promise to care for you,

And to keep you from harm.

From the first bloom of spring

To the darkest winter's night,

I shall be by your side."

Her eyebrows rose as she repeated the words, and he suppressed a sudden giddiness from erupting. It would come to pass, eventually.

He continued, "From this moment onwards,

I will be your friend…and your lover,

And I ask the Gods and Goddesses,

To grant us a long life together,

Until we take our final breath…"

A hush fell after Poppa repeated the last words.

Then she beamed at him. "That was beautiful."

"Lady Poppa, save your soul!"

But they ignored Godefroi's cry.

"That makes me glad, my lady." Hrólfr held her gaze for a long moment, then bent down to kiss her gently on the lips.

They tasted of wine, of sunshine and flowers. He stopped before he went too far and watched as she opened her eyes.

She's too young, he reminded himself.

Hrólfr straightened and nodded to Knud. His friend came forward and pulled the ties from their hands, passing them to Poppa. "Take good care of these, Lady Poppa." Then he held out a small wooden box.

The girl's eyes widened as Hrólfr opened it and removed a small golden cross pendant. "A gift...?"

She lifted her hair, and he leaned forward to tie the leather thong at the back of her neck. The equal-armed object of beaten gold nestled beautifully at the base of her throat. A large, round, dark-red garnet sat in its centre, and the end of each arm was decorated with a smaller, lighter garnet.

When she eventually removed it, she would see the horns of Odin carved on the crossing point on the back. But for now, no one else knew. The pendant combined their two worlds, binding their lives to each other like the ties she still held in her hand.

"Thank you." Tears shimmered in her eyes. "It's beautiful. I...I've never been given such a precious gift."

"Well, then it's time you did."

Seeing her bright smile at the token of her own beliefs, he was glad he'd spared the Frankish smith's life. With this piece, the man had bought his freedom back.

"Now come, wife. We have reason to celebrate." Her hand cradled in his, and their heads held high, they strolled towards the hall.

It would be a long day...

PART TWO

~~~

MARRIAGE

Chapter Seven

Late Winter, AD 895
Bayeux, Neustria

"And don't forget to pay Irmingarde for the bread, Poppa!"

She sighed. "I have paid her already, Father. Now rest!"

Exasperated, she let the curtain to her father's chamber fall back in place and returned to the hall. In the last few weeks, his health had deteriorated. He'd been feeling tired for some time, but at his age, that was not surprising. But recently, his skin paled, and not just with the turn of the season. He'd become thinner.

For the past sennight, Bérengar had stayed abed. It was Poppa's duty to bring him food, but he'd barely touched the warm gruel or the thick meaty broth she fed him. He also took very little ale, even though she nudged him to drink more. He needed his strength, yet how was he to gain it if he refused to eat?

Yet even in his weakened state, he pestered her about every little chore. It was as well that she'd overseen the daily duties in the last few years.

Now, their *majordomus* had sustained an injury in sword-fight training, and with Father sick, pressure was mounting.

Poppa hated having to ask for help, but her mind was made up. She must speak with Sigurd, who Hrólfr left in charge of the Northmen in town. Father would berate her, but she could not do everything on her own. Men did not follow orders given by a young woman.

"Christ's Blood, I need to get away from here," she muttered as she strode towards the side door of the hall.

"What is it, Poppa? Has your father worsened?" Landina called after her.

She turned, not having seen Landina and Pepin in her hurry. They were moving the tables against the wall.

"I'm sorry, Landina. I did not see you. He refused to have the gruel again, so I left it beside his bed. I don't have time to sit with him all day. What are you two doing?"

"We're going to brush the floor and change the rushes…as you asked of us last night."

"Ah, of course." Poppa blinked. She'd forgotten. "Thank you. Have either of you seen Sigurd?"

"Yes, earlier, when he broke his fast," Pepin said. "I think afterwards he was going to head to the shore with a few men. Several longboats have been spotted, and he wanted to make sure they stay away from Bayeux."

Relief flooded through her. Hrólfr had been true to his word and left them in the capable hands of Sigurd, a man she'd not noticed before her husband's departure. The young Northman ensured a nightly watch, kept an eye on the coastline, and had every capable man and boys over ten years of age train in axe and sword fights twice a week, where he also taught them how to remain disciplined in a shield wall.

At Poppa's request, Sigurd took over some of Father's duties, and a new sense of normality set in.

But there was still no sign of her husband!

It was as if he did not exist. Well, occasionally a messenger arrived from his new base at Rouen, but all she received were warm words, hoping she was well. Sigurd shared any other tidings with her.

In the last five years, Hrólfr had gone raiding along the River Seine, before he finally began to build a settlement in the town of Rouen which he'd captured without much resistance. It appeared the locals were very happy with his protection, and his influence in the region was growing.

But Poppa was getting restless. Only once had he visited Bayeux, three years ago. To her surprise, after a surprisingly enjoyable evening spent talking of his adventures, and her chores, he'd made no attempt to touch her.

To her embarrassment, Father had proclaimed her a woman, worthy to be bedded, in front of the gathered crowd in the hall. Yet Hrólfr declined and left two days later. She'd not seen him since.

Sigurd had tried to calm her fury, but eventually gave up, leaving her to Landina to soothe her.

Did Hrólfr not find her appealing? Did he not want sons?

Father had been angry, too, blaming her sharp tongue for her husband's swift departure, but she'd only been polite and friendly towards him.

"I'll see if I can find him, thank you." She took her cloak from its hook behind the door and wrapped it around her, securing it on her shoulder with a clasp. Then she walked briskly through the quiet town.

Grey clouds were looming low, moving fast, with a promise of snow. The wind whipped up, almost ripping the wimple from her head, but she relished the breeze on her skin, even though it was bitingly cold. Fallen leaves and small branches crunched under her leather boots.

As she marched along the path towards the sea, she prayed Sigurd was not down on the beach. With icy patches on the mud, it would be too dangerous for her to tackle the path down the cliffs.

Father's end was nearing, and with it came uncertainty. Had she not been married off to Hrólfr in such a haste, Sigurd would have made a fine lord. A tall, handsome warrior like him garnered respect with his mere presence. But the young man only had eyes for Landina, yet her friend always insulted him.

Besides, Poppa was wed. Not that she felt that way. Her life was certainly not that of a wife, cherished or otherwise.

They must send a messenger to Hrólfr, advising him of Father's impending death, and asking for his plans regarding Sigurd's future role in Bayeux, and hers.

Hrólfr would not become count – the title would be bestowed upon someone else chosen by the king – but he was still lord of Bayeux. Yet if he was happily settled in Rouen, whence he could sail up and down the River Seine whenever he wanted to, what was to happen to her?

Would she have to leave home?

Poppa bit back the tears. Now as not the time for sentimentality. She must set Hrólfr an ultimatum –return as lord of Bayeux, or to have her join him in Rouen, leaving Sigurd in sole charge here.

Sigurd knew her predicament well. He would find the right words to say to Hrólfr without antagonising him.

The first flurries of snow fell when she neared the sea. On the top of the cliffs a little away from the path stood a small group of men. Recognising Sigurd as one of them, she crossed the uneven ground towards them. Here, she had to look out for hidden rabbit warrens or dried up roots, so she watched her footing. It slowed her down, giving her time to think of what to say.

"Lady Poppa," Sigurd exclaimed and waved.

He gestured to the men who promptly split into two groups. Three went eastwards, the others towards the west, greeting her as she passed.

Then Sigurd approached her. "The ships that were sighted early this morning have gone, but they might merely have sailed around the promontory there," he pointed down the coastline. "We will keep a close watch. I must bring more men out, so we appear well-defended to any would-be raider."

Poppa nodded. "A good idea. Recent attacks on nearby settlements don't bode well."

"Oh, they will try." He grinned. "But Bayeux is under Hrólfr's protection, and anyone attempting to seize the town will have to answer to him. His following has grown, with many more men joining from the northern lands." His gaze was fixed on the distant sea.

"Do you miss your homeland?"

"Sometimes." Sigurd shrugged, not revealing more about his past of which she knew very little. "But this is my home now, and I love it here." His arm swept over the land towards the town. "I'd hate to settle elsewhere."

"It grows on you, this place."

He laughed, his usually serious face lighting up. "It really does. You are fortunate to have spent all your life in Bayeux."

The reminder of her situation brought her back to her task. "I am, yes. But with my absent husband preferring his new settlement at Rouen, I might not stay for too much longer."

Sigurd sent her a sharp glance. "Why? Have you heard from Hrólfr?"

Poppa shook her head, uncomfortable with the thought of asking for a favour. "No…but I was hoping you could send a messenger to him."

"Has something happened?"

"I…I think Father is dying."

"He's been dying for many moons."

"That is true. But his condition worsened since last night. He demands Father Godefroi stay with him, so he will be absolved from sin just before he passes from this earth," she explained when Sigurd frowned.

"Ah, sin." The corners of his mouth twitched.

"If he doesn't repent, heaven will be closed to him." Although Poppa could not suppress a small smile. Father with his ruthless ambition and selfish actions throughout his life would have much to tell the priest.

"And that would be a disaster."

She met his gaze. "Yes. Heaven means the same to him as your Valhalla does to you."

"I know. Come, let's walk, and then you can tell me what the messenger should say to Hrólfr."

They'd often discussed religion in the long evenings in the hall, more so since Father had taken to his bed. Sigurd usually sat beside her at the high table, keeping order. She'd found him a willing listener, one who would not talk over her, nor belittle her thoughts. How Landina could not see his kindness, the support he gave them, was beyond her! Not forgetting his handsome looks: his long, light-brown hair that he kept tied back, the twinkle in his eyes – and the wide, open smile.

Poppa decided she would speak with her friend again. Landina must forget the grudge she bore all Northmen who had settled in Bayeux. Even after five years, her tongue was vicious, whenever one spoke to her.

Poppa admired Sigurd's patience as he kept trying to engage with the girl. God only knew why he persisted!

Her mind returned to the present. "As I said, Father won't be long of this earth, Sigurd. We must be prepared. There may be other Frankish lords with an eye on Father's lands; men who have the king's ear."

"Are you concerned for your safety?"

Poppa shrugged. "I'm not thinking about me, but you may be right."

"Young women have been abducted for less than land."

And by your people too…

The words hung unspoken between them, and she quickly shrugged them off. The Franks were no strangers to taking girls as slaves, especially from the Pagan tribes they conquered. A realist, she'd learnt much since her husband left. She'd listened, and formed her own opinions.

"Indeed," she agreed. "Now, could you send a man asking Hrólfr for his plans for Bayeux? Because the moment Father dies, we must be on alert. Hrólfr may even send reinforcements, in case of impending attacks from Bretons or Franks from other towns."

"Of course. It makes sense."

"Thank you. The king may also have his own plans for Father's titles. Now that there is no male heir, and I'm not allowed to inherit, he might impose a man of his choosing."

"Which could mean trouble for us here."

"Indeed."

They slowly crossed the field towards the top of the path that led down the cliffs. Voices drifted up from the beach below. Only now did she realise that it had stopped snowing.

Sigurd stopped. "I will request Hrólfr to come here himself. He must let us have his orders in person."

Poppa snorted. "You are 'requesting' his presence?" she teased.

Sigurd burst out laughing. "Yes. That will get his attention. He has been remiss in his attention towards Bayeux – and towards his wife." He looked down to the beach where several of their guards sat huddled around a fire. The sea – reflecting the dark grey colour of the sky – was a churning mass of waves crashing onto sand and rock.

A shiver ran down her shoulder. Should Hrólfr return, she would perhaps have to travel with him, back to Rouen, by boat. Uncertainty had grown in recent years. Not for the first time, Poppa wondered what married life to a man like Hrólfr would be like.

From what she remembered, he was very different to the friendly, easy-going Sigurd who'd swapped raiding for settled life in a small town, and he seemed content.

Hrólfr was ambitious, like Father, but without the scheming. Or perhaps he was, and she did not know.

Fact was, she knew precious little about her husband. The man was a stranger.

"Thank you. I'd better return home." She waved towards the town.

Sigurd nodded. "Fret not, Poppa." She'd permitted him to drop her title when they were unobserved, like now. It pleased her that he regarded her as a friend. "All will be well." He sent her an encouraging smile, then climbed down the slippery path.

As Poppa retraced her steps, she could not shake off a sense of foreboding. For five long years, she'd been in charge of the hall, and all the people in their household.

She loved Bayeux, knew every nook, every hideaway. No, she did not want to leave.

What am I going to do?

***

A fortnight later
Bayeux, Neustria

Hrólfr stepped from the karve and, together with his men, pulled her ashore. It was with mixed feelings that he landed here again, on the Neustrian coast off Bayeux, bringing reinforcements to help Sigurd defend the town, if needed.

When the messenger had first relayed his friend's words, Hrólfr reacted with anger. Who was the man to tell him to come here in person? It was not as if he had nothing else of importance to do. But he sensed Poppa's words behind the demand, fearing for their safety.

Truth be told, with Bérengar on death's door, other Franks could cause trouble, and attempt to capture the town from his grasp. Perhaps the Norse settlers had grown fat and lazy, no longer able to wield an axe.

Sigurd's added request for reinforcements irked him. Hrólfr needed every man in Rouen; he could scarcely spare any. And especially not for a small, backward place like Bayeux. But the place was not unimportant. It was of strategic advantage, a lookout towards the west.

It had taken him two days to realise that Sigurd was right.

He left his men to secure the karve and went to greet Sigurd. "Your spies must've spotted us."

Sigurd grinned, then clasped his arm firmly. "We're keeping a close eye on any passing longships," he said, "but I was hoping you would come once you got my message."

Hrólfr snorted. "Your order, you mean." But his voice was full of mirth. The sea air had blasted away the last remnants of his anger. Instead, he'd found himself filled with guilt; for leaving Sigurd to keep Bayeux secure, and for ignoring Poppa.

His wife.

He looked around but there was no sign of her.

"Poppa's waiting for you in the hall," Sigurd said, as if he'd read his mind.

"'Poppa', is it now? Not 'the lady Poppa'?" Hrólfr raised an eyebrow. Had his friend become close to her? A shadow clouded his mood.

"Well, yes, of course." Sigurd stepped back. "In company, certainly, but not amongst friends. And we consider each other as such."

"Friends? How can you be friends with a girl?" Hrólfr shook his head, tutting. What was the world coming to? The man was friends with his wife!

94

Sigurd crossed his arms in front of his chest. "When the 'girl' oversees a large hall in a town the size of Bayeux, then yes, I am honoured to call her a friend. We work closely together to keep the peace."

"What?"

Sigurd sighed, then half-turned. "Come, Hrólfr. It seems we have much to talk about. And don't you start being jealous! You've not paid any attention to your wife since your handfasting ceremony. Poppa has grown into a responsible young woman – one who has been waiting for her husband to return."

"Are you berating me?" Unease gripped Hrólfr as he fell into step with Sigurd. How could he be jealous? He barely knew the girl. "I have been occupied."

"No, I'm not." Sigurd's voice bore a hint of frustration. "But you must admit that leaving her to fend for herself all the while you're setting up home in Rouen might be considered somewhat rude."

"She doesn't need me here to run her household."

"That is true. She is perfectly capable of coping with everything thrown at her, something you better prepare yourself for."

They began the climb up towards the clifftop, Sigurd leading the way. Up here, they'd have to shout to hear each other, so they remained silent until they arrived at the top.

Setting off on the path towards town, the two men continued their walk beside each other again.

"How fares Bérengar?" Perhaps the count was recovering, taking some of the strain off his daughter's shoulders.

Sigurd stared ahead, his mouth set in a thin line. Eventually, he spoke. "He died two nights ago."

Hrólfr touched Mjölnir.

This was unexpected. Or perhaps not, and he'd merely refused to accept it. Rouen was far enough away for him to pretend he had no attachments. Since he'd settled in the town, he'd shared his bed with a Frankish thrall who was everything Poppa was not. Playful, seductive; a grown-up woman. One who knew what he needed – and when.

On the other hand, Poppa was a child.

Or was she? Five winters had passed since their handfasting, and he'd only seen her once since that day. He wondered how much she'd changed since. Back then, she'd already been beautiful. To his shame, he realised that the girl must now be at her best child-bearing age.

But Hrólfr was not ready for children. He saw what happened to his friends who settled down. A wife and offspring mellowed them; only a few had shown themselves prepared to join him on raids along the coast. He clenched his teeth.

"That's not good." It was all he could say.

Bérengar's death changed everything. Perhaps Sigurd had been right in summoning him.

"The vultures will soon descend on Bayeux – Northmen and Franks alike. With no one to inherit Bérengar's title, the Frankish king will want to lay claim to the land and put an ally in place."

"Odo can try," Hrólfr said grimly. For years, the man had been a thorn in his side. When he was Count of Paris, he'd thwarted Hrólfr's siege. Now he was King of the West Franks – and unpredictable. "I've brought a score men who will remain here."

Sigurd gave an audible sigh. "That will help us, as will your marriage to Poppa."

The lady Poppa. Hrólfr was not certain why Sigurd being on such friendly terms with his wife should bother him, but it did. Yet he himself had shown no interest in her.

I've been busy.

"Yes, that's true. It may even be the main reason that stops Odo. Since we settled in Rouen, he's not approached us, nor has he tried to attack. I still don't trust him, though."

"Are you planning to take her with you when you return?" Sigurd's glance was inquisitive. Did he want the girl for himself?

Were they lovers?

Hrólfr's imagination was running away with him. Desperate to stop those unwanted thoughts, he nodded.

"Given potential threats to the town, I think it's best she comes with me."

And away from you…

But to Hrólfr's surprise, Sigurd slapped his back. "Finally, though I'm not sure how she'll react. She's used to running the household here in relative freedom."

"With you at her side…"

"Are you jealous?" Sigurd chuckled, then quickly turned sober again. "You've left her for too long, Hrólfr. No," he raised his hand when Hrólfr opened his mouth to counter him, "you know it's the truth. She's a young lady bearing much responsibility."

Hrólfr shrugged. "She'll have plenty of that in Rouen. But her departure means there will be more work for you."

Having reached the first houses, they turned into the central lane that led to Bérengar's hall.

"I don't mind." Sigurd nodded at a passing guard. "The count has already left many of his administrative duties to me. I've been solving disputes, punishing crimes, and keeping the peace. Well, on his and your behalf." He grinned. "Here we are."

They approached Bérengar's hall, and the queasiness in Hrólfr's stomach increased. Was he ready to take Poppa with him? Bayeux was safe in Sigurd's hands.

He ran a hand through his unbound hair. It had become knotted in the sea breeze, and he swore as he pushed his fingers to untangle the knots. Eventually, noticing Sigurd's smirk, he gave up.

Taking a deep breath, he walked through the door that Sigurd held open, his eyes only slowly adjusting to the dim light inside the hall. He blinked as he looked around.

"You have returned, lord." Pepin rushed forward, bearing a cup of something that sloshed all over his hand in his eagerness.

Hrólfr smiled. The lad had grown; he was now tall, wiry, and held himself with an air of responsibility. Gone was the child with the big, fearful eyes.

But what surprised him the most was the warm welcome,

something he'd not expected from a thrall.

"Pepin, let me look at you!" He took the offered cup and drank deeply, the cool ale welcome after the journey. "You've grown into a man."

The lad stretched to his full height, beaming at him. "Please enter. It's good to see you returned."

Pepin's enthusiasm reminded Hrólfr of his own youth. How self-assured had he been! How arrogant!

"Thank you." Hrólfr glanced from Pepin to Sigurd and back. "So tell me, where is your mistress?"

It was better to have it done with. A conversation with Poppa was long overdue. Hrólfr brushed aside as guilt pricked his conscience.

He'd been very busy.

"Oh, Lady Poppa is just changing. She'd been out counting geese when we received word of your arrival."

His eyebrows shot up. "She was doing what?" Had he heard right?

Pepin giggled. "She was counting the geese, and the goats and chickens too. For the books. She keeps a record of everything the hall owns, including each animal." Price shone through his voice.

"Ah, that's…commendable." He knew Franks were fastidious with their administration, but he'd not expected a woman to be so meticulous. "Has she been doing that for long?"

"Ever since Count Bérengar began to feel unwell, although he usually took a servant with him who dealt with the animals." Sigurd said as they walked towards the dais. "Lady Poppa sees it as her duty to account for each coin spent, and each animal slaughtered." He lowered his voice. "It may be a useful skill to take advantage of in your household in Rouen."

Hrólfr frowned. Did he need to account for each goose? What had he let himself in for? And why had he not intervened? It would seem Poppa established herself securely in her role as lady of the hall.

Then the curtain to the private quarters was pushed aside,

and she entered the main hall. He swallowed hard. Was that really the girl who'd screamed at him for allowing her friend to be taken away?

The vision in front of him was one of a true lady. A Frankish lady. His wife.

Her straight posture revealed a poise she must have gained in recent winters. An overgown of rich green linen suited her well. In the back of his mind lurked a memory of her wearing the colour before. Large eyes stared at him, and he realised that he was as much under her scrutiny as she was under his.

Clearing his throat, he passed the cup to Pepin and strode towards her. The silence in the room unnerved him. Aware that Sigurd and Pepin were watching them closely, Hrólfr squared his shoulders.

When he came closer, her eyes were cool, distanced.

The blame was not hers. It was his. Heat crept into his cheeks.

"Poppa."

"Hrólfr." She'd learnt to roll the 'r' properly in his absence. Most likely, he had Sigurd to thank for that. But it only served to increase his sense of guilt.

"I am sorry to hear of your father's death." The words came easy to him. Truth was, he did not care. Nor did she appear too saddened, and he remembered her strained relationship with Bérengar.

"Thank you. We had been expecting it for over a sennight, so when he passed, it did not come as a shock. Let's get you settled." She gestured towards the dais. "How was your journey?" Her tone was polite, yet it sent chills down his spine. In her own way, she was castigating him for leaving her alone for so long.

As he followed Poppa, his eyes raked down her body. The skirts of her gown swayed slightly with each step, but her wimple covered all her hair. The respectable daughter of a count, and lady of the hall.

No longer a child, she was a woman of status, of responsibility.

Then it hit him. Poppa had become independent.

Shaking his head, Hrólfr realised that he'd done Poppa a great disservice by ignoring her for so long. She did not deserve to be tied to him.

I do not deserve her…

Chapter Eight

Early March, AD 896
Bayeux, Neustria

Landina closed the last lid and secured it. All Poppa's belongings were stored in four large chests – her whole life reduced to this.

Poppa blinked back the tears and looked around the hall. It was bustling with men preparing to set off. The sun had not yet risen, yet everyone was packing their meagre belongings, ready to take to the waves again.

The waves. Nausea rose in her throat. Never having travelled by boat, she was uncertain how she would feel. Would she suffer from the seasickness? The thought of vomiting in front of Hrólfr and his men disturbed her. No, she must not fall ill.

So she'd eaten very little the night before, and refused to break her fast this morning, apart from a small cup of ale. She'd heard that wine was not recommended prior to a sea journey, so she'd refrained from it too.

"That's everything," Landina said, her voice sullen. These last few days, her friend's anger had grown again.

The poor girl could not hide her dislike of Hrólfr, and it was not the first time that Poppa wondered if it was wise to bring Landina to Rouen. Landina had never accepted his treatment of Ranulf, allowing the boy to be taken to the north by his friend, Leif. No word had reached them as to how Ranulf fared.

For all the girls knew, he could be dead.

It was not a thought Poppa accepted easily. Her own feelings towards her husband were still torn. Hrólfr was a man of honour. Yet he'd neglected her for years, only to turn

101

up and demand she join him in Rouen. His lame excuses – the building of a new hall and securing the town from attacks – had not convinced her, but in the end, she had no choice but to comply.

Walking through the partition into the hall, Poppa wished her friend would accept Sigurd's recent offer of marriage – but so far Landina had thrown the whispered words of love and affection back in his face and insulted him for his origins. Then she'd stormed off in the foulest mood.

It was a sensible proposition, one that would see the girl safe. Sigurd was a good man, not responsible for Ranulf's fate.

But he was still one of *them*!

As Poppa watched the men leave the hall in small groups, to prepare the karve for departure, a sense of loss hit her. The sentiment was stronger than when Father died. Somehow, she'd almost been grateful, for it permitted her to forge her own future.

But then, Hrólfr returned.

Their reunion had been polite, yet distanced. She understood how girls would become smitten with him – he was tall, with broad shoulders and a wide chest, and long, muscular legs. His blond hair fell over his shoulders, and he often kept it loosely tied back. But most of all, she'd remembered his piercing blue eyes. Hazy like a lake on a hot summer's day. Eyes that had convinced her, five years earlier, that he cared a little for her.

Then he'd left, showing no interest in her.

Now, she avoided looking at him. It was safer that way. She did not have to make it easy for the man.

Remembering her friend, she decided to try one more time. "Are you sure you really wish to leave Bayeux? We'll be surrounded by Northmen in Rouen."

"Yes." Landina drew her mouth into a thin line, disapproval seeping from her cold gaze. "There's nothing left here for me." She hiccupped.

Poppa braced her arms in front of her. "And Sigurd?"

"What about him?" her friend hissed.

"He's always been kind to you. I think he'd care for you well."

Landina stamped her foot. "I don't need anyone to look after me. Now I go and pack my own things, then we can follow the men." She disappeared into the private quarters behind the curtain.

"She has not changed her mind, then." Sigurd's voice drifted over to her from the side door. He must have come in during her conversation.

The sadness in his eyes broke Poppa's heart. Why could Landina not see beyond his origins, to the kind man Sigurd truly was?

"No," she whispered. "I'm sorry."

He nodded, then stepped aside to let Hrólfr enter. "Well, I'll have to make sure to visit you."

"Why, of course." Hrólfr slapped Sigurd's back. "You'll always be welcome at our hearth."

Poppa had not dared to tell her husband about Sigurd's feelings towards her friend. It was for the man himself to do; or not.

Hrólfr approached her, and she fiddled with her belt. He'd forgotten all about her. She should not feel nervous. "Are you ready?" His gaze went over to the chests lined up on the dais.

"Yes, but Landina is just collecting her belongings."

"Good. I'll fetch some men to carry these to the karve." He looked her up and down. "Do make sure you are wrapped up warm. The wind is biting on board."

He left with a curt nod, and the atmosphere in the room calmed.

Sigurd, hovering by the side door, smiled as Landina emerged.

Poppa took her fur-lined cloak from the rack by the main door and wrapped herself into it. She was already wearing her warmest, long-sleeved gown of thick, dark brown wool, and two shifts beneath. And the high, tightly laced boots with their fur lining would keep her feet warm. Or so she hoped.

If they did not get wet…

Busy with her cloak, she surreptitiously watched her two

friends. Over recent years, Sigurd had become a friend. In the five summers since the attack, he'd been nothing but respectful and supportive, especially during her father's recent illness. It hurt her that Landina could not see the good in the man. The silly girl would want for nothing.

Their murmured words stayed out of her reach, but her heart sank when she watched Sigurd reach out, only for Landina to evade him.

Yet, Poppa could swear Landina was watching the Northman when she thought herself unobserved. So why was she behaving so badly, rejecting a chance at happiness?

Perhaps she did notice Sigurd's good side after all.

Poppa lowered her gaze and stepped outside, pulling the door quietly shut behind her. She sent a little prayer heavenward in the hope that Landina would see sense and stay.

To Poppa's disappointment it was not long before her friend joined her outside, followed by Sigurd carrying the big bundle containing her clothes.

"So you are decided?" she asked her when they approached.

To her surprise, Landina blushed, the perpetual frown temporarily abandoned. "Yes, I am. I can't possibly leave you to go on your own." She pushed her chin up in defiance, but her eyes were glazed with moisture. "Rouen is bigger than Bayeux, and you will need someone to look out for you."

"But I'm sure there are women…" But Poppa knew what Landina meant and squeezed her hands in thanks. But she was still intrigued by the change in Landina's demeanour.

"I'll be visiting you, come spring," Sigurd said. "We must keep an eye along the coast for any trouble, so don't think you're rid of me that soon."

"Wonderful." Poppa beamed. "But what of Bayeux?"

"Don't fret. The town will be safe. We have plenty of men to defend it." His confidence was catching; she believed him.

And perhaps distance would help Landina decide…

"Ah, there you all are." Hrólfr's voice sounded from

behind her, and she turned around. "Are you ready? Light is rising, and we must be on our way to reach the Signa in time."

"Of course," Poppa said, not admitting she had no inkling of why that was important. "Yes, we are."

"Good." He instructed the twelve men who'd followed him – local men who would not travel with them – to collect her belongings. Once they returned, carrying the heavy chests between them, he gestured up the lane. "Let's go, then."

It was late afternoon by the time they reached the mouth of the Seine – or Signa as Hrólfr called the river – and began their journey up the winding waterway.

Poppa and Landina sat huddled together at the centre of the ship, beside the mast, protected from the worst elements by a canvas. Despite this, the cold damp had been seeping through her layers of clothing and into her bones. Her ears were hurting from the cold wind, despite the hood pulled far down to cover much of her face. Her crates were stored beside them, making it impossible to stretch her legs unless she stood up.

And with the rolling of the waves, Poppa had no intention to get up and risk falling overboard, but she peeked through the open side of their makeshift tent to watch rolling fields either side of the river.

Landina was humming an old lullaby. Her eyes were closed, and she rested her head on Poppa's shoulder.

Poppa smiled when Hrólfr looked in on them, raising an eyebrow. She put a finger to her mouth so he would stay silent, and he nodded.

"Soon," he mouthed, then he pointed ahead, and moved out of her sight, opening the gap just a little wider to allow her to get a better view.

Thick green forests covered both shores as the river narrowed. The sound of metal drawn from scabbards reached her ear. The men were preparing for something.

An attack? But from where?

Suddenly, the trees seemed threatening, as if hiding an

invisible enemy. She waved with her free arm to get Hrólfr's attention, and he crouched beside her.

"What's happening?" she whispered.

"We saw smoke rising through the trees, like from campfires."

"Campfires?" Her mind went blank. "But whose?"

"Danes." His mouth was set.

"Do you think it's someone you know?" Curiosity crushed the fear that threatened to overwhelm her. How strange that all these different groups of men from the northern countries did not only fight Franks, Angles, and Saxons, but also each other.

Seeing the sturdy sword at his hip reassured her. The men would keep her and Landina safe.

For what seemed like an age, Poppa watched the shore for signs of movement, but no boats were launched, no cries of attack sounded. Yet the tension amongst the men, as they rowed with their weapons beside them, remained palpable.

Eventually, Hrólfr pointed out the first houses of Rouen. Then a wooden palisade came into view.

Poppa released a long sigh. Finally, they arrived.

Now, she was looking forward to a large fire to warm her frozen bones, though she could not shake of a strong sense of trepidation. This place was to be her new home, with danger lurking from all sides?

***

April, AD 896
Rouen, Neustria

Hrólfr leaned back in his elaborately carved chair, stretching his legs. Torches cast the hall into a flickering display of light and shadows. Rows of tables filled the open space, and every seat was taken. Sounds of laughter filled the room, and it gladdened him that people enjoyed the feast.

For the first time since his return from Bayeux he'd permitted a gathering of this size.

It was a long overdue recognition of his wife's arrival.

But in recent weeks, he'd led repeated forays into the woods on either side of the Signa. Yet whilst they found traces of deserted camps, they did not see any Danes.

This concerned him greatly. If they were indeed Norse, why did they not reveal themselves to him? It was well known that he resided in Rouen, and if any Northmen were looking for somewhere to settle, he'd happily help. But whoever it was, the fact that they were hiding from him raised the hairs at the back of his neck.

It meant only one thing. They were looking for trouble.

That was the reason he could not completely enjoy the feasting. His mind strayed back to those deserted campfires. Hrólfr shook his head to rid himself off his morose thoughts. Whatever was going on outside the gates of Rouen, tonight, he owed Poppa his full attention. The guards would alert him of any danger.

He turned half-way to look at Poppa sitting beside him, sinking into the plump cushions of her smaller chair.

At that moment, she bit a morsel of succulent meat off a bone and chewed it slowly. She seemed content, having thrown herself into the organisation of his home straight after their arrival. It came natural to her, and within days, the settlers, warriors and thralls alike followed her orders.

But tonight, there was a nervousness about her. Hrólfr had an inkling. Ever since they'd met again, he often felt her eyes on him. A pang of guilt nagged him.

So far, he'd not made any attempt to share his wife's bed, but instead remained in his own quarters, next door to the lavish rooms he'd prepared for her. Being watchful of attack, day or night, required him to rise at a given moment's notice, and he did not wish to disrupt her sleep. Or so he told himself...

He took a sip of Rhenish wine from his drinking horn and watched his hearth warriors tuck into their meal. This morning, they'd gone out to hunt for the first time since their return, and their prey of wild boar, deer and rabbit provided a much-needed boost to everyone's morale.

They might not have caught up with the new arrivals, but at least they would go to bed with full bellies tonight. Fresh deer tasted different from salted, dried beef. And the wine Poppa had distributed helped it go down well.

Poppa leaned over to him. "Have you ordered some food to be set aside for the men on watch tonight?"

Hrólfr opened his mouth, then closed it again, shaking his head. He'd forgotten.

She smirked. "Why am I not surprised?" A flick of her hand brought Pepin rushing forward.

The boy had been delighted to join them in Rouen, having followed on a second ship, and he'd already proved himself. As Poppa's right hand in the coordination of the kitchens, he'd helped her create a system of hierarchy that appeared to work very well. The boy would make it to *majordomus* one day.

"Yes, Lady Poppa?" He leaned closer to hear her better over the noise in the hall.

"Please see to it that there is enough meat and fresh bread left for the guards when they come off duty. Tonight, every man shall eat well."

"Yes, of course. I'll have the kitchen maids keep some platters aside."

She smiled. "Thank you, Pepin. Oh, and make sure you eat too. Take your time. I can pour our wine. Leave it here." She pointed towards the jug brimming with wine he was holding.

He set it down on the table and gave a small bow. "Thank you, Lady Poppa. You're very kind. I'll return soon."

"Take your time!" she repeated, laughing, after his retreating figure.

"Pepin takes his responsibilities serious," Hrólfr said. "He's a good man."

"Oh, I'd be lost without him. I barely need to utter the word, and off he goes, putting everything in place." She sent him a sideways glance, with wariness in her gaze. "I would like to reward him, but I don't know how."

"It's a nice thought, Poppa. How about a finely carved cutting knife? His is quite old, I've noticed."

108

Her eyes lit up, and she clapped her hands together. "What a wonderful idea! I shall ask Carloman to make one for Pepin."

"Please do. He always carves beautiful hilts for the weapons he forges. We'll pay him, of course."

"Thank you. I hope it will please Pepin."

"What will?" Knud, sitting on Poppa's left, leaned over.

She smiled at him, and Hrólfr was relieved that, after initial reluctance, his wife appreciated the hard work Knud had put in to make the settlement at Rouen a safe place for them to live. Their defences, whilst not complete, were already impressive.

"We're going to have a cutting knife made for Pepin; one with a finely-carved handle."

Knud nodded. "It shows your appreciation, and the lad has really been working hard." His gaze met Hrólfr's and not for the first time gave him pause for thought.

"Yes, I agree. But so have you…" Poppa disrupted his musings.

Knud chuckled. "Don't fret on my behalf, Lady Poppa. I have everything I need."

Later that night, the effect of the wine had taken its toll, and after much merriment, men and women began to return to their homes. The hall quietened.

Hrólfr pushed back his chair as he waved off Knud and some of his men.

Pepin and several other thralls emptied tables of cups, bowls and trenchers.

Landina disappeared up the stairs to the private quarters.

Poppa had given her a small chamber beside her own. His was on the opposite side, the size of both hers and her friend's combined. It was meant to be for him and Poppa, but so far, he'd not encouraged her to join him.

On arrival in Rouen, setting her up separately had seemed the easier option, to give her space to settle in. But now, he wondered what she actually made of the separation. She'd not once mentioned it to him.

Because tonight, they'd talked and laughed together; the first time completely at ease with one another. It was a positive sign. Perhaps the time was right for the next step in their marriage?

Then why did he feel like an untried young lad? His mouth twitched at the thought. Never had he been this shy about a woman. But Poppa was not any woman. She was his wife – a beautiful and intelligent one. In the short time they'd lived under one roof, he'd seen glimpses of her personality. And he liked what he saw. Poppa was kind and caring, but also firm when folk were sluggish or lazy. She was fair and did not judge, nor was her punishment too severe.

The wine filled him with daring. As she rose to retire, he gently clasped her hand and looked up at her. "Stay with me, Poppa."

Flicking him a quick glance, she sat. "But only for a moment. I'm quite weary." She stifled a yawn.

Whether it was real, or to avoid the marriage bed, he knew not. Did she guess his intentions?

With slow, deliberate strokes, his fingers began to caress the soft skin of her hands. The tips of her fingers were slightly calloused – Poppa did not shy away from physical work if needed. Another trait he admired in her.

"Wh… What are you doing?" Her voice was barely above a whisper. He brushed away a stray lock of hair that had fallen over her eyes. Hues of auburn danced in the light of the torch on the wall behind them.

"I thought it may be time to be…together."

"Together?" Her eyes widened and her breathing quickened. So she'd not expected this.

Would she ever? He must press his advantage.

"Yes, as I said. You could join me in the big chamber, which is meant to be yours as well, you know."

Her cheeks turned into the becoming shade of a spring rose. She nodded.

"But I must prepare." She touched her hair. "I look a mess."

"Not at all." He kissed the back of her hand. "You are the

most beautiful woman in all of Neustria."

The colour on her cheeks deepened, and she averted her gaze.

"But by all means, prepare. I think Landina awaits you already."

After a quick nod, she stood. Her hands were trembling. "I shall be with you shortly."

He gave her what he hoped was an encouraging smile. "I'll be waiting."

Once she'd disappeared through the door, he emptied his drinking horn, then bid Pepin, who was still clearing up tables, goodnight.

After reflection, he looked into the closest pitcher and found it half-full of wine. He took it and went to a side table to pick up two unused cups. Then he went upstairs to his chamber.

Looking around, he winced. Mud-stained hose lay on the floor beside a dirty tunic. The lid of his clothes' chest stood open, revealing chaos inside.

This happens when you don't want anyone tidying after you.

Hrólfr felt like a boy about to face a mother's wrath. Quickly, he set down the pitcher and cups on a small table beside the bed, then shoved the dirty clothes and a stray belt that lay on the bed into the chest and slammed the lid shut. He heaved the covers from the straw-filled mattress and shook them out in a corner behind the door, before he put them, one over the other, back in place.

Why was he so concerned? Poppa had likely been in this chamber. The mattress was always fresh, and every time he'd returned from a foray, he'd found his dirty clothes washed and folded up in his chest. Only for him to mess it all up again, uncaring.

I must do better.

With a sigh, he sat on the bed and untied his boots. Fortunately, he'd had a swim – and a quick wash – in a shallow part of the river early this morning. His mind wandering, he put the boots beside the chest.

Was he nervous? He laughed, but without mirth. No. He'd bedded women before. Women who knew what they were doing; who proved willing bed mates.

Even Åsa, the pretty jarl's daughter, all those winters ago on the isle of Birsay, when they were both young and curious, had been daring. Sometimes, he wondered how her life had turned out since then. Perhaps Leif would stumble across her at Jarl Sigurd's court.

With a sigh, he brushed the memories from his time spent on Orkneyjar away. He filled both cups with wine. Then he reclined on his bed and waited.

Moments later, a hesitant tap sounded on the thin door. The wall partitions between the chambers did not allow for solid wooden doors, but in time he'd make sure they'd be replaced.

"Come in." He put his cup on the floor beside the bed and stood, the hem of his tunic falling down to his thighs.

Poppa slid through the gap and secured the latch. Sending him a shy smile, she fidgeted with strands of her long hair that cascaded loose over her shoulders. She wore only a light shift that reached to her knees, revealing long, slender legs.

"Here," he said calmly and handed her a full cup of wine. "This will help."

The corners of her mouth twitched. "Have I not had enough yet?"

Hrólfr laughed. "If you think so…"

But despite her brave expression, she took a few tentative sips. She avoided to look at him; instead, her gaze was scanning the room.

He held out his hand and she took it but remained standing. After she'd downed the rest of her wine, he put her cup on the floor. Her breathing hitched, as if she'd never thought this moment would come.

Their eyes met, and he smiled. "That's better." But still her body trembled.

Pulling her closer, he ran his hands along up the outside of her thighs, and then up the enticing curve of her hips beneath her shift. "Take it off."

"What? Why?" She covered her mouth with her hand, then whispered, "I was told it wasn't necessary to…to…"

"By whom?" Those Christians with their strange ideas, but Poppa was an innocent, after all. She would not know otherwise. "Please? I want to see my wife, not have her hiding in her night shift."

"But the Church forbids it."

Hrólfr stopped himself from rolling his eyes. Instead, he grinned. "But the Church also says you should obey your husband in all matters…"

"Hmm. If you insist." But before she moved, he grabbed the hem of her shift and slowly lifted it up, rising as he did so until their bodies stood close. He cast her shift aside, then pulled up his own tunic which joined hers on the floor.

Poppa had not moved back. The woman was brave. Her warm breath caressed his chest, and he took her hands in this. Her eyes were closed now, as if she was embarrassed. But as he looked at her, all he saw was feminine beauty. Long legs leading up to shapely hips, a narrow waist, and perfect full breasts that cried out to be touched. She shook her head, and her long tresses covered them, as if she'd sensed his thoughts.

"You're beautiful, Poppa." His voice hitched, and her eyes flew open.

"Umm, if what you see pleases you…"

He let out a held breath. "It pleases me very much." He kissed the tips of her fingers, then placed her hands on his chest. "And your Church is so wrong."

A shade of pink covered her cheeks. She seemed happy with his words.

Leaning forward, he blew light kisses over her brow, her temple and, finally, their lips touched. Gently at first, he forced himself to go at her pace.

Take it slow.

His body began to react to her touch, and he pulled her tight against him as his tongue explored the sweet taste of her mouth. Hints of mint and wine mingled into an exciting blend.

"Poppa." His hand raked through her hair while the other slid down her back, cupping her firm bottom.

It was time for the next step.

Pulling her down on the bed with him, and he stretched out beside her, as she lay on her back. Then his slow exploration of her body continued as she gasped beneath his touch, her eyes fluttered closed. A whimper escaped her when his tongue flicked over a puckered nipple.

Hrólfr smiled as her back arched against him. She was learning fast.

And they had all night…

Chapter Nine

April, AD 902
Kingdom of East Anglia

Hrólfr sat under the awning in front of his hall, sharpening the edge of his sword. A cold wind swept in from the sea. Despite the blinding sunshine, a chill crept up his legs. Early this morning, a hard frost had covered the ground, and even the normally warming rays could not dispel the sense of iciness.

Poppa was still resting, preferring a later start these days. He did not begrudge her the small comfort of their warm bed. After he rose, he'd lit a fire in the hearth, so their small hall was warm and welcoming when she emerged from their chamber.

Shortly after their arrival on these shores, he'd built the wooden structure that had become their new home. Now it housed not only him and Poppa, but also a dozen of their friends. They'd followed him on the flight across the Narrow Sea and helped him build the hall, and, in return, he provided them with a roof over their head – they bedded down in the hall at night – and food in their bellies.

As he carefully worked over new chinks the sword had received in a recent skirmish against the West Saxons, he could not help but wonder if Eiríkr, ruler over the Eastern Angles and Danes, was the right man to hold this vast area together.

"He's certainly no Guthrum," he mumbled to himself, tutting.

"Who?" Poppa appeared beside him, placing a hand on his shoulder.

Hrólfr looked up, his gaze falling on her rounded belly.

After four winters, she was finally with child. And he would ensure she was safe from attack to deliver it.

The impending birth, maybe three or four moons away, was the main reason he'd taken up settlement in a hamlet close to the coast, at a fair distance from any West Saxon incursions that their King Edward made into East Anglia in response to swift attacks from the Danes.

Attacks he'd taken part in. Well, not really a full assault, but rather small scuffles along the borders.

How petty it all seemed! Neither Edward nor Eiríkr gained an advantage. Like two cocks in a ring, the two kings preened in front of their followers, plotting to oust the other.

By now, Hrólfr was tired of supporting the Dane, but unless he was able to reclaim Rouen, he had no alternative. He'd received no warning of a Frankish attack on his town, and when it came, his men were not prepared for such an assault. The thought that his beautiful home was under the control of Robert, Margrave of Neustria, irked him every day.

And that he'd had no choice but to flee with his little family. But he would have his revenge. In the meantime, he was stuck between the two fronts here.

"Eiríkr. His bark is louder than his bite." He kept his voice low so only Poppa could hear him, but still glanced around. The Danes here were a strange lot; one moment content to live alongside the Saxons, the next gagging to attack them. "Guthrum had managed to establish a relatively peaceful base for all here, but Eiríkr risks everything over a whim. We don't have enough men to challenge King Edward."

"Is the fool planning another raid?" She pointed at his sword. "Is that why you…?"

"Yes. He's called upon us again now winter has passed." Nodding, Hrólfr laid his sword down on a blanket and wiped his hands on his tunic. "From what I've heard, Æthelwold the troublemaker is on his way here, looking for support to his claim to the West Saxon kingdom again. Ha!" He gave a mirthless laugh. "As if the drunk has any chance."

"You've met him before, this Æthelwold, haven't you?"

"Yes. It was years ago, before I came to Neustria. His head

was full of dreams of *his* kingdom that his uncle, King Alfred, had snatched from his grasp. The man is a fool. A dangerous one should he gain the support of the Danes in Northumbria and here." A sigh escaped him. "But enough talk of kings and their plans. How is our son faring today?"

Hrólfr could not forget how Poppa lost a child two summers ago, the first time her womb had quickened since they began to live as man and wife. But the Gods had other plans. After carrying the babe for six moons, she'd lost it after the frantic flight from Rouen to Anglia, leaving her body exhausted. For over a sennight, she'd hovered between the worlds, her feverish ramblings scarier than any foe he'd faced in battle.

The memory had come unbidden, and he brushed it aside. He needed no reminders of that wretched time. The guilt he felt would never go away. Nor would the anger at Robert of Neustria who'd chased them from their home in his cowardly attack.

It was the will of the Gods...

He touched Mjölnir still snug at the base of his neck.

No. It was the actions of an enemy.

Poppa patted her belly. "He's fine. Last night, he was a little restless, but he's settled now. Just as well. I have errands to run."

"Have you broken your fast yet?"

"I'm not hungry, Hrólfr. I'll eat when I return from my visit to Ealswith." She kissed him, then wrapped her cloak tighter around her.

He rose. "I can come with you. The ground is treacherous in places."

Poppa stared at the frosty path that led through the village. The black ice was churned up in places in the trail of carts and donkeys that had gone to the fields at dawn, leaving a muddy, slippery mess. "Thank you. It looks slippery."

He wrapped his arm around her waist, and together they made their way along the side of the path, passing several huts made from wattle and daub, very like their own. A few times, her booted feet slipped on hidden ice that had not yet melted away, and he held her tight against his side.

Eventually, they reached the home of Ealswith, a Saxon seamstress Poppa had befriended. A proud widow, she barely made ends meet for herself and her son, Leofwin, a boy of six winters. Poppa ensured that the young woman always had paid work to keep her going.

But in recent days, Ealswith had become tired, her limbs heavy. Unable to focus on her stitching, she'd taken to her bed on Poppa's orders.

A smile played on his lips. No one in the village ever ignored his wife's orders. Her word was followed without complaint or hesitation. In the end, the woman rested, and Poppa did her sowing for her in the afternoons when daylight allowed her to work out of doors.

"When do you wish to return? I can come back."

She shook her head. "I'll be fine by then. Leofwin can accompany me."

Hrólfr snorted. "The boy's barely able to walk..." But he knew her mind was made up. She did not want him to fuss.

Poppa laughed and punched his upper arm, and he yelped in mock pain.

"You're impossible! Leofwin is old enough to help in the fields when he's not looking after his mother. So of course he can make sure I get home safely. You do what you must, and I shall see you later."

She planted a light kiss on his cheek, then knocked on Ealswith's door. Moments later, Leofwin opened it and let her in.

Hrólfr returned home, deep in thought. He stared at the huts as he passed. People were poor, and life was harsh enough without the ambitions of pretenders to a throne far away from here. Yet Eiríkr called all men of fighting age to join him. The man did not care about the wives and children left behind, or widows like Ealswith whose husband had died during the most recent skirmish.

Edgar had received a swift burial, but Eiríkr did not even see fit to give the widow a coin.

Not for the first time, Hrólfr wondered why they stayed.

118

But where would he go? Word from Neustria did improve his mood either. Sigurd had trouble with the Franks, but so far, he and his small band of men had managed to keep Bayeux safe from attack. It was the big towns the Franks were after. Rouen. Chartres. Nantes.

Riches were found there, not in small villages.

Perhaps he should take Poppa back to Bayeux, then try to recover Rouen from there? But with the child soon to be born, she would not be in a condition to cross the Narrow Sea anytime soon. Perhaps in late summer, before the autumn storms arrived.

In the meantime, he would have to support Eiríkr in his forays. Loot was distributed evenly, and despite their humble abode, Hrólfr had amassed a nice haul which he'd buried in a secret place away from the huts. Should their village come under attack after all, no one would find it.

Outside his hall, he lowered himself on the stool and picked up his sword again. With a sigh, he set to work.

***

July, AD 902
Kingdom of East Anglia

"Sweet Mother of God!"

"Not long now, Lady Poppa." Ealswith dabbed her forehead with a damp cloth, the water trickling down Poppa's temple. "Your son seems eager."

"You think so?" She strained, gasping for breath. "He's taking his bloody time!"

"Ealswith is right, lady." Áslaug's calm voice did not soothe her, although the old wisewoman seemed to know what she was doing. "I can see his little head already. Don't forget to breathe! 'Tis important. Now push again."

Instead, Poppa screamed as agony tore through her body. Why had no one told her it would hurt so much? More tears ran down her face, and Ealswith wiped them away gently.

"I just want it to end…" Poppa whined.

Áslaug smiled over the bulk of Poppa's round belly. "The Gods are listening. Your lad is nearly there. Keep telling them!"

After almost a full day spent pushing, Poppa did not care about the Dane's heathen words. If God – any god – eased her pain this very moment, then she did not care which of them helped her. "Please…" she begged, before she pushed once more. Her head felt like it was going to burst, and she bit down hard on the leather strip Áslaug had given her.

Eventually, a victory cry emerged from the crone, and relief flooded through Poppa as her child's little body slid from her womb.

"It's a fine boy, lady!" The wisewoman's voice was full of pride. "Ealswith, give me a hand here."

Later, as she lay on clean linens, her son suckling at her breast, Poppa marvelled at the little wonder in her arms – and at the way a Saxon Christian and a Danish heathen had helped a Frankish woman bring him safely into their world. Why were men attacking each other when they could all live together, in peace, supporting one another?

She sighed then closed her eyes against the unfamiliar pain of her nipple. Her son drank greedily. He would turn into a fine warrior one day. Or a man of peace.

Given his father, who knew!

Hrólfr missed his son's birth. Several weeks earlier, he'd joined Eiríkr and that wastrel, Æthelwold. She'd raged at him, but to no avail. He'd gone reluctantly, hating to leave her at this time. But his experience was needed, and the king of the East Angles left him no choice.

"Oh, little one, your father just can't help himself." Gently, she stroked the soft cheek. "Perhaps your arrival will convince him to settle and stop this fighting nonsense."

But Poppa doubted it.

"Lady?" Ealswith returned with a tray bearing a bowl of something steaming. She set it down on a small table. Their bedchamber was tiny compared to their home in Rouen. There was barely enough space for their bed, and a table and two stools. Along a wall, six chests contained all they were able to rescue before they fled Rouen.

Poppa swallowed back the tears that threatened every time she remembered their ill-fated journey.

Smiling, Ealswith took the now sleeping babe from her and tucked him into the blankets in the little cot his father had built. Then she picked up the bowl and sat on the edge of Poppa's bed. "Here, lady. You need to build up your strength."

"I'm not hungry." Poppa craved sleep, something her demanding son deprived her of so far.

But Ealswith shook her head. "Oh no, Lady Poppa. You can sleep after you've eaten some chicken broth."

Poppa kept her eyes closed and shook her head.

"If you take a few sips now, just a few, I'll stay here and look after the little one, so you can sleep. That sounds fair, doesn't it?"

Holy Mother of God, the woman was persistent. Opening her eyes, Poppa propped herself on her elbows and let Ealswith feed her spoonfuls of thick, meaty liquid. She chewed on the small cuts of chicken.

Slowly, her wits returned. The seamstress was right, she admitted. Eventually, she declined any more and lay back.

Ealswith put the bowl on the floor, then adjusted Poppa's cover. It was high summer, yet her body felt cool with exhaustion. She let her friend fuss over her and closed her eyes.

The last thing Poppa remembered was the creaking of the chair beside the cot. Ealswith was true to her word, keeping watch over the babe.

With a smile on her face, Poppa fell asleep.

Autumn, AD 902
Kingdom of East Anglia

"They're coming back. Finally! They're coming!"

The cry went through the settlement. Poppa dropped her needlework, lifted William from his cot, and rushed outside.

121

The boy let out a squeal at the abrupt disruption to his sleep. Poppa bounced him up and down until his complaints turned into giggles.

With the old men and young boys in the fields, the women and children gathered in the centre of the village. In the distance, the cloud of dust grew larger.

"Is it really them?" Poppa frowned, but beside her, Áslaug nodded sagely.

"Aye. The Gods told me."

But Áslaug's Gods could be wrong, could they not? What if the band approaching them were West Saxon attackers? It was well known that many villages in the kingdom were deserted, with all the fighting men having followed Eiríkr. She did not want her baby to die, so she sent a small, silent prayer heavenwards.

The crowd had grown quiet, as if they held the same misgivings. Some murmured to each other, casting glances at their humble homes.

Then Poppa recognised him.

"God be praised," she whispered. She planted a long kiss on William's chubby cheek. "Your father has returned, my boy."

Tears pricked her eyes as the riders came closer, with Hrólfr in the lead. Behind the riders, other men from the village followed on foot. Around Poppa, the women were squealing with relief.

The men on horseback halted beside the stables and dismounted.

Poppa waited until Hrólfr had handed over the reins to a boy, then she rushed towards him, a broad smile on her face.

His eyes widened when he spotted William. He opened his arms, and, with the babe nestled against her chest, she stepped into his embrace, letting his warmth wash over her. His tunic smelled of sweat and dust, and his hair and face were grimy with dirt. But it did not matter. God had returned her husband safely.

After an urgent kiss, he stood back and held her at arm's length. With wonder in his gaze, he stared at William.

"Who do we have here?" His forefinger trailed across the boy's cheek and chin.

"Your son. William."

He raised an eyebrow. "William?"

Her heart pounding in her ears, Poppa nodded. "Yes. With you absent, I had to choose a name for him. He was born two months ago!"

"Of course. I see." But he did not seem certain. Then he searched her face, his eyes trailing down and back up her body. "And you? Are you well?"

"Yes, I am now. I suffered from a light fever following the birth, but Áslaug and Ealswith cared for me. They have been wonderful."

"Then I must thank them. I was wrought with concern."

Poppa snorted. "Really? I'd have thought you needed your wits about to focus on warfare...or whatever it was that kept you all from coming home."

Wrapping his arm around her, he sighed, all humour gone. "If it was safe to cross the Narrow Sea before the coming storms, I'd take you back to Neustria." His voice low, he glanced around, but no one was within earshot. Many other couples were absorbed in their own reunions. "We lost several men, sadly."

Four women wailing at the edge of the crowd told her who. "That's a huge blow for the village."

"Yes. And with Æthelwold continuing to whisper nonsense in Eiríkr's ear, we'll soon be on the move again. That fool of a king believes everything the scheming West Saxon says."

Hrólfr turned and took his pack from the saddle, then allowed the boy, who'd been collecting more reins, to lead his horse away with the others. "Thank you."

Poppa's mind was in turmoil. "I was hoping you'd be able to stay for a bit longer. You missed so much of William's early weeks."

"I know. Come, let's go home. I want to take a proper look at my son, and I can't do that when I carry all this stuff."

"And you'll need a wash too," she pointed out, wrinkling her nose.

But the news of yet another impending departure had blunted her joy.

Much later, long after night had settled, Poppa snuggled against him, content to breathe in his scent. He'd relished it when she rinsed his sore body with hot water infused with scented herbs, while William was snoozing happily. As if the little boy knew their little family was complete.

Hrólfr's skin bore fresh cuts and bruises, but he brushed off when she voiced her concern. After a quick meal of ale, bread and cheese, he cradled his son in his arms. Eventually, their son dozed off, and was soon settled in his cot.

With relief, they'd turned to each other, only partly aware that their frantic moves could wake their child at any moment. Their lovemaking had been fierce at first, then gentle as their bodies melted into each other. His need for her was always greatest after a campaign, and, relieved he'd returned safely, Poppa welcomed his hunger, and his body.

Now, a flutter of pleasure settled in her heart. She'd missed him so much. As she lay, her head resting on his chest, her hand caressing the soft sprinkling of hair, she adjusted her breathing to his. Slow and steady, and reassuring like his heartbeat.

Poppa closed her eyes. It would not be long until he had to leave again, but for now, he was here, with her. It mattered not whether they were in East Anglia or Neustria.

As long as they were together…

Chapter Ten

Hrólfr huddled deeper into his cloak, but even the thick fur could not keep away the biting winds that swept over the flat land. Around him, fellow warriors were riding crouched over their mounts, head down low over their horses' necks to avoid the worst of the sting. A whiff of sleet hung in the air, and dark clouds gathered above them.

He scanned the countryside. It was a grim sight. Meadows lay desolate, logged with filthy water; the bare, thin branches of the birch trees on either side of the track a reminder of the season. The horses' hooves made slurping noises in the churned-up mud.

In this foul weather, he should be at his hearthside, with Poppa and William, not out here, exposed to the forces of nature. For the last four days, they'd ridden through sleet and hail in search of West Saxon raiders, but so far, the turds had evaded them. Now that winter arrived, he thought about the futility of their action. Their clothes, tents and saddles were sodden, the men's mood sour.

But Eiríkr and Æthelwold were fired up by messages of gathered West Saxons, and they were keen to meet them in battle. Hrólfr glared at the leaders who rode mere yards ahead of him. Despite the conditions, they joked and laughed as if this were but a mere excursion through summer fields – a far cry from the reality he witnessed around him.

He swore as sleet hit his eyes, the sharp, icy sting stoking his temper. With the damp back of his hand, he wiped his eyes in a futile move. His already bad mood darkened further when a man on horseback came galloping towards them.

Several guards positioned themselves in a semi-circle in front of Eiríkr and Æthelwold. Hrólfr's hand went to the hilt of his sword. But as the rider approached, he recognised the man as one of their own who'd been sent to watch the movement on the border.

"Halt!" The king held up his right arm, and the men reined in their horses. From behind him, he heard sighs of relief. Those not on horseback were even worse off. He glared at the king's back.

The guards made way for the messenger to pass. A brief, lively exchange followed. After he sent the man away, Eiríkr called Hrólfr and several local *haulds* to him.

He grinned. "Great tidings! Edward the Usurper is barely two miles away, behind that that small wood of birch trees." His fist beat the air, and the men followed his lead. "We got him!"

Only Hrólfr was skeptical, but he kept his doubts to himself. King Edward would have his own spies scanning the wetlands, and he would have long since been notified of their pitiful advance.

"So what do we do now?" asked Oscetel, a *hauld* from a village further north on the coast.

Æthelwold snorted. "What do we do? Why, we attack, of course!" he yelled.

A cry went up, quickly hushed by Eiríkr who sent Æthelwold a dark glance.

"Be quiet! Do you want their sentries to hear us? We must sneak up on them. The later they realise how close we are, the more to our advantage it is." The King of the East Anglians looked each man in the face. "Now spread word to those behind you, quietly. We move on and surprise Edward."

The *haulds* nodded as Æthelwold drew his mouth into a thin line at the unspoken reprimand. The man was everything Hrólfr detested: scheming, backstabbing, lazy, opinionated, and full of his own self-importance.

Yet here he was, fighting the claimant's battle because he'd promised Eiríkr his help.

What am I doing here?

126

Not for the first time did he wish he'd sailed for Neustria before the autumn storms arrived, but William had developed a cough, and Poppa was adamant they would not travel until the boy was fit and healthy.

And given her own experience of their crossing to reach East Anglia, he could not blame her, even though he knew she detested his absences. He hated them too.

Yes, he was a warrior, happy to fight for a valid reason, but Æthelwold's cause was flimsy at most. It was hopeless. Despite Edward's early struggles in gathering supporters, the West Saxon king was now enjoying his role, and his raids into East Anglia were proof of his growing confidence.

Not that Æthelwold would see it that way.

Hrólfr sighed as he nudged his stallion – a gift from Eiríkr for his service – forward into a walk, following the two leaders and the *haulds*. He understood the lords' allegiance. After all, they were duty-bound to their king.

"Not only are we soaked and cold, our weapons damp, and our blades blunted, but now we're meant to do battle without a rest, after walking for hours?" a man walking beside him mumbled.

Hrólfr sent him a quick glance. His boots were muddy, the cloak roughly thrown over his shoulders threadbare. Then he looked at the other men walking behind. Some were from his village. Tired, exhausted from the cold, they put on brave faces.

"Yes. It's what we must do, or everything we've done so far will have been in vain," he said, keeping his voice gruff. It was his role to keep the men going, before they drifted away, back home, or elsewhere. "So when we approach the camp, shed your cloaks, and keep your weapons and shields close."

"Will we form a shield wall?"

He shrugged. "I don't know. It depends whether they spot us or not, and if there's enough time. You've seen the messenger head off again. Hopefully, once we've skirted that copse here, we'll have a better view."

With one hand, he unclasped his cloak, securing the clasp

in the thick fabric. Then he rolled up the cloak and placed it in front of him, across the wide back of his mount. Slowly, he donned his helm, guiding the horse with his thighs.

As they skirted the birch trees, the land opened in front of them. In the distance, a moving mass shifted in the hazy light. Was it fog? Or the West Saxons?

"A rider, from the right," someone called out.

Hrólfr stared as their messenger raced to meet them again, bent over his gelding. Was the man injured? Then he straightened, breathing heavily.

"Warriors, my lords. Many of them. Over there, waiting for us. But Edward himself has gone. He's ridden westwards."

"He's done what?" Æthelwold's face turned puce, and Hrólfr suppressed a grin. "No…no…no! We can't let him escape." He turned to Eiríkr. "We must go after him."

"To do that, lord, you will need to go through that *fyrd* over there. Even you can see that they've blocked our path."

"Then we must do what's needed! Run them through and go after Edward." Holding his axe aloft, Æthelwold urged his stallion forward.

"What? Wait!" But Eiríkr's cry went unanswered as Æthelwold stormed off without a backward glance.

Hrólfr gritted his teeth. "The fool will get us all killed."

The king glanced at him, then sighed. "We can't leave him to fight on his own, can we? Men of East Anglia," he raised his voice, "follow me!"

"No shield wall, then…" Hrólfr muttered. But the noise of the crowd around him drowned out his words. Kicking his horse in the flanks, he touched Mjölnir, then focused on the enemy waiting ahead.

Hrólfr's shield arm jarred at yet another blow from an axe. His opponent was a broad man beyond his prime, as tall as he was, but the man's movements were slowing. Yet his aim was good, and the force he used to bring his weapon down, strong.

Having abandoned his horse before he joined the melée,

Hrólfr waded through mud and water-logged earth, stumbling over dead bodies as their number grew. With Edward and West Saxons warriors fleeing, only a large group of fighting men remained, but Hrólfr had no time to wonder who they were.

There was no time to exchange any words, either, as their enemies were keen on slaughter. Hired mercenaries, most likely.

Planting his boots firmly into the ground, he pushed his attacker away with his shield. The man briefly lost his balance, and Hrólfr saw his chance. As he took a step forward, followed swiftly by another, he sent him sprawling backwards over the torso of a dead man.

The warrior swore, sliding backwards on his arse, axe held aloft.

Ah. The soft lilt he recognised from his journeys to Lundene. "You're from Kent?"

The man spat on the ground, then jumped to his feet. "Aye. And here to slay Danes." His agility surprised Hrólfr. Without doubt, a seasoned warrior. He respected the man's prowess.

Now he must kill him.

"Are you? Let's see how that's going, shall we?"

Hrólfr took a deep breath and, with the scent of blood in his nose, he advanced towards the enemy.

Daylight was fading when, at last, the men from Kent fled the meadow. A yell went up, and Hrólfr answered it, as did the East Anglians around him. They had won.

The boggy ground was littered with dead – or dying – bodies. Limbs lay cut off where they had fallen. Shards from broken shields stuck out here and there. The weapons of the defeated were theirs to take. And there were plenty.

He stepped over the men, making sure no one survived. A quick end at the pointy end of his sword was more merciful than leaving them to suffer a long, slow death. As he went, he picked up knives, swords, and a few axes.

Then a cry reached his ears, and the wailing grew louder.

Looking for the source, he frowned. A group of East Anglians were gathered at the far end of the field. Others, closer to him, were leaning over something on the ground.

Carrying the weapons under one arm, he went towards that group first. They were men who'd arrived with Æthelwold. And they looked lost, bewildered.

"What happened?" He drew closer, and their circle opened to admit him.

"Christ have mercy," one man said, kneeling beside a body. "Where is the priest?"

"I'll fetch him," another said and ran off.

Hrólfr nodded slowly. This would change everything.

Before him lay Æthelwold's prone body. He'd taken an axe to the neck where blood had begun to dry. A knife stuck out from the ribs, right where his heart would be.

Someone ensured the pretender to the West Saxon throne was most assuredly dead.

"See his body looked after." As the men set to the task, he turned towards the wailing group of Danes.

Was Eiríkr injured? Scanning the field, he could not see the king's banner.

Then he spotted it lying in the mud. He let out a slow long breath.

"Lord Hrólfr." One of the king's household warriors came over, shaking his head.

"How fares the king?" Hrólfr asked.

The sombre expression on the other man's told him the truth before he even answered. "He's losing much blood. He has a large gash in his stomach. We don't dare remove the sword."

"His stomach?" He patted the man's shoulder. They both knew the reality. It did not matter whether they left the sword in the wound or withdrew it. Either way, Eiríkr would bleed to death.

Suddenly, their victory tasted bitter.

Later that night, after they'd set up camp a couple of miles away from the field of battle, Hrólfr sat on the damp earth, extending his cold hands towards the fire.

He'd been amongst the first to keep watch, to ensure the men of Kent, or Edward and his West Saxons, did not surprise them in the dark. But all was calm around them.

Too wound up to sleep at the end of his shift, he pondered the events of the day. Had there been any point in that battle?

Æthelwold's ruthless ambition had not only got himself killed. No, he'd dragged King Eiríkr with him to death, and about four score others. Good warriors and ordinary men who now lay slain beneath a pile of earth. It had been difficult, digging up holes large enough to ensure the mortal remains would not easily be dug up by foxes. To add to their work, the priest had insisted that Christians could not be interred alongside Danes, so they separated their dead prior to burial.

Hrólfr grimaced. He wanted to wash the blood off his skin, and the mud. But a nearby stream was bitterly cold, and he was not prepared to die for a sense of cleanliness.

If only Eiríkr had not indulged the pretender. For months, they'd followed him do the other man's bidding. It had not brought them fortunes nor seen their borders safe.

No, Hrólfr was done with Danes and West Saxons. Let them sort out their differences amongst themselves. He was ready to face the Franks again.

On his return to their village, he would take Poppa and William, and the men loyal to him who'd survived this futile campaign, and they would find a safe route across the Narrow Sea.

It was time to return to Neustria.

***

April, AD 903
Bayeux, Neustria

Poppa sighed contentedly as she observed the people gathered in her old hall in their honour. It was many years since she'd last seen some of those who now gathered here.

Men and women were raising their cups and drinking

131

horns in echoing calls of welcome.

Beside her on the dais, Landina smiled. She had prepared a feast, and she seemed pleased with the outcome. Now that all the leftover food had been removed, everyone began to relax under the influence of ale and mead.

Pepin, in his role as *majordomus*, ensured everything had run smoothly. Since their flight from Rouen, he'd kept the hall in her name. Poppa beamed as she watched him with a cup of something in his hand, speaking with some of the locals.

Looking at her old friend by her side, Poppa was relieved Landina found happiness as Sigurd's handfasted wife, and the responsibility of the hall had done her good. Yet a sense of sadness was still lurking beneath her friend's smile.

No word from Ranulf had reached them, even though travellers returned from the Orcades with tidings from Leif. Landina told her she was still thinking about her brother every day.

Last night, they'd talked into the early hours. After silence had fallen, they'd sat by the fireside, a cup of mead in hand, catching up. They only returned to their beds long after their men had gone to sleep.

Today, Landina and Sigurd's young daughter, Emma, were fussing over William since dawn. And because she would not leave the little boy's side come the evening, both were now fast asleep together in the large bedchamber at the back of the hall. Now, a maid was keeping watch over them.

The children had been a joy to observe, and Emma's quiet patience when faced with William's outbursts was moving. The girl was caring, her sweet nature endearing to all. Poppa had immediately warmed to her.

Two years earlier, Sigurd had the private quarters rebuilt. Where there used to be flimsy partitions, solid wooden walls now separated the chambers, and the curtains had been replaced with doors, for more privacy. Just like in the hall in Rouen. Poppa approved of the changes. Her friends had turned the old hall into a comfortable home.

Although he'd offered her and Hrólfr the big chamber,

they'd declined. Poppa was happy to return to her old chamber, even though it was tight with her husband and a babe. But she had no complaints.

The hall was also much improved. New trestle tables replaced the rickety ones, and new, sturdier sconces were fitted to the walls. They held the torches far more securely, not risking burning down the house anymore. The smoke from the central hearth escaped more easily through a new opening. Sigurd even had the roof re-thatched.

While she was delighted, Hrólfr seemed lost for words. Did it remind him too much of Rouen, of their old life there? She watched her husband deep in conversation with his old friend. Having picked up his drinking horn, he'd kissed her temple, then left his seat beside her and joined Sigurd.

The previous evening, the two men spoke about what had been happening across Neustria, the Frankish king, the Bretons, and attacks from Danes which seemed to have become fewer, but not stopped altogether.

As she strained her ears, Poppa was certain Hrólfr was trying to get Sigurd and his followers on his side for a new attack on Rouen. Her husband had spoken of little else on their journey back to Neustria. Therefore, it did not surprise her too much.

Ever since he'd come back after the skirmish against King Edward's Kentish followers, his thoughts had focused with renewed energy on regaining control over the town. He wanted to challenge King Charles of the West Franks into letting him and his men settle there again.

Sigurd told them that, in their absence, Rouen had been under attack from several small groups of Danes, and Hrólfr formed a plan how to keep them at bay.

Poppa sipped at the chilled Rhenish wine, then glanced at her husband's profile as he spoke animatedly with Sigurd. Truth be told, Hrólfr was keen to move on, even though they'd arrived mere days ago. But Poppa suspected that he would have to bide his time – not easy for a man who was used to command warriors into action. There was also the question of his age.

Not long ago, he'd passed his fortieth year. The grooves around his eyes had deepened, and he'd gained a little in weight in East Anglia. Still an impressive warrior to face, she could not shake off the sense that Hrólfr wanted everything in order before he grew too old. Yet only God – or his Gods – knew what lay in store.

Her mind wandering, she touched the cross pendant he'd given her as a wedding gift. The garnets were gleaming in the torchlight. It was the one token that combined both their faiths – the shape of the cross for hers, and, carved on the back in tiny strokes, Odin's horns. Her most precious possession, she guarded it closely, often only wearing it beneath her shift as not to draw attention to it.

Like a secret between her and Hrólfr. She smiled. Then she listened in again.

Here, in Bayeux, men obeyed Sigurd, and although he'd reassured Hrólfr that he was still his man, the situation they'd found themselves suggested a more shared command. She smirked. It would do her husband good to have someone as level-headed as Sigurd to spar with. As old friends, they'd always shared the same perspective, and she was certain that, eventually, Sigurd would help Hrólfr in regaining Rouen.

As would Knud who was apparently staying in a settlement on the River Seine, having established a base there. It would be like in old times.

She brushed the memory of their attack that fateful Easter Sunday away and turned to Landina. "Sigurd will enjoy forcing Hrólfr into a waiting game," she whispered.

Landina giggled and leaned towards Poppa. "Yes, I think he will. He's so used to getting his way that he'll find it difficult to follow another."

"They'll have to learn to work with each other, heeding each other's counsel. After the disaster in East Anglia, it's probably wise to wait. Hrólfr said he'll send spies into north-eastern Neustria and beyond, possibly even to Burgundy, as the rumours about the challenges to Charles' power grow."

"I don't understand the man. He never gets any peace." Landina grinned. "I'm serious. They elected him to the position, and now they all hate him. Someone try to understand men!"

Poppa nodded. "You're right. The world would look very different if us women ruled."

"Ha, you bet!" Landina raised her cup and took a sip. "Just imagine what we would do in power…"

"Hmm." Poppa tilted her head. "There'd certainly be less bloodshed, and none of that ridiculous posturing, like cocks in a ring, taunting each other."

"We would talk things through, then come to an agreement."

"Indeed."

They looked at each other and burst into laughter.

Sigurd looked over from beside Landina. "What are you two plotting now?" But his eyes sparkled, and his hand linked with Landina's on her lap.

A sense of happiness filled Poppa. "Nothing," she said, the corners of her mouth still quivering. She exchanged a long glance with Landina.

"What Poppa said." Her friend nudged Sigurd's side with her elbow.

"Tsk, tsk. I could've sworn you're up to no good."

"Mere feeble women like us? Never!" But Poppa's raised eyebrows did not fool Sigurd.

Nor her husband, who seemed to have listened in from their friend's far side. "Who's meek?" Hrólfr asked. "Not you, my lovely lady, for certain."

"I'm the meekest of them all," Poppa said, but she could not hold back a giggle.

Sigurd snorted. "That applies to neither of you."

Hrólfr returned to her side, and they spent the rest of the evening in comfortable banter. Snuggled into Hrólfr's arm, Poppa listened to the skáld.

The tales of heroes long gone, of hardships and glory, told in her familiar childhood hall, made her feel content for the first time in many years.

She had all she needed here: Hrólfr, little William, her friends Landina and Sigurd.

But having met young Emma, Poppa yearned for a daughter. If only God would bless her with a girl of her own.

It would bring her complete fulfilment.

With a sigh, she smiled at her husband from beneath her lashes. He winked back at her.

Tonight, Poppa swore, they would try again…

Chapter Eleven

June, AD 905
Vire, Neustria

Hrólfr sat in a bustling hall in the small town of Vire, his drinking horn filled with wine from Septimania, far to the south. Hints of cherries and sunshine lingered on his tongue. Not even in Rouen had he tasted such delightful wine.

Not even the rain that accompanied their attack could dent his mood. Four towns in the last nine days had fallen to him. The hoards of silver, silks and furs, and precious stones they'd taken from churches and stores of the wealthy merchants made for rich pickings.

Everything was kept secured by a handful of trusted guards. On the morrow, he would issue every warrior with his due reward; an equal share of all the spoils, as promised.

He took a large draught, letting the warm liquid slowly glide down his throat.

Here, further inland, the women of the conquered places were more accommodating. Where they'd not fled, they remained to gain their own advantage from this change in circumstances. As always, he'd threatened punishment for any man in his group who tried to rape an unwilling girl. But as for those females who chose to stay, he let each decide her own fate.

His gaze slid across the hall. Six torches cast a meagre light across the large room. Every bench and stool were taken. Men were fired up by the skirmish, by bloodlust and fury. And now, in the afterglow of the fighting, they followed entirely different urges.

The Frankish men here worked in many useful professions. They did not know how to fight, and so they'd either swiftly lost their lives – or given themselves up. Those were his prisoners, held under strict watch, whilst Hrólfr, Sigurd, Knud, and the other group leaders decided their fate.

Hrólfr did not seek the death of those men. His goal was to control these parts of Neustria, between the king's seat in Paris, the fickle Bretons, and the untrustworthy Burgundians who changed allegiances whenever it suited them. One time, appeasing King Charles; another time, offering Hrólfr a truce. Their unreliable nature frustrated him.

No, he needed these prisoners to work the fields, to slaughter animals, to bake and cook. Even warriors had to eat.

Earlier that evening, the leaders held a small *thing*; the council consisted of himself and eleven of his most trusted men. Some argued that only dead Franks were good Franks, but the very thought sat uncomfortably with him.

Between them, he and Sigurd had slowly convinced the others.

No more bloodshed today. Instead, they would suggest a trade. Which had brought them to the rich merchants who swiftly approached him, fearful for their wares. Now these were men he held in low esteem. They had survived – where they had been reasonable – but their properties and goods were confiscated.

Hrólfr snorted. It would do those fat pigs good to go on a fast for a few weeks.

"What are you laughing at?" Sigurd asked, his eyes glazed over. Like every man in the hall, he had also consumed more of the rich Septimanian wine than they should have done.

Silently, Hrólfr swore that this would be his last for the night. He grinned. "I was just thinking about the merchants who came to us before we sacked Vire."

Sigurd burst out laughing. "In their finery, followed by their browbeaten thralls? I never thought someone who traded with people from as far afield as Miklagard or the lands of the Rus could be lacking so much sense."

"You mean stupid." Hrólfr pursed his lips. "Yes, their display was rather…off-putting."

Letting out a slow, long breath, Hrólfr stared ahead, but not paying attention to the drunken men, with their fumbling hands beneath women's gowns.

Tonight was the first time they celebrated. The men needed something to spend the energy on which had kept them going for weeks. Surveying valleys and hillside towns, watching from a distance, keeping hidden from sight until their put their plan into action and attacked, one town after another.

It was no wonder the men were looking for something to release the pent-up energy. And he?

Hrólfr blinked. He'd not looked at another woman since he first bedded Poppa. For ten winters, she'd shared his life, given birth to his son, waited for his return from campaigning in Neustria and in East Anglia. And he'd stayed true to her. No, he had no intention of changing that, even though his body was crying out for release. Let the men have their fun! Perhaps he should retire, alone.

Sighing, he eyed the contents of his drinking horn. It was half-empty. He should not really have any more wine, should he?

But before he could lift the horn to his mouth, the door burst open, and a young man of barely sixteen winters barged in.

"Lord Hrólfr?" the youngster shouted.

Recognising him as one of Pepin's kitchen thralls, Hrólfr waved him over.

"Lord," the lad's breath came in short gasp as he leaned over the table, lowering his voice. "I bear tidings from Lady Poppa."

A cold fist squeezed Hrólfr's heart. Not again! Poppa had been with child for three moons when he left. Had she died? No, the tidings were from her, so she would be alive, would she not?

His hand sought Mjölnir at the base of his neck, and the cold bloodstone gave him comfort.

Beside him, his friends fell silent. All eyes were on the messenger.

"Then speak." His voice sounded rougher than he'd intended, and he almost apologised when the boy gasped.

"I'm sorry to say but…" He kept his gaze lowered, for some reason unable to meet Hrólfr's eye. "But the lady Poppa lost the child she was carrying. 'Twas three days ago. I…I'm sorry, lord."

Hrólfr stared ahead, his mind numb. Sigurd squeezed his shoulder, and he nodded in silent acknowledgment. "The Gods willed it, though I can't fathom their reasons."

He emptied his drinking horn, as Knud called the boy over and handed him a cup.

The second child lost since the previous summer. The third since they'd begun to live as man and wife. The Gods must hate him. They knew how much Poppa yearned for another child, a girl. He'd even be thrilled with a daughter, as long as she survived!

No longer feeling like feasting, Hrólfr mumbled an excuse and left the hall, waving Knud away when he offered to join him.

He needed to be alone.

As he walked the deserted streets of Vire, his head pounded. Had he drunk more than four horns of wine? The thrall who'd served them tonight had replenished it often. Massaging his temple, he deeply breathed in the humid night air, but it only brought with it the stench of decaying corpses and burnt houses. How he missed the breeze!

He headed towards the edge of town. Surely, it would be more bearable there. Soon, he left the buildings behind and walked into the darkness. Only a sliver of moonlight peeked through the clouds.

As Hrólfr stood staring into the dark treeline of a nearby forest barely a mile from Vire, a guard hailed him, then moved on, and his steps receded soon.

Hrólfr found a large rock and sat. Cradling his head in his hands, his mind tore through the fury inside his heart.

Grateful for a young, healthy son, he'd not spent any more time thinking about children. But Poppa did.

Deep down, she was still uncertain whether their marriage was valid. Although she'd asked him oftentimes, he could not bring himself to join her church. Could one god alone wield so much power when in Hrólfr's world there was a whole bunch of them, each with their own calling?

Each with their own faults.

Had his Gods deserted him, because he'd been neglecting them? Perhaps they did not see him and Poppa as truly wedded, her being a Christian.

Was that why the babes had died before they could live?

Part of him wished he'd be by her side, grieving with her. Yet he was also relieved to be far away. The situation called for other women to support her. There was little comfort he could give.

His hand clasped Mjölnir, but the usual reassurance did not come. Now, for the first time, he felt nothing.

They had truly deserted him.

Questions over questions whirled inside his head, but he found no answers. When in the distance the first light of dawn broke, he shook himself out of his reverie. A new day lay ahead, with more challenges to face. None the wiser, he sighed.

At least, the fresh night air cleared his head. Silence had fallen over the vanquished town. People in their homes were asleep. Even those celebrating had gone quiet. As he walked back to the hall, he saw light in a hut he was passing. From within, laughter reached his ears, the voices male and female.

So some were still celebrating. He grimaced. In the past, he would have joined his men. Tonight, he left them to it.

He had a child to mourn.

***

May, AD 907
Bayeux, Neustria

Comfortably cushioned, Poppa reclined on a blanket, feeding Geirlaug, her infant daughter.

141

Close by, little William threw pebbles into the waves that lapped over the stony beach under the watchful eye of Magda, a servant girl who'd been looking after Landina's daughter, Emma.

Her heart swelled with immense pride as she watched the delight in her five-year-old son's face whenever a stone hit the water. They usually sank immediately, but that did not dent his joy.

But when her eyes fell on the chubby cheeks of her daughter, she realised the girl held a special place in her heart. God be thanked, both children were hale, with good appetites.

When Geirlaug, now fully sated, smacked her lips, Poppa covered her sore breast again. Then she lay the bundle onto the thick fur coverlet they'd brought with them. Within an instant, Geirlaug was soundly asleep, her rosebud mouth blowing little bubbles in the air.

Poppa smiled, and gently stroked her daughter's hair that already framed her round face in thick, dark curls.

"Mother, look!" William shouted, and Poppa shielded her eyes from the sun as she gazed over to where he stood.

"Yes, my sweeting. I'm looking."

"Watch what I can do!" And he threw a large stone into the waves as they approached. Water splashed high, dousing him in fine mist.

"Well done!" She laughed at his happy face, safe in the knowledge that Magda would pull him back should the water reach him.

Leaving them to their play, she lay on her side, her arm draped around the babe. Poppa breathed in the salty sea air, relishing the rays of sunshine warming her. It had rained almost every day since the feast of Easter, keeping them confined in their homes. Now, the sun made a welcome change.

She closed her eyes, tilted her face towards the sun, and let her thoughts wander.

Grateful for a chance to escape the hall after so many weeks, she still could not shake off a sense of worry.

Last night, young Emma complained about stomach cramps. She'd thrown up her meal, and during the night, she'd developed a fever.

This morning, Landina went to feed Emma a few spoonfuls of broth. Poppa had offered to sit with her, but Landina declined with the excuse that the small chamber would be crowded.

She agreed. It was not good for the sick child to have anyone hovering, prodding you where you were sore. Poppa remembered the most recent time she'd suffered from a fever. Her head had felt like splitting, and the slightest noise from those fussing over her caused her more discomfort. No, Emma deserved a calm environment to help her recover.

Deep down, Poppa was relieved. She'd been keen to take her children out into the sunshine, to let them breathe the fresh air of the sea. After being cooped up, it was their first chance.

But a sliver of guilt remained.

She sighed. It did not help that Sigurd was away. He and Hrólfr had taken the boats up the River Seine. Yet again were they trying to recapture Rouen. Word reached her that they'd gained control over much of the land on either side of the river and were closing in on the town.

Poppa had wanted to send a messenger with tidings of Emma's fever, but Landina refused. The girl's father had more important issues to deal with.

But Poppa was not only concerned for Emma. Landina was carrying a babe. Poppa knew that her friend's dearest wish was for another child, but she'd not even fallen pregnant since Emma's birth.

Landina had put on a brave face when Geirlaug was born. Since that day, Landina withdrew from her. The carefree friendship they'd enjoyed for so many years no longer existed.

Poppa suspected that was one of the reasons Landina had declined her help this morning. There was nothing she could do for the moment, but she could not shake off a sense of overwhelming sadness.

Under the sun's strong rays, a sense of sleepiness came over Poppa. Just for a little while, she thought. *Then I'll get up and play with William.*

"Lady Poppa! Lady Poppa, please wake!"

The voice was female, the tone, urgent.

Poppa blinked, blinded by a sharp light. Where was she?

Beside her, Geirlaug began to wail. With jolt, she opened her eyes fully, immediately shielding them from the glare of the sun. Her bones hurt.

She was lying on a blanket on the beach.

"Finally, she's woken." Magda removed her hand from Poppa's shoulder.

Who was she talking to?

"Lady, you must return home," a man said.

She sat up, to find Pepin standing in front of her, his face creased. He was agitated.

"I do? Why? And what are you doing out here, Pepin? Could you not have sent a messenger?"

"There was no time to find someone, Lady Poppa. Please hurry." He reached out his hand, and she let him pull her to her feet, then she picked up Geirlaug whose whimpering was growing louder.

Swiftly, Pepin rolled up the blanket, trapping the cushions inside.

"What warrants this, Pepin? Are we under attack?" She gazed around, relieved to find William hand in hand with Magda. His little face was sad.

"'Tis Emma." Pepin's voice broke. "She died."

"What? How? That can't be." Poppa's mind was whirling. "We left not long ago, and Emma was resting…"

Magda shifted on her feet. "'Tis mid-afternoon. You were fast asleep, as was little William after his playtime, I did not wish to rouse you."

Mid-afternoon? As if in response, her stomach rumbled. She sent the girl a reassuring smile. "You're not to blame, Madga. I thank you for your consideration." Assured that Pepin had collected all their belongings, Poppa turned to him.

"Now, tell me all on the walk back. We must hurry."

"No need to walk, lady. I brought horses."

The sun stood low in the sky when they reached Bayeux. Leaving the children with Magda, Poppa rushed through the deserted hall into the private quarters. The sound of sobbing reached her from Landina's bedchamber. Tentatively, she nudged the door slightly.

Emma was laid out on her small bed, one hand placed over the other. Her pale face still held the sheen of the fever, but instead of cries and thrashing limbs pushing the covers away, her little body lay still. Too still.

Landina kneeled, her head rested on her daughter's shoulder. Was she asleep? Had exhaustion overcome her?

Poppa's heart broke for her friend. "Landina?" She pushed the door open fully and stepped into the room.

"Arghh." A pitiful wailing emerged from her friend's mouth as she turned to look at her. "Oh Poppa! What am I going to do without Emma?" She collapsed onto the floor, her fist pounding the wooden boards. "Why is God punishing me? Why?"

Poppa knelt beside her friend and rocked her like a babe in her arms. "I…" She let the tears roll as she watched Emma's calm face. As if the girl were asleep. "She looks so peaceful." The moment the words left her lips, Poppa realised she'd said the wrong thing.

Landina extracted herself, using the bed's wooden frame to pull herself upright. Her eyes were blazing. "Emma was never peaceful. She was trouble, and loud, and never did as she was told!"

"I…"

"Spare your false words of sympathy, Poppa!" Landina hissed. "My Emma was not peaceful. That," she pointed with a shaky hand at the body, "is not my daughter. Emma is never quiet!"

Poppa reached for her, but Landina slapped her arm away.

"Leave me be!"

"I loved Emma too, like my own."

In a swift move, Landina pushed Poppa against the wall. She pressed her lower arm against Poppa's throat. "But…she…is…not…yours. She's mine."

Black spots appeared in Poppa's vision, and she tried to push Landina away, but her friend tightened her grip. "Of course," she croaked. "But—"

"No 'but', Poppa. I have lost my daughter. You have two children. Don't tell me you didn't feel a sense of relief, knowing yours are safe whereas mine…mine…is dead!" Landina screamed, then heaved herself away and fled the room.

The door slammed shut behind her, shaking the wooden partitions.

Her body trembling, Poppa slid down the wall and reached for her throat. Luckily, she was not hurt. Only her pride was.

Tears streamed down her face. "What happened to Landina?" she muttered.

Her friend had turned into a stranger.

Poppa stared at Emma's body. Despite their fight, she remained eerily serene. Nothing would ever disturb the girl again.

Geirlaug's birth had brought their ancient friendship to an end, but Emma's death turned Landina into a stranger.

As realisation hit her, and she let out a shuddering breath. "Oh, Landina."

Poppa covered her eyes with her hands. She let the tears stream down her face, mourning not only Emma, but also the loss of her childhood friend.

When Pepin found her, much later, night had fallen. He had Emma's body placed into a newly made coffin and taken to the church.

Of Landina, there was no sign.

Pepin sent men looking for her. They searched the whole town, but she'd disappeared. No one had seen a distraught woman. Sigurd's wife. But darkness had fallen, and it was impossible to scour the countryside beyond the houses. Beaten by the moonless night, the search party soon returned.

In the meantime, Poppa and Magda had withdrawn to her chamber with the children. Little Geirlaug mumbled in her sleep and William snored loudly.

The silence of the night did not bring her comfort. Her unease over Landina's safety was too strong. On the pallet beside the bed, Magda turned over restively. No. Tonight, neither of them would rest.

Outside, the birds began to chirp when Poppa finally fell into a restless sleep, a child cradled in each arm.

Chapter Twelve

Day of the Dead, December 17th, AD 907
Bayeux, Neustria

A low mist lay over the fields as Poppa passed the last of the houses and headed towards the rising sun. The mud from the sleet that had arrived with blustery winds yesterday clung to her boots. But this morning, the sky looked brighter, and Poppa took deep breaths of the fresh air.

Hrólfr had offered to accompany her, but she'd declined. This was her own duty.

She owed Landina her full attention.

As Poppa entered the small cemetery on the edge of Bayeux, the mist began to lift, and the blinding rays of the sun warmed her face. She smiled. It was a sign, she was certain.

Perhaps, finally, her friend had forgiven her.

Usually, Poppa's first visit on this Day of the Dead – the feast day when the souls of the departed must be honoured – would be to Father's tomb in the easternmost corner. But today, Father had to wait.

Instead, she headed to the northern side where the simple graves were found; earthen mounds covering plain coffins that held nothing but the bones of their occupants. The dead here wore no elaborate tunics and held no crosses decorated with precious stones in their hands, like Bérengar did in his beautifully carved sarcophagus.

But Landina had nothing of value to take with her. Except her daughter…

Bare, simple crosses, unadorned by any names, marked the mounds. Folk could not read, so the expense would have been a waste. Families knew where to find their loved ones.

Landina and Emma shared the same grave, and the same wooden cross. It was at Poppa's insistence that their names were carved into it.

As she read them out loud, Poppa remembered her lessons with Father Peter. Ranulf and Landina had always teased her, thinking it a waste of time. It seemed like a different life.

It was a different life!

Crouching at the base of the mound, Poppa placed a hand on the beaten earth. It was damp beneath her fingers, but it was a connection with the ground. By touching it, she felt closer to her old friend.

"How are you both today?" She sighed. "Home is so quiet without you. Too quiet. You probably see everything that's going on, but I'll tell you anyway. After all, my visit here has been long overdue."

With a sense of guilt, she remembered the last time she came had been during the busy harvest season. It had rained heavily, and she'd caught a chill after having helped in the fields for too long.

"Hrólfr is back home for the winter. It's good to have him here – there are many repairs to be done, and he needs to coordinate them. He can't leave everything to poor Pepin, only to complain on his return that something isn't to his taste. Men, eh?!"

She let out a harsh laugh. Glancing around, relief flooded through her when she found she was still alone. Poppa preferred it this way. It was her only chance to speak with her friend.

"As for Sigurd…he's now settled at the mouth of the Seine, near a most beautiful beach. You would have loved it there. 'Tis a shame you can't see it. Or perhaps you can, and you know this already." As sadness washed over her, she let her thoughts wander. "He has yet to accept your passing, my dearest friend. It was hard for him in the summer, staying in Bayeux where everything reminds him of you. Only once has he been to the cliffs, to leave this town." And he'd not been the only one. "To be honest, I don't go to the sea these days. I can't bear to look at the spot where they found your body."

Tears pooled in her eyes at the memory.

At first, Father Godefroi suspected Landina had taken her own life and refused a Christian burial. How dared he suggest she'd thrown herself to her death? She must have taken a wrong step in her upset state.

It was a tragic accident. Or not?

But deep down, Poppa was still uncertain.

Regardless of what the truth was – for Landina had taken it to the grave – Poppa was sure God did not begrudge Landina and her daughter their small space here. Emma was an innocent, and she needed to be with her mother. Separating them would have been cruel. They died within hours of each other, their bond unbreakable.

Yet the horrible man insisted. How could he call himself a man of God?

Poppa sniffed.

When Hrólfr, on his hurried return two days later, threatened Father Godefroi to string him up from his feet and dangle him over the hearth in the hall, the priest had – with a murmur of protest – relented and granted Landina and Emma a Christian burial. Sigurd was drowning his sorrows in mead, but Poppa had no doubt he would have roasted the priest alive if the man had not agreed. Even though Sigurd did not share his wife's faith, he'd always respected it.

"So I think a new beginning, in a different settlement, will do him good."

Poppa hoped her friend understood.

"And if you're concerned that he's taken another wife, don't fret. He's not even looking at other women. The poor man is still mourning your…passing."

Her mood darkened further.

"Hrólfr told me Sigurd has grown more and more withdrawn. Instead of joining the other Northmen in his new hall, he spends much time with the captives they make during their raids. Fellow Franks, and whoever else is unfortunate enough to fall into their hands." She wiped away a tear. "I think he seeks company like ours, yours and mine. Frankish people. He's still suffering, keeping away even from his friends. Could you not…I mean…appear to him, to let him know you still care?"

Poppa startled, surprised at her own idea. Was she talking nonsense? Fortunately, she was still alone. She did not want to risk any Christians overhearing her talk of appearing ghosts.

"Your soul needs calm, rest. So does his. Yours in Heaven, and Sigurd's here on earth, haunted. You could take Emma with you." She smiled. "I'm certain he'd love the reassurance that you're both well."

Poppa brushed away intrusive doubts. No, she was not conjuring up the dead. Father Godefroi would chastise her for such a suggestion, but she merely wished to help ease Sigurd's pain.

"The stupid priest is not here." After another careful look around, her smile turned into a grin. "I dare you, my friend."

Just then, the sun rose over the wall that surrounded the graveyard, and a ray of light shone onto the cross bearing Landina's and Emma's names.

Poppa's heart soared. God was listening. Did he approve?

A sense of happiness washed through her, and she blinked back tears that threatened to burst from her eyes again, but this time with joy. "Thank you, lord. And you, dear friend. I…I miss you every day. You – and Emma. William is too sensible to ever be as mischievous as you, little girl. Perhaps little Geirlaug will follow in her footsteps. I'd love that."

The wind carried the sound of voices to her. It must be the first townspeople to come and honour the souls of their dead.

Her time with her friend was over. She rose, brushing the earth from her cold fingers. Only now did she realise that her body felt icy.

"I will visit soon again, I promise." She lifted her cross pendant from beneath her cloak and kissed it. "Be blessed, Landina and Emma. The love of God will light your way. Oh, and don't forget Sigurd…"

Midwinter, December 25th, AD 907
Bayeux, Neustria

The torches cast a warm light across the hall. Outside, a storm was raging. Snow drifted in from the sea. But still, many came to join them for the feast days. As every winter, their celebration was one that brought both their traditions together, Poppa's commemoration of the birth of Christ and Hrólfr's Jul.

Late last night, she'd attended mass with members of her household. Father Godefroi's sermon had been dull and long, as expected. It seemed to her he was comparing their home of Bayeux to the fabled city of Babylon, full of sin. It was a clear attack on her husband and their marriage.

Poppa suppressed a snort once or twice, and, following mass, duly thanked the priest for his reflections.

In memory of the solemn spirit of Christ, she'd held back the scathing comments that sat on her tongue all through his ramblings. Instead, she'd smiled, then proceeded to ignore him.

Now, the hall was filled with the sound of many voices. Franks and Normans sat side by side. Hrólfr's and Sigurd's men were well liked here, and the Frankish locals – many arrived during their absence – had realised that they posed no threat to them.

The scent of roast meat, accompanied by a hint of rosemary, wafted through the large room. It made her mouth water.

From side door that led to the kitchen building, Pepin was overseeing the servants who brought in trays of food, enough to feed them all twice over. Ale flowed freely; the pitchers regularly replenished. The larder was well-stocked after the autumn slaughter, and tonight, everyone should feel sated and content.

The platters placed in front of Poppa on their trestle table held not only the succulent meat in its herb sauce, but also freshly baked breads and boiled turnips.

Beside her, Hrólfr spoke quietly with Sigurd, seated to his

right, who had arrived the day before, much to their surprise.

Poppa was pleased to see him smile again, the lines on his face less furrowed than when she'd seen him last, following the death of his wife and daughter. Something good must have occurred.

"Lady Poppa?" Pepin hovered between her and Knud, bending over the table to make sure she heard him over the clamour in the hall. "Everything is served."

"Thank you, Pepin. The meat smells wonderful. Make sure you have your own portion too."

"Yes, lady, I shall." Quietly, he withdrew into the shadows behind them.

She nudged Hrólfr's arm, and he turned towards her. "We are ready to begin."

"Ah, finally. I've been eyeing up that meat for what seems like forever."

She smiled when he stood and called for silence. "Friends, we welcome you to our hall, to eat and drink to your heart's content. Tonight, we celebrate Jul," he pointed at a group of Northmen at a nearby table, "and the birth of Christ," he gestured to Poppa and several other Christians. "We feast together, in peace and harmony."

A shout went up from the far end of the hall. "Get on with it, Hrólfr. The deer's getting cold feet."

Laughter echoed around the room. Her husband smirked at her, then faced the crowd again. "Now that would be reason for rebellion, and we can't have that. Enjoy your food and drink!"

Hrólfr sat again and Poppa began to ladle chunks of meat onto their shared trencher. It was important to combine their different heritage and faiths. Sharing meant accepting. And that was crucial.

A skáld struck up a tune on his lute to accompany the meal, and voices faded as folk helped themselves.

Hrólfr nudged her. "You won't believe what Sigurd just told me." He rolled his eyes. "I think he may be jesting."

Poppa kept her expression neutral. "Tell me, then I'll let you know if I believe it."

He laughed. "He's going to get himself drowned."

"Drowned?" She sent him a sideways glance. "What do you mean?"

Leaning back, he gestured for Sigurd to share his news with her. "Go ahead."

She eyed her friend curiously.

"It will please you, Poppa, to hear that I will convert to your faith."

Her eyes widened. "You will become a Christian?"

Sigurd beamed. "Yes. Before I return to my settlement, Father Godefroi will baptise me. On the morrow, in fact."

"Here? In our church?" When had he arranged that?

Then she remembered that she spotted him near the church the night before, after mass. But she'd never guessed that he'd gone to speak with the priest.

Pride washed through her. Her good friend's soul would be safe. Then there was only Hrólfr to convince, but all her attempts so far had ended in disappointment.

"I'm so pleased for you, Sigurd. What brought on this... change?"

He looked down at his hands for a moment, as if lost in thought, far away from here. Then he met her gaze directly. "Landina and Emma appeared to me, in a dream. It was in the night of the feast of the departed."

"The commemoration of souls?" A shiver prickled at her neck.

"Yes."

"Tell me what happened...only if you wish," she added hastily, not wishing to presume.

Hrólfr snorted. "Do you believe him?"

He raised an eyebrow and smirked, then he stared from one to the other.

"You are serious, aren't you?" He sobered when Sigurd nodded.

"Yes, I do believe him," Poppa said, sending Sigurd an encouraging smile.

At the same time, she silently thanked God for his help. He had indeed listened.

"Well, I went to bed late, like every night. I'd been drinking mead. Too much mead, as always." A shadow crossed his gaze. "But then, in the middle of the night, I woke. Hm. I think I did." He glanced around but apart from Poppa and Hrólfr, no one was listening. Still, he lowered his voice. "Or perhaps it was a dream. But right there, in my bedchamber, stood Landina and Emma, hand in hand. They were clad in silken dresses that had been decorated with precious stones. Their faces shone; they radiated contentment. Then Landina spoke. Her voice was warm. It... it felt real."

Poppa nodded, her food forgotten. Hrólfr sat between them in silence, listening intently, all humour vanished from his face.

Sigurd took a draught of ale, then continued. "She...she said that they were in a beautiful place, full of sunshine and happiness. But they were missing me." Furiously, he blinked back tears. "Like I miss them, every day. Then she told me that, one day, we would all be together again, as a family. But I could only join them in their paradise, yes, that's what she called it, a paradise...if I believed in it."

"But you do," Hrólfr interjected. "Our *Folkvang* resembles the Christians' paradise, if you're chosen, instead of going to Valhalla."

"I know." Sigurd stared back at him. "But Landina is not in Freyja's realm, nor in Odin's great hall, but in her own God's. So we would never be together after death."

"And that's why you want to part ways with our Gods – who have always stood by you?" Hrólfr's muscles tensed; he was simmering with suppressed anger.

Poppa merely placed a hand on her husband's arm. "Sigurd is right, Hrólfr. Our paradise is not yours. Your Gods don't mingle with mine. Landina and Emma are in our paradise. They can't cross over."

"Perhaps it's possible they—"

"My mind is made up, Hrólfr. I'm sorry if you find it impossible in your heart to support the idea. But I'd rather believe in one God who will see me united with my family than a bunch of warring brats who might play tricks on me, so I'll be trapped in the afterlife without my girls." His mouth formed a firm, determined line.

"Brats? You call our Gods brats?" After his initial shock, Hrólfr's body began to shake. A moment later, he was leaning forward, chuckling loudly. He patted his friend on the shoulder. "Oh boy, you'll likely be glad to be out of their reach after your drowning." He wiped away a tear from the corner of his eye. "They'd string you up by the balls."

Despite herself, Poppa giggled. Eventually, even Sigurd joined in the laughter.

"Are we allowed to attend your baptism, Sigurd?" Poppa asked. "You will need someone who acts as your godfather."

"It would be an honour to have you there, Poppa. But I already have a godfather." He grinned. "I asked Ragno."

"The blacksmith?" Her eyes widened.

"Yes. He has been a great support for many winters, and, as you know, he joined me in my new settlement."

Poppa nodded. Ragno was a good fifteen years older than Sigurd. It had been hard to find a worthy successor in Bayeux following the smith's departure, but fortunately there was a young lad who'd assisted him, and who turned out to be skilled enough to take over the responsibility. "Ragno will become your godfather?"

"Yes," Sigurd repeated.

She reached out beyond her husband and pressed her friend's hand. "I'm so pleased for you."

"Thank you. I knew you'd understand." He sent a tentative glance towards Hrólfr, who sighed.

"You're a grown man, Sigurd. It is your decision if you want to leave the brats, as you call them, behind. And of course you will always have my friendship, whatever you believe in." The corners of his mouth twitched. "I may just have to appease the brats on your behalf…"

Dizzy with happiness, Poppa returned her attention to the tasty food on her trencher, and she cut off a chunk of venison. She was so pleased.

The rest of the evening passed in friendly banter.

Later, after the platters had been removed, everyone listened when the skáld sang of warriors, of maidens, and of adventures in lands far to the north in both their tongues.

Poppa brushed aside the brief memory of Ranulf that the man's words evoked. To her shame, she'd completely forgotten about him. The next time a group of Northmen were heading for Orkneyjar, she would send word of Landina's passing. If Ranulf was still alive, he should receive the message.

But in the meantime, she enjoyed the warm, spiced ale that Pepin had prepared for her only and leaned back into the soft furs of her chair.

Sigurd would be a Christian. No longer was Landina's soul tormented. Her ruse had worked.

Contentedly, Poppa sighed.

Her friend would be at peace. And Poppa's heart felt lighter.

***

Spring, AD 911
Rouen, Neustria

"The damned man has deceived us!" Hrólfr's fist slammed on the table, sending drinking horns flying. As he watched his own smash to the floor, a sense of dread hit him. He stared at the shards, then waved away the thrall who'd rushed forward to collect the offending pieces. "Leave it!"

The youth shrank into a corner of Hrólfr's private chamber on the upper floor of the old hall which he used for small meetings with trusted friends. It kept prying eyes and pricked ears at bay.

Hrólfr paced the room, clenching and unclenching his hands. Had the Gods deserted him? Or was Loki up to one of his games?

Yet he did not feel like playing.

Anger surged through him at the latest tidings.

A score men on their way to Chartres had been waylaid by

the Burgundians. They were hanged, and their bellies ripped open as the noose was tightened very slowly around their necks. They were not granted a quick death. Their entrails were burnt in front of their eyes, and all weapons taken.

He pinched the bridge of his nose. Like that, they would never enter Odin's great hall. They would never join their fellow warriors. He let out a sharp breath.

Only one witness, who had one eye gouged out and his right hand cut off, was sent back to tell the tale. He'd arrived thin and weak, not having dared to seek shelter along the way.

"It looks that way," Knud said. Having caught his own horn in time, he swallowed its contents and put it on a shelf on the wall, well out of reach of Hrólfr's fury.

"Richard's message from last week about a truce was all lies. And I dared believe him."

"We needed the time to pause, to regain our strength. You had no choice."

But Hrólfr was not so certain. Perhaps his head was addled. He was nearing fifty winters, after all. His hair was greying at the temples, and he was out of breath more and more often during weapons training. It did not bode well.

Perhaps his time would come soon, and younger men would follow his path. But William was not yet ten winters old and needed much guidance. No, Hrólfr was not ready to leave this earth yet.

"We need to teach him a lesson. Send a messenger to Sigurd and the other leaders along the coast. I want them all to gather here."

"Why?"

"Richard is in Chartres until the summer, is he not? We'll challenge him there."

"In battle?" Knud sent him a sharp glance. "Is that wise?"

"If needed, yes." Hrólfr glared at his friend. "But perhaps a siege will do. It's a rich town; what treasures we can find there!"

"But it's also very well-defended since the last attack by Danes. I've heard their walls are impenetrable."

Why was Knud so sceptical? It was not like him. "We can but try. Men can be bribed to open gates..."

"Shouldn't we secure Rouen first? We'd have to leave men behind, to guard the hall."

"You're right. A group of men will keep the town safe from the claws of the Frankish king."

Between them, King Charles of the Franks and Duke Richard of Burgundy kept creating trouble for Hrólfr since the onset of spring. Dropping their usual style of warfare – pitched battles – they were instead sending search parties to intercept small groups of Northmen – Norse and Danes – travelling through Neustria. Some were Hrólfr's enemies, for which he was grateful, but others had been his allies. He owed them his support.

The attacks tended to happen unexpectedly, and the Franks and Burgundians, together with hired mercenaries from Aquitania in the far south, showed no mercy. They killed cowardly, sometimes even at night, slaughtering sleeping men, to avoid facing the Norse in a fair fight.

Then Richard had offered a truce – only to break it within eight days. The terms sounded reasonable, and Hrólfr believed the duke.

He snorted. The man would soon find out who held power in Neustria. Burgundy might be a powerful duchy, but it needed defending all the time. Since his return from Anglia, Hrólfr and his followers had taken control of the lands from the mouth of the River Signa and westwards along the coast, towards Brittany, and southwards, to the borders of Richard's domain. Many towns and new settlements agreed to Hrólfr's terms and enjoyed his protection. He no longer took captives to sell as thralls. If the men worked the land, practiced their skills, and learned to fight and defend their villages, they were far more useful to him than huts full of defenceless women. Only a small number of hostages, treated well and fairly despite their captivity, ensured their continued support. It worked.

But now these murdering raiders were running loose, causing fresh trouble. No, he could not accept their insolence.

Richard of Burgundy must be taught a lesson.

He gestured for the thrall to fill a new drinking horn, then he took a deep draught. A smile formed on his lips.

"You have a plan?" Knud raised an eyebrow in question, and Hrólfr nodded. His friend knew him well.

"Good. I'll fetch messengers right away."

As the door fell shut behind Knud, Hrólfr reclined in his chair, stretching his long legs. A sigh escaped him. Age was catching up with him fast, but he was not ready to give up the fight just yet. Life would be boring without it.

He merely needed to take things a little easier…

PART THREE

~~

BETRAYAL

Chapter Thirteen

July 20th, AD 911
Near Chartres, Duchy of Burgundy

The summer sun was beating down on them as the men sat on their cloaks in the dried mud, breaking their fast. Every line on the sunburnt faces was covered in dirt, hair sticking together in clumps.

After two days of heavy rains and thunderstorms, it dried up early morning, but the damage was obvious. The camp had been turned into a large quagmire, and there was no clean or dry space to be found, not even inside the tents.

Several of the warriors injured during their last attempt at breaking through the gates into the town had died, their wounds festering so quickly in the humid air, they'd had no chance.

Hrólfr nodded to the men, mostly Danes who had followed his call, in encouragement, but he was not surprised at their averted gazes. He was as frustrated as they were. Ignoring how the mud squelched under his filthy boots, he marched on until he reached his tent. He opened the flap and tied it back to let the breeze enter the stuffy interior.

Here, the floor was almost as churned up as outside. With a sigh, he poured himself some ale into a clay cup and sat on a stool behind the large table covered with maps and drawings of the walls surrounding the town of Chartres. Staring at them deep in thought, he took several long draughts.

How did he get it so wrong? He slammed the now empty vessel onto the table, which shook under the force. He'd been raiding towns and villages in Neustria for well over a score years, yet he'd utterly underestimated the defensive barriers.

Whoever built it held knowledge way beyond Hrólfr's experience.

He should not be impressed, but he was. There was much to learn here. On the inside must be a walkway high up where men were seen patrolling. It was also from where they shot arrows and threw pots of boiling water at his shield walls when they tried to destroy the gates with the battering ram. But even the gates were too solid to splinter.

He'd never seen anything like it.

Not only did the scalding water severely injure his men, but it also meant that within the perimeter, they had plenty of fresh water. And from the way they acted, also enough grains to feed themselves for some time yet.

It was no surprise his warriors were disgruntled. Some drifted away across the fields towards the north, back to the coast, and beyond. Only yesterday, a group of Norse from the Kattegat had taken their boat and sailed down the Autura River towards Rouen, and ultimately, along the Signa into the Narrow Sea. The flat lands of Anglia seemed more appealing than a solid wall the height of a giant.

A wall that was impossible to breach.

Torn between his admiration for the builders and his own frustration at his failure to break through it, he'd run out of ideas. Hrólfr stared at the drawings, then swept the parchments onto the floor with his arm.

"Argh!"

"Ah, you're back." Sigurd entered, grinning, and helped himself to a cup of ale. "I thought I saw you return. All is well with the ships?"

Hrólfr nodded, then held out his cup for Sigurd to fill. "Yes. The guards are paying close attention to any movements from the town. How are your men?"

Sigurd snorted. "Like yours, as well as can be expected. They'll be spending most of today making sure their weapons won't grow rusty. And—" He cocked his head.

Hrólfr heard it too.

A roar from somewhere nearby. Like an angry swarm of bees.

"What is that?" Sigurd put his cup down and hovered in the entrance, gazing out. Hrólfr stood beside him, baffled.

A cry went up outside, followed by others. Then the clashing of metal reached them.

"By Odin's old bones, we're under attack! Gather your men and get word to Knud and the other leaders."

He grabbed his shield and drew his sword.

His friend was already striding through the camp, but all around him, men were scurrying to get to their discarded shields and helmets.

Had they all been too careless, drunk on the summer's heat – and ale?

Knud rushed towards him. "Men, scores and scores of them!" He halted, catching his breath. "From the main gate, the mercenaries are riding out, followed by what looks like peasants armed with pitchforks. They're nearly upon us."

"How did we miss them?" Hrólfr issued the order to withdraw to the boats. They would have to leave the tents and all their belongings behind. Already, the roar became stronger, louder.

More clashes of metal reached them.

"Withdraw! To the ships!" Knud yelled, and the message was relayed from warrior to warrior, most barely clothed in their tunics. If they were lucky, they had their swords on them. If not...

"To the ships!" Hrólfr howled, urging the men forward. Nearby, Sigurd and a small group of his warriors were fighting off attackers. But behind those, many more were approaching fast. Soon, some of the Danes were caught up in the rush, fighting a losing battle.

As Knud urged the men to flee to the boats, which lay moored barely half a mile from their camp, Hrólfr ran across to aid Sigurd.

With the momentum of speed on his side, he knocked down a stocky fighter who stumbled backwards over the torso of a fallen mercenary. Fending off the wild stabs from his opponent's sword with his shield, Hrólfr pressed his advantage and slashed the man's exposed thigh.

167

Ignoring the howls emanating from him, Hrólfr ducked and pushed his own sword deep into the attacker's throat. He withdrew his sword, and blood gushed from the wound, splattering his arms and tunic.

Retracing his steps, he sidled up to Sigurd. "Come now. We must hurry." He pointed at riders approaching the entrance of their camp. "Call your men and follow me!"

After they've finally rid themselves of the early attackers, Hrólfr weaved his way through the sea of tents, Sigurd and three survivors on his heels. Here, the ropes of the tents were too close for horses to gallop through safely. Behind him, he heard swearing and shouting.

"What did just happen?" Sigurd asked between short breaths.

"I wish I knew."

Soon, they left the camp behind, but now, they were in open countryside. Fields lined either side of the road that led north. They had to cross them to reach the river.

But out here, enemies on horseback held the advantage.

They lengthened their strides as they crossed the fields. Not long, and the masts of their ships appeared as they lay anchored on the Autura River.

Hrólfr slowed and glanced over his shoulder. The riders had now cleared the tents and, followed by a rabble of running mercenaries and what looked like a bunch of poorly armed peasants, made swift progress towards him.

He swore under his breath. This was bad.

Swiftly, he caught up with his friends and fellow warriors.

"They will be upon us before we reach the ships," he shouted to Sigurd. "We'll have to face them when they get closer."

"Dangerous with those horses, unless we find a way to make them rear up."

The rhythm of his booted feet pounding onto the ground reverberated through his head, and it began to ache. But that would be the least of his concerns. He might equally die here.

Then he spotted, to their left, a roped-in area where a score cows were grazing, watching the fleeing Northmen pass.

"The rope!" Hrólfr shouted. "Cut the rope! Chase the herd this way." He gesticulated to Knud, who quickly understood. He ordered a few to follow him and, using their swords, they sliced through the ropes. Then they rounded up the herd and sent them in the direction of the riders.

Hrólfr urged his men forward, ordering them to get the ships ready to leave, then he slowed down to join Knud.

The heavy beasts did not want to move, so a few slaps on their rumps finally made them trundle across the field. A few more slaps, accompanied by frantic shouting, and the cows began to run in panic – straight into the path of the attackers

"To the ships!" Knud ordered, everyone raced towards the water's edge.

As they approached the riverside, Hrólfr risked a glance. As planned, the frightened animals were scampering across the field, and the riders were forced to detour around them, trying to get the skittish horses under control.

"It worked." Knud slapped him on the back. "Now let's board and be away from here."

They embarked on their separate ships, and as soon as the last man's feet hit the planks, they pushed off.

Finally, the riders were advancing, but by the time they reached the river, the ships were well away.

A few carelessly thrown spears splashed into the water, but it was already too late.

"To Rouen!" Hrólfr ordered. He was still breathing heavily with exhaustion, but it would not do to show weakness in front of the men who had escaped with him. "Row, brave warriors of Odin! Row!"

A sennight later
Rouen, Neustria

"Hrólfr? Hrólfr!" Sigurd's voice reached him in his private chamber above the hall.

"Up here, Sigurd." He pulled a clean tunic over his head and looped the belt around his hip.

Steps pounded on the wooden stairs, and a moment later,

Sigurd's tall frame obscured the narrow door. "I'm glad to find you home." He paused to catch his breath.

"Whatever is the matter?" Hrólfr sat on his bed and put on his boots. He'd had them cleaned the previous day, relieved most of the mud had come loose.

"A delegation has arrived."

"A what? Who sent them?"

"King Charles!" A broad grin split Sigurd's face. "And some Burgundians, too, by the way it looks. Apparently, they've come to negotiate."

"Have they, now? Then we must ensure they're well received."

"I've instructed your *majordomus* already, with your permission."

"Of course. Thank you." Hrólfr nodded. "I would like you to be by my side, at all times, during these talks. You share their faith; it might help matters."

Sigurd laughed. "Anything to make them do what we want, eh?"

"Indeed. Come!"

Soon after, a group of Frankish courtiers entered, followed by the Burgundians. Hrólfr gave a lazy smile. The Franks were known for their stylish clothing, yet they looked like peasants compared to the flamboyant delegation from Burgundy. Their tunics were richly embroidered – not with gold thread, like the king's closest advisors – but with the most colourful patterns.

He had to grant it to them – they dressed for the occasion. Hrólfr was relieved that he'd just changed into clean tunic and hose, although he looked modest compared to the visitors.

But he had an inkling of what they wanted. Despite the hasty retreat at Chartres, he'd kept the upper hand. They'd escaped with only a small number of casualties. The Burgundian rout had failed.

Now, King Charles and Duke Richard knew he was here to stay. Leaning back in his well-cushioned chair, he bid them welcome.

Then he spotted a vision of light between the men: a young woman, barely in the first flush of womanhood. Beneath a sheer veil held in place with a golden circlet, her long, golden hair shone in the light of the candles, and her exquisitely cut gown accentuated her womanly forms. She seemed not to walk but to glide across the hall.

Who was this vision? Not for many winters had he seen a woman so enticing.

Then her pale grey gaze met his, and he was lost.

Leaning forward, Hrólfr smiled. Negotiations had just become more appealing.

***

Late July, AD 911
Bayeux, Neustria

"You have done what?"

Tears stung Poppa's eyes, and she angrily wiped them away with the back of her hand. No. She would not cry in front of him.

The rumours were true. She should have paid attention, not laughed them off as malicious gossip. But it sounded so surreal.

Not only had Hrólfr finally converted to the Christian faith, but also, he'd wed some Frankish princess, in a Christian ceremony.

Married by a priest!

Poppa had lost count of the many years she'd tried to convince him to join her in Christianity, and to have their wedding blessed under God, but Hrólfr always resisted. Even Sigurd's attempts, following his own conversion, had served for naught.

For as long as she'd known him, Hrólfr had not been religious; he'd often ignored his Norse Gods. Apart from the Thor's Hammer amulet, which was at this moment conspicuous in its absence, he did not own anything that linked him to this old faith.

And he'd not celebrated the feasts either. Yet he could never explain to her his reluctance to converting.

Now he dared stand in front of her with a sheepish grin on his face, arms raised in front of him in an attempt to calm her.

"How could you!" With the full force of her fury, she slapped him.

He merely nodded, not even trying to defend himself. "I deserve this."

"Yes, you do."

He hovered over her in their bedchamber, but it was Poppa who was threatening him. As if he sensed it, he sat on the edge of their bed. "Poppa…"

"Don't 'Poppa' me! I am your wife. You are already wed."

He sighed. "It was part of the negotiation, to seal our agreement. I didn't know King Charles was to offer his daughter until—"

"A girl born to one of his concubines." Poppa's breath came in short puffs. Never in her life had she been so angry.

So disappointed.

"Gisela is a king's daughter, whether you like it or not. It is a great honour. I'm no longer a Northman raiding these lands. I am jarl – or earl, as Charles calls it – of the coastal region of Neustria, of all the settlers here, all the way to the border of Brittany. As a man in such a strategic position, I must be beyond reproach."

"An honour? But you are already wed." But even repeating it did not make it valid. Theirs was a handfasted union between Frank and Norse. It was not a union of two Christians.

"Not in a manner acceptable to King Charles or Duke Richard."

"Ah. So you've become a Christian to hump the daughter of a whore – legally, in the eyes of God. *My* God!" She swallowed hard. "The harlot is now a countess. Not I, your wife of a score years, who supported you in all your adventures."

Her dreams were crushed, and it hurt. The pain of his betrayal made her feel sick; her heart was breaking.

Clearly, he'd never cared for her, whatever sweet words he may have whispered in her ears. Their love-making had been false; the contentment she'd always felt, destroyed.

What have I done wrong?

Her fury turned into desperation. "What about our children? What about William and Geirlaug?"

William had been in Rouen with his father, to become a warrior. Poppa was fretting over his safety ever since, but she realised her son was growing into a young man. A man who was already able to read, thanks to Father Godefroi's lessons. As for Geirlaug, she'd been staying in Bayeux, also receiving an education, and Poppa had no intention of changing the status quo.

"Ah yes. It's one of the reasons I'm here, to tell you."

Poppa scoffed. "There is more? What is going to happen to my son?"

"William has been baptised, at the same ceremony as I."

"What?" She steadied herself at the wall. When he rose and reached out to her, she slapped his hand away. "You had him baptised without my presence? How could you?"

He lowered his gaze, no longer able to meet hers. "Because Gisela was—"

"That whore was at *my* son's christening?" Anger surged through Poppa's veins again. "The one thing I've been begging you for years – to convert, and to have our children join God's fold, to save their souls, and you denied me the honour of being there? I'm his mother!"

With a sigh, Hrólfr glanced up. "You can attend Geirlaug's ceremony. Father Godefroi will be delighted to perform it, I've no doubt."

"Oh, how gracious of you. Of course, a daughter is of less importance, so not the big event that must have been your own baptism." But inwardly, she was pleased for the girl. As soon as Hrólfr left, she'd organise it. "Though what I actually meant was…my lord jarl…who will be your heir? After all, you're no longer the youngest. And you have a fine son already!" She pinned him down with a sharp look.

A broad smile swept across his face.

Here was a man of middle age, still handsome, muscular, with his wits about him. A man she'd loved ever since they first met, even though she'd not known it then.

The man who now betrayed her. She hardened her resolve and continued to glare at him.

"Have no fear, Poppa. I have already announced William as my heir. Nothing will change that."

"And what if… what if…" She could not force herself to speak the words, never mind think of her husband in bed with that harlot.

"If Gisela bears a son?" He raised his eyebrow, all humour gone from his face.

Was it her imagination, or was there truly a sense of sadness about him?

It was probably wishful thinking. Fiddling with her belt, she nodded, her throat constricted.

"Then William will take precedent. It's a fact I had added to the agreement with the king. It's set in stone."

Relief coursed through her. Even though she'd likely be forgotten in the new line of jarls of whatever, at least her son's future was secure.

"That is the one thing you've done right then. Now, begone!"

He stood, trying to reach out to her again. "Poppa, I—"

Opening the door, she stood back. "Get out! This hall is mine by right of my father, Count Bérengar. You've told me all you had to say, so go on…return to your harlot!"

With a sigh, Hrólfr walked slowly towards her, until he stopped barely inches in front of her. Her gaze fixed on the far wall, she refused to look at him.

"We shouldn't leave it like this," he said, his voice low.

"Well." Her tone was as sarcastic as she could make it. "You should have thought about it before you wed for glory and power…my lord jarl."

Cupping her face, he tilted it until she was forced to look him in the eye. "It was not easy to reach this agreement, Poppa. I'm getting too old for raids. Now, we can settle in Rouen, and keep the lower Signa region free from attacks

174

from marauding Danes. The Franks will stop pestering us, too. That's what I agreed to. It means we can live in peace. You don't have to fear any more attacks on Bayeux. We—"

Her eyes blazing, she pushed his hand away. "It means I no longer live with my husband, the man who refused to convert to marry me in the eyes of Holy Mother Church; the man who refused to have our children baptised – until now. The man whose life I shared, with whom I would have travelled to the ends of the world to find a safe haven. That's what I take away from your agreement, my lord. It's the harsh truth. I…I don't care about the rest. Now go!"

"I've always loved you, Poppa." Hrólfr tilted his head, but she ignored the sorrow in his eyes. "I will visit you."

"Don't trouble yourself! I don't want to see you ever again. Enjoy your newfound power, my lord jarl. Go and hump your harlot! You will leave…us…alone!"

Before he could say another word, she pushed his tall bulk out of the door, then slammed it shut. Leaning against it, she slid down until she sat on the wooden planks.

Finally, Poppa let the tears flow…

Chapter Fourteen

"Now, take a swing, son." Hrólfr grinned as William hit Knud's shoulder with the flat of his sword, stopping short at the nape of Knud's muscular neck. "Yes!"

The ageing warrior raised his hands in mock defeat. "I yield, young lord."

At almost ten-and-seven, William was already as tall as Hrólfr, and towering over Knud by half a head. But his shoulders still needed to broaden, although perhaps it turned out that – like with his dark brown hair and eyes – he'd also inherited Bérengar's slim shape.

Hrólfr hoped that was not the case. William needed to become a strong warrior to command men and gain their respect. The boy would be jarl one day, or earl, as King Charles kept saying; he was heir to a large area of Neustria: the earldom of the Normans now stretched from the Signa to the border with Brittany, and inland.

Despite challenges, both sides honoured their agreement. Hrólfr kept the Danes away, and Charles ensured the Franks left him and the settled Northmen in peace. The region was turning prosperous again, its fields tilled, new trade routes opened. People had begun to feel safe. His own younger self would have hated it – he'd regarded it as boring. But at almost sixty winters, Hrólfr was grateful he had a hall that was not in danger of any raids.

But all that land would one day be William's to defend. Not yet, though. The lad still had much to learn.

"That's enough practice for today, I dare say. Poor Knud will need a whole pitcher of ale to get over his failure."

The older man snorted in response. "Oh yes. This little rascal," he pointed at William, "will one day become a great leader. He can't deny his Norse blood. But today, I let him win…"

"No, you didn't!" Laughing, William sheathed his sword, then joined Knud as they walked to where Hrólfr stood on the edge of the practice yard. "You were simply not fast enough, old man!" But the twinkle in his eyes showed that he was winding Knud up.

Hrólfr's friend was proud to train his son and other boys who wanted to learn how to fight. Each morning, the yard was filled with the clash of metal on metal, the cries of orders, and the rigorous formation of shield walls.

But today, in the spring drizzle and high winds, it was only those two who braved the Gods.

The weather. The elements. Not the ancient Gods.

It had been a long time since Hrólfr even thought about his past. These days, his daily life was consumed by negotiations with Danish raiders, establishing the strategic defence of his lands, going to church – if only to please the new archbishop of Rouen, not his wife – and dispensing justice.

No longer did he ride out to face down potential enemies. His men did this now. Near the mouth of the Signa, or Seine as he was told by the king to call it now, Sigurd had established a small settlement that served as a great line of defence. His spies patrolled up and down the coastline.

From his hall in Rouen, Hrólfr had created a large group of informers. But as he was not getting any younger, William had recently been present during these meetings. It was time the boy learnt how to administer an earldom.

A warrior as well as an able administrator, that's what his son would be.

As they approached the hall, Gisela's high-pitched screaming drowned out everything else. It sounded like she was chastising a thrall. If it were deserved, he would have no objection.

But by now, he knew his wife. Where the woman could not find a reason that suited her, she'd create one.

"I'll be in my hut, then, resting my ancient bones…" Knud rolled his eyes, turning on his heel in the direction of his home.

Hrólfr sighed and opened the door – and wished he had stayed at the yard.

Beside him, William groaned. "I'll grab my fishing rod, Father. I'm soaked already, so might as well catch us a treat for dinner."

Without a glance at the two women by the hearth in the centre, William took the stairs to their private quarters two steps at a time and disappeared.

"You clumsy girl!" A sharp slap echoed around the empty room. "Now brush up the ashes and wipe the floor clean. Then get out of my sight before I decide to sell you to the Moors!"

Gisela's screeching hurt his ears, and Hrólfr was considering turning around when she spotted him and rushed towards him.

"There you are, Rouf. Finally! I've been looking for you."

"I was at the practice yard, with William. Why? Has anything happened?"

He glanced around but the hall was deserted apart from the sniffing thrall who had the thankless task of scooping up ashes that had fallen out of the hearth.

His wife stared at him, her grey eyes cold. "Does something have to happen for you to be in your own home? With me?"

He shrugged. "I watched my son practice swordplay. That's important."

"I see. And I'm not." Her mouth formed a thin line.

"Gisela, you are in charge of the hall and the household. I dare think it keeps you busy. I can't sit around all day, growing fat and useless."

"But there are chores to be done by the lord." She crossed her arms beneath her small breasts.

Breasts that a long time ago lost their appeal, just like the woman herself had. In fact, not a day went by when he did not regret this farce of a marriage.

178

Charles had been clever, tying Hrólfr to him through his daughter. But the King of the Franks did not have to live with her every day.

"Then get Pepin to organise whatever requires doing. As *majordomus*, it's his responsibility."

"How convenient for you!" she hissed.

Taking a deep breath, Hrólfr clenched and unclenched his fists. He would never countenance violence against women, but by God – any god – Gisela had often brought him close.

"I need to change before I meet with the cloth traders. Make sure the Rhenish wine is chilled for our guests and have some pastries served." He passed her but swung around close behind her. "Oh, and if I see you slap a thrall over a simple accident again, I'll lock you up."

She snarled over her shoulder. "Father would never let you get away with that."

He leaned close to her ear, almost recoiling from the sickly-sweet scent of the water she bathed in every morning, and whispered, "Your father is not here..."

Later that night, Hrólfr reclined in his fur-covered chair, his legs stretched out in front of him. The trestle tables had been dismantled, and a calm descended on the hall. Men were sitting in small groups, drinking ale, talking, and playing board games.

His wife had withdrawn early to their chamber – a chamber he avoided these days. Her maid accompanied her, and he knew just the kind of gossip that would go on whilst the women were sewing or embroidering until it was time to sleep. Gisela hated everything here: his hall, the Norse settlers, and the bustling, growing town of Rouen.

It would never match Paris.

He grimaced. No, Rouen was a far more beautiful place to live than the stinking, overcrowded capital of the Frankish kingdom.

For the last four winters, he and his wife led separate lives. She had not once fallen pregnant when she was willing to share her bed with him, in the early months of their marriage.

Now, Gisela was bitter, blaming him and his old beliefs for their lack of children, calling him a heathen, a ruthless conqueror, a raider. She was still young and beautiful, yet her perpetual expression of disappointment, even disgust made her appear older.

Gisela wanted to be seen as a martyr, one who suffered terribly for her faith; a woman who lived with the enemy, for God. And everyone who crossed her path was at the receiving end of her sharp tongue.

Yet, had he not given up everything to be a true husband to her? Had he not turned this hall into a welcoming home? Did she not have thralls doing her bidding from sunrise till sunset?

Pepin supervised the household in her name. The woman did not have to lift a finger.

A stinging pain shot into his temple, and for a moment, he closed his eyes.

Had he been a fool? Or was his personal unhappiness a fair price to pay for peace?

Glancing around the hall, he watched men sitting together. These warriors did not have huts to return to. They slept in the hall, on simple pallets, washed themselves in the horse trough or in the Signa…the Seine!

Apart from the usual crowd, a small group of Northmen had settled in a corner. They'd only recently joined his hearth, arriving by boat from the Kattegat. Tired of the fighting between rival kings, they'd offered their swords to Hrólfr.

The young men were playing dice over a few cups of ale. Their faces and posture showed youthful confidence, and the arrogance that came with it. Highly skilled warriors, these six were just the types of men he needed to expand the settlement of Norse people. In due course, they would likely choose wives amongst the Frankish communities. Whether the men decided to convert to Christianity was not for him to concern himself with. Here, in the land he was forging, followers of both faiths lived side by side.

And it was all thanks to him.

A sense of pride shot through him, quickly dashed. This peace had come at a high price. His marriage, or rather, marriages. Because despite his conversion, he still considered himself wed to Poppa. And to Gisela.

What did that make him? A man with two wives? He grinned and scratched his beard.

"What brought that smile to your face, Hrólfr?" Knud settled in Gisela's chair beside his.

If she'd seen it, she'd scold him. But Hrólfr did not care.

A thrall came forward from the shadows and offered to refill their cups.

Cocking his head, Hrólfr picked up his cup brimming with a deep red Septimanian wine and stared at it, baffled. When had he stopped using a drinking horn? Damn, his memory deserted him. "I've just been thinking about my wives." He took a draught, then set the cup down.

Knud snorted. "Your *wives*? Don't let that priest know you're considering yourself still wed to both ladies." A glint in his friend's eye told him the truth.

No, the Church and Her servants would not take his words kindly. And if Hrólfr hated one thing, it was to be berated by a man who was always with his nose in the Scriptures.

In that respect, at least, he still felt like a heathen. Like Knud.

"Oh, Father Anselm knows my views well, as does the archbishop who doesn't miss a chance to tell me to drop William as my successor." He rolled his eyes.

"So, who would the good archbishop prefer? Gisela hasn't borne you a son...yet."

"And likely never will, truth be told. The woman is as cold as the grave. And William remains my heir."

A frown appeared on Knud's brow.

"Not you, too?" Hrólfr had heard rumours of Frankish opposition to his son. An opposition simply based on his birth, not on William's prowess or intelligence.

"What? Oh no. But perhaps it would be wise to take the boy with you to negotiations, first, for him to listen, and perhaps later, to share his counsel? That way, everyone discovers that your son is perfectly capable of handling the earldom."

Hrólfr pondered Knud's words. His friend's well-meant advice was always worth listening to. Knud would never utter the false words you might want to hear. He was not a King Charles. The old warrior spoke his mind.

Perhaps Knud was right, and Hrólfr should give William some responsibilities. A chance to share his own load, and for others to see that his son was a worthy leader to follow.

And if the boy did well, perhaps Hrólfr could sit back and enjoy his life's dusk, the time before night fell once and for all over his adventures.

The time before he died.

***

September, AD 919
Bayeux, Neustria

"Lady Poppa." The messenger kneeled before her as if she were a queen. It could only mean one thing.

Straightening her back, Poppa sighed. "Rise, and tell me what my husband wants now?"

"How did you..."

She raised an eyebrow.

The young man, not much older than William, flushed, his face taking on a strong hue of red that reached his blond hair. She sincerely hoped that Hrólfr would never consider sending this friendly young man on an errant that required a face that revealed nothing. This one could not hide any secrets.

"Well, never mind," he mumbled, rising. "Lord Hrólfr bids me to tell you that he shall be arriving by nightfall."

Poppa's humour fled. "Why?" She stared at him. "What does he want from us?"

"I... He did not share this information, lady."

"No, I suppose he would not. Erm, Claudia?" She waved the servant girl who'd been hovering out of earshot over.

"Please see to it that this fine young man is fed and watered. And whilst you're in the kitchen, order two pigs slaughtered. And have our guest accommodation prepared. The Earl of the Normans will be arriving soon, with several of his men, I assume."

She looked questioningly at the messenger, and he nodded. "If that is all…?"

"Yes, Lady Poppa. Thank you." The messenger inclined his head, then followed Claudia out the side door.

Left alone, Poppa let out a long breath. She'd not seen Hrólfr for over a year when she'd made it very clear – again – that she refused to be his concubine.

Eight years after he wed that woman, Gisela, as part of his agreement with King Charles, and it still seemed that Hrólfr had not found happiness in the harlot's arms. Nor had she given him a child.

A wry smile played on Poppa's lips. Deep down, she was elated to hear of the discord between him and his other wife.

Poppa would never forget how he'd betrayed her, brushed aside her loyalty, and trampled on her concerns for their children's safety.

Recent tidings of William's involvement in his father's campaigns and negotiations had given her much pride, even though she could never suppress a sense of danger.

She longed to see him, but that would mean travelling to Rouen – where that illegitimate whore sat like a fat, ugly spider in the centre of her web.

No, despite Hrólfr's pleas and her own sadness at not being able to see her son grow into a man, she would never set foot in the town until that woman was gone.

With a sigh, she rose, wondering where her daughter was. The morning lessons should have been finished by now, so she would be out, doing some chores.

Poppa left the hall through the main door, arriving on the large square in front. It was bustling with arriving or departing traders, their carts pulled by tired-looking donkeys.

She glanced around, but her gaze only met Alva's.

Now the wife of a weaver from Chartres who'd settled in

Bayeux six years earlier, the old baker's daughter was no brighter than on that terrible day when Hrólfr and his Northmen had raided the town. It had been Alva who revealed Poppa's status to the attackers. For some reason Poppa could not fathom, Alva always seemed jealous of her.

Now, the woman waddled over, wide hips swaying as she struggled to walk. Her fondness of pastries was well known.

I guess that's the fate of being a baker's daughter.

"Lost something, Poppa?" Not for Alva to give Poppa the reverence she deserved.

She let the slight slip. "Not really. I'm merely looking for Adela. Have you seen her?"

The baker's wife sent her a snide grin. "You mean Geirlaug? She's probably tumbling in the hay with some young raider… Like mother, like daughter."

Poppa rolled her eyes. *Please, God, give me strength.*

"Adela Geirlaug is more of a Christian than you are, Alva. I'll find her. Don't concern yourself." She left the woman standing and strode along the main road. It always surprised her, the hatred some locals still felt, after all these years. Was the peace they enjoyed not enough?

Soon, she reached the hut where Adela's best friend, Aregund, lived with her parents. Gusts of cold wind tugged at her gown. It was not the kind of weather to play outside. The grey sky would soon release the first autumn storms, possibly even tonight.

Knocking on the door, she listened to any sounds from inside. Was that laughter?

A moment later, the door was pulled open and a grinning Aregund appeared. The freckles on her nose had not yet faded, but she already wore several layers of clothing.

Poppa approved. The sensible Frankish girl was a good influence on Adela.

"Good day, Lady Poppa." The girl smiled. "Please come in."

At ten-and-four, Aregund was two years older than Adela. She'd been one of the first to call Poppa's daughter by her baptism name, no longer using the Norse, Geirlaug.

It had taken Poppa years to get used to it, yet the children adjusted far more quickly.

I'm getting old…

She brushed away the uncomfortable thought. "Thank you, Aregund. Is my daughter with you?"

"Yes, I'm here. Has something happened?" Poppa appeared from behind the curtained off section of the large room that held two big chairs and a stool, a small trestle table, and an assortment of copper cooking pots and jars of beaten earthenware tidily set around the unlit fire pit.

A chill hung in the air here. Could the family not afford to light a fire?

Poppa decided she would look into it. She smiled at her daughter. "Only that your father is on his way to visit us."

"Whatever for?" Adela crossed her arms.

Suppressing a smirk, Poppa said, "That, we shall discover upon his arrival. If you wouldn't mind returning home with me, you can help me set up the hall."

"If I must…" Her daughter slowly walked towards her, nudging her friend.

Aregund snorted, then offered, "I can help too, if you wish. My parents are both out, collecting wood. They won't be back for a while yet."

Poppa nodded. "That would be kind. Thank you. Then let's go and show these Northmen what a well-kept Frankish hall looks like."

As they walked back, the girls were skipping beside Poppa, giggling.

Oh, to be so young again. So innocent.

Not for the first time, Poppa prayed that her daughter's fate would not match her own.

Adela deserved better than a husband who betrayed her.

Night had fallen when Hrólfr and his companions arrived. Just in time, as, moments later, the heavens opened, and the downpour soaked men and horses. A flurry of action ensued.

Claudia showed the men where they could spend the nights. Soon, the large hut near the hall that was reserved for

185

guests had teemed with men discarding wet cloaks and tunics, and the girl had fled to the hall.

Sending the girl off to change her soaked wimple, Poppa dreaded to think of the smell in the hut. The place would have to be aired for days after the men left! A dozen warriors were to share the confined space, but at least they would find a warm fire and dry pallets on fresh rushes.

Now, the hall glowed in the light of scores of candles. Shadows danced on the walls. Hrólfr's followers, which included some Northmen she'd not met before, were a noisy bunch, but she did not begrudge them their exuberance. Most were hearth warriors who stayed at Hrólfr's hall at Rouen, only accompanying him if he went someplace. Which, these days, did not happen too often, according to rumours.

Sending William an indulgent smile, she patted his arm. When he'd dismounted earlier, she barely recognised him. He had grown into a handsome young man, resembling her father in his younger years, a full head taller than herself. His posture was one befitting his position as Hrólfr's heir. Head held high, his dark brown eyes glowing, with wide shoulders and a straight back, he began to look like a leader. Slimmer than his father, who'd gained weight since she last saw him.

His gaze met hers. "You have exceeded our expectation, Mother. The hall is in fine condition, and your larder appears to be brimming." He lowered his voice. "Perhaps we should send some of those Danes over by boat to relieve you of some of your stock." The twinkle in his eyes told her he was jesting.

"They would be welcome and put to work immediately! Fear not, my son. We are well defended here."

He laughed, watching her admiringly. "I have no doubt. No one would dare challenge the famous Lady Poppa."

"I'm inclined to believe you. Well, as long as your father protects her property." She settled back into her seat, but even though she said the words, she did not need Hrólfr to defend Bayeux. Sigurd's trained Norse had long taken care of it, keeping a constant watch on the shoreline. None of it was her husband's doing. At least not directly.

186

But she knew that, with Hrólfr being Earl of the Normans, as the Northmen were now referred to by the Frankish nobles, expanding the land granted to him mile by mile, it was ultimately his influence and importance that mattered.

Hrólfr was the deterrent.

But William was the future.

"I hear you attend negotiations with your father. Is that so?" Poppa kept her voice calm, but a slight shakiness betrayed her pride. Had it not been for all the men in the room, she'd have gathered her son into her arms and told him what a wonderful young man he was.

Instead, as befitting the daughter of a count and erstwhile wife of an earl, she maintained her dignity and kept a certain distance.

Not that William would appreciate motherly outbursts of pride and love. The corner of her mouth twitched. It would have made quite the spectacle.

"Yes, Mother." If he could straighten his back even further, he did just that. "I'm learning much about diplomacy and when to use pressure and when…bribes."

Poppa laughed out loud. "Your teacher is the best. He's had many years of experience. Follow his lead, and you will be successful as he is. If not more successful…" A long glance hung between them as time stood still.

Then William gave a slight nod. "I understand, and I will try my best."

"That's all I ask of you, son. I'm incredibly proud of you."

"Look, William!" Leaning forward, Adela interrupted from his left. "The skáld will begin his tale soon." She nestled close beside him, and Poppa pulled away.

It was time to let her children catch up with each other. It pleased her to see William indulge his sister.

Not hearing their shared words, she watched her daughter's face light up. Between them, her son's posture showed he was relaxed.

Their first meeting in years could have been awkward, dismissive even. Instead, they had forged a close bond in a few short hours.

"I can't believe how much Geirlaug...umm, Adela has grown again."

Hrólfr's voice startled her out of her observations. So much so, she was almost cross with him. But he shared Poppa's look of pride as he watched them.

"I've been wondering for years as to how you would think of your daughter, Hrólfr. And now I know." Poppa straightened in her seat and eyed her empty cup. As soon as she raised it, Claudia rushed forward to fill it.

She waited until the servant girl had withdrawn, then took a sip of the rich Rhenish wine her husband had brought with him. A gift from the Duke of Burgundy, apparently.

A gift in return for what?

She brushed the question aside. "Geirlaug. I've not used her birth name for a long time. Have I mentioned that she used to call herself Adela Geirlaug for years?"

He shook his head. "No, I don't think so. I only remember what you tell me in your letters." A frown appeared on his brow.

Poppa let her eyes roam over his face. Deep grooves covered his forehead; lines crossed his pale skin. Grey streaks ran through his thick blond hair that he wore loosely tied at his nape. Ha! He refused to turn fully into a Frank, not imitating their style, and for that, she was grateful. But with peace came a calmer life. Hrólfr was no more a warrior roaming the countryside, fending off invaders. Now, he had men who followed his orders. And so, he'd lost his healthy, tanned glow, his raw masculinity.

And with it, a piece of his soul, she thought. His reason for being.

Despite the years of their separation, he was still the only man she cared for. The only one she loved, even though his betrayal cut deep. Once, shortly after he set up his new wife in Rouen, he'd offered to release Poppa, so that she could wed another – a suggestion she had flatly refused to countenance. No, in her eyes – and in God's, whatever the priests said – she would always remain his first wife. Not that scheming whore...

At the memory of Gisela, her mood soured, and she quickly locked her feelings away. As the skáld began to hum, she leaned over to Hrólfr.

"What do you want this time?" she asked, her voice low.

"You." His eyes met hers, and she drew in a sharp breath. Gone were the arrogance, the self-confidence he'd displayed the last time they met. Instead, in their light blue depths she saw sadness, and longing. Then he blinked and looked away, and the moment was gone.

Then you have wasted your time coming here...

But she did not say those words out loud. He appeared lost. In the past?

Poppa sipped her wine and, like everyone else in the hushed room, listened to the skáld's tales. Watching the men, she wondered how many of them preferred a life of adventure, of conquest.

The kind of life a young Hrólfr had led.

With a sigh, she took his warm hand, and he pressed hers, their fingers entwined. A calm glance passed between them.

Tonight, she would be kind to him, relieve him of the burdens that seemed to haunt him for a few precious hours.

On the morrow, she would tell him to return to Rouen.

Without her.

Chapter Fifteen

October, AD 919
Bayeux, Neustria

Hrólfr did not leave. Poppa never asked him to.

Instead, he and his men helped with the harvest, as did everyone else who was not needed for other duties. Now, the grain stores were full. Soon, the time would come to slaughter animals, and to cure their meat for the winter.

Poppa put a stopper on yet another vessel brimming with the sweet-smelling juice of freshly-pressed apples and put it on a shelf in the windowless adjoining room beside the three score others they had filled over the last few days. They would stay here for a good fortnight, then the first *sicera* would be ready for drinking.

Even the children helped collect the fruits, pilfering the occasional treat along the way. She gave a wry smile when she remembered several sore tummies and cries of woe. Adela was one of those affected. She enjoyed sweet treats too much! An infusion of *mentha* leaves in boiled spring water eventually eased the pains.

Although she did not like to see her daughter ill, she had to learn, like the other children. It felt still strange, sometimes, to think of Geirlaug as Adela, but given the girl's adventurous streak, there would always remain a trace of the wild Norse Geirlaug in her.

Beside Poppa, Magda pushed the press down again, and more juice ran into the tray below. The plump woman's cheeks were red with exhaustion, but her eyes were bright. "This is the last juice from this lot." She pointed at an empty crate which had not long earlier been filled with ripe apples.

"And that's enough for today, Magda. We've done well."

Poppa scooped up the dregs into a small pitcher which she planned to take to the hall. The children would love them, thinned with spring water, with their evening meal. "Let's leave those two crates for the morrow."

Magda wiped her brow with her sleeve, then nodded. "The *sicera* will last for at least two years if we use it sparingly."

"Wonderful. And only on feast days or for important visitors. Everyone else gets the usual ale." Poppa grinned, then handed the pitcher of apple juice to her friend.

They'd long stopped preparing mead. Norse traditions were fading, and ale was so much weaker.

Although Magda was a servant – she'd first looked after William, and then after Adela when she was still little – Poppa had become reliant on the woman's assistance in running the household. Magda was over ten years younger than her, and never shied away from any tasks.

Laughing, the two women left the storeroom and sauntered towards the hall.

Of course, Poppa had not objected when Hrólfr decided to stay, despite her early intentions to see him gone. He'd postponed his departure week by week, always finding yet another excuse. The ease with which they reverted to their old daily life had surprised her at first, and her feelings were still muddled.

As if there was no wife waiting for him in Rouen...

But there was, and she could not deny the shadow Gisela cast over the precious hours they spent together. When Hrólfr first began to tell her about his life in Rouen, Poppa had been adamant she did not want to know anything that was somehow linked to Gisela. It was a hard for him, and the name slipped from his lips on more than one occasion. Every time, Poppa abruptly changed the subject.

Now, he remembered not to mention the harlot in her presence.

The days went by quickly, as they always did. They spent hours talking, playing board games or listening to the skáld – who'd remained in Bayeux. His wife hated the man, especially as she had never cared to learn the Norse tongue, like Poppa had over many years.

The Countess of the Normans seemed to embody the very essence of a Frankish lady, and Poppa found it unnerving that she herself now identified more strongly with Hrólfr's old customs than those of her own faith. And even though time had passed since he'd become a Christian, he would always remain a Northman at heart. Wild, adventurous – and hard to control.

Poppa had one important advantage over the king's illegitimate daughter: she knew her husband better.

A cry went up from the road that led towards the east, and Poppa stopped in her tracks. Mud spurting high under the horse's hooves, a rider was approaching at speed. Swiftly, she pulled Magda out of reach of the frantic animal.

Seeing her, the man slowed down before he came to a halt beside her. The horse's breath steamed from its wet nose in fast bursts. He must have been riding hard and far.

"Lady Poppa. I bear a message for Lord Hrólfr, but you might wish to hear it too." Despite the chill in the autumn air, the man's face and neck were covered in sweat.

Now she recognised him for one of the Danish warriors who'd recently returned to Rouen with William. "Come into the hall, Leikr, and then you can give us your tidings." She waved to a boy loitering nearby. "Walter, take the horse to the stables, then quickly find Hrólfr and send him to the hall."

With a mien of importance, the boy took the reins from the messenger and gave Poppa a wan smile before he walked off with his head held high.

Poppa had just settled into her chair by the fire when Hrólfr strode into the hall. Having no need of Magda, she'd sent her to rest in her own home.

Leikr, the messenger, sat on a bench on the far side of the fire pit, taking large gulps from a cup of ale.

Hrólfr's eyes went from her to the man, and he joined them. "Leikr? What brings you to us? Has something happened to William?"

To Poppa's relief, the young Dane shook his head.

Leikr moved to stand up, but Hrólfr bid him stay seated with a flick of his hand. "No, lord. 'Tis concerning Lady Gisela."

Hrólfr slumped into his carved chair and sank into the thick furs, his brows furrowed. "What has she done now?" His tone was flat.

A shudder ran down her spine, but Poppa held her breath, waiting for Leikr to continue.

The Dane put the cup beside him on the bench, then leaned forward, elbows on his thighs. "She's on her way here. William tried to stop her, but she evaded us."

"What?" Hrólfr roared. "God's teeth! Why would she do that?"

But Poppa knew, and Leikr's next words confirmed her suspicions.

"When we returned without you, the countess was mad." He sent Poppa an apologetic look. "I'm sorry, Lady Poppa, if my tidings upset you. Lady Gisela raged for several days, screaming, and throwing things at everyone. William avoided her. We kept watch, but clearly not close enough. The next we heard was that she had taken several members of her personal guard and set off in the direction of Bayeux. She was adamant she wanted to...to..." He stared at the beaten floor.

The woman be damned! "What does she want?"

Poppa tried to keep her voice calm. None of this was the messenger's fault.

Leikr finally met her gaze, unblinking. "She wants to tell you to leave her husband alone." He picked up the cup and emptied it.

"Oh, what a mess!" Hrólfr's shoulders shook, and he covered his face with one hand.

Poppa realised he was laughing. Her anger evaporated, and she grinned.

Leikr stared at them, mouth agape.

"Then let her try!" A sense of pride surged through her. She would not give in to the begging whore.

193

"I assume you overtook them?"

The Dane nodded. "Yes, two days ago. I heard they stayed at a convent for a couple of nights, to allow her to rest. During that time, I passed them, unseen."

"We can expect her on the morrow, then?" Poppa asked.

Leikr nodded. "Yes, at the earliest."

"So Gisela doesn't know you're here?" Hrólfr had regained his composure, but his eyes were still glowing with mirth.

Leikr shook his head. "I took great care not to be seen."

"You did well, young man. Perhaps stay here until I return to Rouen? You can sleep in the hall if you wish."

"That's kind of you." Leikr rose. "Now, if you don't mind…I'll check on the horse."

"Of course," Poppa said. "And…thank you."

After the door had fallen shut behind the messenger, the silence in the hall pressed down on Poppa. She turned to look at Hrólfr who was reclining, stretching his legs. "I've been expecting something like this."

"Then you are wiser than I am." He sighed. "But then, we both know that already…"

Poppa laughed, the sound loud in her ears, then she calmed, breathing evenly. Was she prepared for this confrontation? She let out a long breath.

"But let's be serious, Poppa. I worry about you," Hrólfr whispered, all laughter gone. The lines on his forehead deepened when he frowned. Suddenly, he looked his age. "The woman has a malicious streak. Whatever the circumstances, always make sure you are never alone with her."

Chapter Sixteen

October, AD 919
Bayeux, Neustria

Not for the first time did Poppa feel stomach-sick. She swallowed down the bile, keen not to show anyone – least of all Hrólfr – how affected she was.

Today was the day Gisela would arrive. Leikr, who'd gone to check on their progress, had returned a short while ago.

Gisela and her retainers were less than half a day's ride away.

Around Poppa, brown leaves were swirling in the autumn winds that swept in from the sea. She gazed across the fields to where the shore lay.

Sometimes, she wanted to run away from it all; or tell Hrólfr to leave her be, once and for all.

But she'd made her bed, and now she must lay in it. It was her own fault for allowing the wretched man to come back into her life. Recent years had passed well, peacefully and calmly as Sigurd's men kept the coast clear of attack. Now, the Northmen chose other sites to land, she heard. They headed east, to the land of the Rus, and even to Byzantium! On his last visit in the summer, Sigurd regaled her with their tales of adventure.

Turning away from the view, she took the muddy lane back into town. Since Hrólfr's return, he'd been paying her much attention. He'd gone hunting for fresh meat and furs, had repairs done to her home, and fitted more sconces for torches to make the hall brighter.

Now, it was was warm and inviting, ready for winter. Inviting to all except for the woman who'd invited herself – Gisela.

Poppa sighed. "I'd better go back before she arrives in my absence," she muttered to herself as she waved at the butcher's son who, dragging a small cart behind him, ran errands for his father.

Everyone was preparing for winter. The nights were already cold, with frost not far off. A constant layer of moisture settled everywhere. Her boots dragged through the bed of leaves, crunching them underfoot. How lovely would it be if someone could clear them all off the muddy lanes! Leaves just made the ground more slippery when it rained again.

Perhaps Hrólfr could spare a man to remove them? She grinned, an idea forming in her head. He'd come to regret returning to Bayeux...

A commotion outside the hall made her increase her pace. Under no circumstance did she want to be caught running, but she also wanted to be at her hall when the woman arrived. It was her home, after all, which now, thanks to Hrólfr and his talented companions, looked even more impressive.

Several riders dismounted on the small square but there was no litter. Surely, the princess would not travel on horseback.

Hrólfr emerged from the hall just as she approached the door. He moved to stand beside her, watching as fifteen men tried to get their horses taken away. Several boys had come forward, keen on a small token or coin. Poppa grinned. The inhabitants of Bayeux were nothing if not clever. A sense of pride washed through her.

"I don't see her."

Poppa raised an eyebrow. Hrólfr couldn't even speak his wife's name. "You know well that some guards travel ahead. She'll be here any moment."

He took her hand in his and leaned closer. "How are you feeling about this?"

She bit back a nasty comment, but instead put a smile on her face. "I'm fine, husband." She met his gaze, and he laughed.

196

"You'll always be my only love," he whispered in her ear, his hot breath brushing her cool skin.

The words warmed her heart.

Let Gisela come and claim the man she married in the eyes of the Church! Poppa shared a bond with Hrólfr that could never be severed, whatever the circumstance.

Then, a movement caught her attention, and she sobered. A litter carried between two horses arrived, followed by more riders. Hrólfr bellowed orders to have everyone attended to.

Her heart beat steadily in her ears, and Poppa took deep breaths. This was the moment she'd been dreading ever since Hrólfr's wretched agreement with King Charles all those years ago. She wished she was somewhere else on this earth right now.

The curtain of the litter was pushed aside, and a woman alighted. Lithe and tall, her long hair gleaming golden beneath a thin veil, Gisela immediately displayed a beauty Poppa felt lacking in herself. She let go of Hrólfr's hand and folded her own hands tightly in front of her.

This was going to be more challenging than expected.

***

Hrólfr's mind whirled as he watched two footmen helping Gisela and a maid from the litter. Around him, men stared in awe.

Gisela was beautiful, he admitted to himself. Her delicate frame and features commanded all male attention, and she received it. At least, from those men who had not met with her wrath.

His retainers remained polite yet distanced. And he knew why. Despite her beauty and meek appearance, Gisela had a sharp tongue and a quick temper.

The beauty that beguiled every stranger at first never reached her mind. Men envied him, not thinking beyond the bed chamber, but even there, her enticing body could not raise a fire in him. Within days of their marriage, she used it to blackmail him.

But her intentions backfired, and he had not taken her to his bed for many winters, preferring the company of his men in the hall, or solitude, to her scolding.

Now, her cool grey gaze roamed across the small square, then settled on him. Then she spotted Poppa beside him. The glare she sent her could freeze a lake.

If looks could kill...

But as if unaffected, Poppa stood still, her back straight, head raised. There was a brave, proud woman! His wife. He had yet to see her shy away from a challenge, and here, she met the biggest one of all head-on.

"Welcome to Bayeux, Lady Gisela." Poppa's voice – loud and firm, without a hint of the nerves she must feel – rang across the square. "Please come inside. You must be weary from your journey." She gestured towards the door.

Gisela sauntered forward in languid movement, clutching the fox wrap around her shoulders. Ignoring Poppa, she came to a halt in front of Hrólfr and looked up at him. "Good afternoon, husband. We have missed you." Her fingers slid down his chest.

He took a step back, uncertain of how to react. Why did this woman always make things so difficult?

"Where is William?" he asked instead.

"You could at least bid me welcome, Rouf."

He hated the way she over-pronounced his name the Frankish way, mocking his origins.

"You invited yourself, Gisela." He crossed his arms.

Beside him, Poppa bristled. She rolled her eyes then turned away, addressing Gisela's guards. "Please come within for a warming cup of ale."

After a hesitant glance at their lady who did not react, they followed Poppa into the hall.

"Are you coming?" Hrólfr asked Gisela.

She drew her generous mouth into a thin line of disapproval.

Knowing the signs only too well, he sighed. "You're here now, so you may as well. Or freeze to death. The choice is yours."

Without another look at her, he followed the others into the warm belly of the hall.

"How dare you leave me standing there!" Inside the threshold, Gisela caught up with him, grabbing his arm.

Hrólfr turned sharply, and she bumped into him. He steadied her, then quickly dropped his hands. "I offered. You didn't move. If you wish to cause a scene, go ahead. But remember you are a guest in this hall. It belongs to Poppa who has kindly bid you welcome. Now behave like an adult, not a spoilt child."

Gisela laughed, the sound harsh in his ears. "Poppa's hall? It should be mine!" She scrutinised the interior, obviously looking for faults – and finding none. "Although I wouldn't really want a poky little place like this. Now, where are my quarters? Up there?" She pointed to the steps.

Aware that silence had fallen, with everyone watching their exchange, Hrólfr shook his head. "No. You're to stay in a guest house, behind the hall. It is more…private."

His wife scoffed. "Ha! For whom? Not me, that is certain. Let poor Gisela stay in a pigsty whilst you're humping your whore in the luxury of the hall?"

Silently counting down from five to one, Hrólfr tried to calm himself, but the woman always riled him up.

To his surprise, Poppa joined them. "When you are finished with your little public disagreement, come and have a cup of spiced wine. If this is not to your liking, lady, then feel free to retire to the guest house. You shall find it cosy and warm."

Gisela drew in a sharp breath. "How dare you speak to me like that, you—"

"What?" Hands on her hips, Poppa took a step closer to Gisela. "This is my home, and, as Hrólfr said, you are a guest. My hall is always welcoming strangers, even those we may not wish to visit. But I will not be insulted on my own doorstep. So, if you do not want to be my guest, you can remain in the guest house until you leave. I can have food and wine brought to you, and you will not have to suffer my company. Or I, yours, for that matter."

A sense of pride surged through Hrólfr. After all these years, Poppa was still a force to be reckoned with. He'd known it from the first moment he'd set eyes on her younger self, back in the old church on that fateful Easter Sunday.

Her mind worked like his, and with a clarity he'd not felt in many winters, he realised that he had done this incredible woman the gravest disfavour. No, never should he have wed King Charles' daughter, however tempting the prize may have seemed at the time. He should have fought for the land, like his forebears had done on other shores, not sold his soul for ambition, and lust.

Poppa should have been beside him, as countess. His wife. His one true love.

A sigh escaped him, and he found both women staring at him. Clearing his throat, he said, "Poppa is right, Gisela. Stop seeking trouble. Either join us or leave."

Poppa nodded, then turned on her heel. He followed, catching up with her at the high table.

"Can I pour you some wine?" Picking up the pitcher brimming with spiced wine, he waited for her response.

"Yes, please." She held her cup out to him, and he poured it for her before filling his drinking horn which he'd found again.

In unison, they took a few sips, then he gestured to her cushioned chair. Her gaze raking the room, she eventually lowered herself, wriggling into the cushions.

He also sat, stretching his legs in front of him. The awkwardness he'd felt on Gisela's arrival had shifted to irritation. The woman was known for her over-reactions, and he had to hand it to Poppa – she dealt with the situation with grace and fairness, but also with a blunt honesty.

Moments later, Gisela joined them, a rueful smile on her face. He was not fooled, but still waved to a thrall to fill a finely painted cup for her.

Poppa had guessed Gisela's expensive taste.

The king's daughter took the comfortable seat on his left and leaned towards him. "I apologise, Rouf. I am fatigued from the long journey."

"Then apologise to Poppa. It was her you insulted, not me. I'm used to the sting of your tongue."

For a moment, Gisela's mouth dropped, her features looking harsh in the flickering light of the fire. Then she beamed and, meeting Poppa's cool gaze, she said, "Please accept my sincere apologies, Lady Poppa. I appreciate the warmth of your hall."

Poppa's mouth twitched. She was intelligent enough to realise Gisela was as false as a snake. "There is no need to apologise, Lady Gisela. You are always welcome in Bayeux."

Hrólfr felt like bursting into laughter. Instead, a coughing fit wracked him; the third time today. Damned age!

Poppa certainly won this first encounter. But he was still concerned for her safety, even though he'd ordered his men to watch her when he was not present.

He sobered, and his breathing slowed. He wondered the real intent behind Gisela's visit. The woman stopped at nothing.

How could he stop her?

Chapter Seventeen

Early November, AD 919
Bayeux, Neustria

It had been a week since Gisela's arrival, and the woman infuriated Poppa more and more each day.

Not content with staying in the guest hut Poppa had furnished lavishly for her, the princess had insisted on staying in the private quarters in the hall. This meant, of course, that she would witness everything that went on. Poppa vacated her own large room, putting it at Gisela's disposal, and moved into the small chamber opposite.

It meant one major adjustment, though. For the duration of Gisela's stay, Poppa had decided that Hrólfr should have separate lodgings. The last thing she wanted was for Gisela to walk in on them in bed together. The Church frowned upon such behaviour, and Poppa did not want to give her a reason for even deeper hostility. It was enough that the woman knew what was going on – she did not have to witness it.

Hrólfr had grumbled and raged, but complied in the end, and moved into the guest hut intended for his wife.

Poppa, meanwhile, asked Claudia to stay in her bedchamber whenever Gisela was upstairs. The thought of a stranger searching through her personal belongings made her skin crawl. She would not put it past the woman – or her maid – to dig around.

The days passed quickly. Gisela settled in and began to order the servants around as if it was her own home.

Poppa held her tongue. It was not for long, she hoped.

To her surprise, Gisela had not tried to seduce Hrólfr, but merely exchanged polite words with him. To Poppa, it seemed like a ruse.

The woman had arrived with one intention – to take her husband back, and perhaps oust her rival once and for all.

Poppa would not give her the satisfaction of moving aside, though.

But try as she might, Poppa could not shake off her shadow. Gisela was everywhere, and shared her opinion on everything, whether she was asked it or not. For the last couple of days, Poppa was close to losing her patience. This was her home, her hall.

Yet this woman had forced her way in and tried to turn it into her own.

What was her ultimate intention? Take control of Bayeux in her stead?

If the woman hated Rouen, she'd like the calm of Poppa's hometown even less.

After another sleepless night spent going over recent events, Poppa had enough. She needed space to breathe, to think. And the only place she'd find it was the beach.

Then, on her return, she would confront the woman and tell her to go back.

She dressed quietly, plaited her hair in a long braid, and wrapped herself into her warm, fur-lined cloak. The nights were chilly, and whilst she was seeking fresh air, she was not willing to risk frostbite this early in the morning.

On tiptoes, she left her chamber and made her way past several snoring figures sleeping on pallets on the floor towards the door. She drew back the bolt and stepped outside. Cold wind stung her cheeks, and she pulled the hood low over her head. Relieved that she'd brought her woollen mittens, she held the cloak tightly around her middle and walked away from the hall. At the end of the lane, she turned right, following the path that led to the sea.

The dry ground crunched beneath her boots; her tread heavy as she maintained a fast walking pace. To the east, the early light of dawn kissed the fields. Her breath came in short bursts as the exertion took its toll, but Poppa did not slow down. It felt good – the cold breeze, the damp in the air, the scent of the sea.

Out here, all was calm and peaceful. At this early hour, no one was about. The fields lay bare following the harvest, and the wind swept briskly across the empty landscape.

Finally, she reached the cliffs, and halted at the top of the path that led down to the beach. The sun still hid behind a layer of low cloud. For a moment, she stared at the waves crashing into the sand as the sea heaved and fell at a steady rhythm. Two longships lay moored not far from the shore, lights bobbing in the wind. It had been Sigurd who'd advised her always to have men guarding their ships, even if they were not used. She'd heeded his advice all these years. It had been a blessing when a fleet of Danish longships had approached the shoreline. Their attack had been repelled before they even began.

With a tinge of regret, she remembered that she'd not heard from him in many months. Poppa vowed to send a messenger on her return home.

A crunching sound behind her made her spin around. Her blood froze.

"Gisela. What are you doing here?" Poppa glanced up and down the cliffside, but no one else was about.

Had Hrólfr not said she should never be alone with the princess? A sense of dread settled in her stomach, and she slowly inched away from the sheer drop.

"Good morning, Poppa." Gisela's gaze went towards the ships, then back to meet Poppa's. The smile she gave was false. "Like you, I could not sleep. So when I saw you leave, I thought I could do with a walk, too. To clear one's head, you know?"

Poppa nodded. "Well, here we are." She pointed at the cove. "This is where our ships land…when you don't travel across the countryside from Rouen, I mean."

Gisela stepped closer, glancing over the edge. "Interesting. You seem to like this spot, or why come out here so early?"

"Yes." Poppa shifted, continuing to face Gisela. She would not be caught with her back to the woman. "You are right. I love it here. It's where I retreat to when I wish to be alone."

But for once, she wished it were not so.

Yet on the ships, everything was quiet still, and no one would venture out here from town without a good reason.

"It's quite a distance, though." Gisela shifted her feet. "I thought the walk would never end."

"Well, you didn't have to follow me all the way…"

Perhaps she should go back. Clearly, the woman had sneaked up on her with a purpose. A shudder ran down her spine. It was as well she heard the approach, or her broken body may now be lying below in the sand.

Was that Gisela's plan? To kill her?

Cold grey eyes were watching her. Calculating. Plotting.

Nonsense, Poppa! Pull yourself together.

Gisela smirked. "I was merely curious; that's all."

"I think I will return home."

The woman had walked nearly two miles to the coast in her wake. Whatever she wanted, she could share it on their walk back.

"He loves you."

The voice was tinged with sadness, but Poppa did not intend to fall into Gisela's trap.

"Why did you really follow me?" She folded her arms, all patience gone.

The woman's eyes widened. "Oh, I'm so sorry. Have I offended you?"

Poppa sighed. "No. Not yet. Why?"

"I wanted to talk with you – away from everyone. Away from Rouf."

"Leave Hrólfr out of it. He is the one who got us into this mess."

"A mess you call it?" Gisela laughed harshly; the sound carried away swiftly by the wind. "I wed him on the order of my father. Do you think I was happy to get married to a heathen?"

"I wouldn't want to speculate, Gisela."

"Very funny!" The woman's mouth formed a thin line, then she continued, "I'd dreamed of living in Paris, like my half-siblings. But whilst they bask in luxury – having been born legitimate – I have to make do with that hovel."

"What hovel?" Poppa frowned. "You mean Rouen? But the hall is lovely."

Gisela snorted. It was the most unusual behaviour for a princess of Francia. "You call that place lovely? Well, perhaps you would think so, coming from a village as you do."

"Bayeux is a town," Poppa pointed out.

"But it's not Paris. Rouen is growing, yes, but nowhere near the sumptuous splendour of the palaces and gardens of Paris."

Poppa hated her ignorance. She'd never visited Paris, so she was at a disadvantage.

Maintaining her silence, she merely shifted her weight from one foot to the other. The cold had begun to seep into her bones.

It was truly time to go home.

"Wait!" Gisela called out as Poppa made to turn away. "You can't just leave me here, alone."

Fumbling in the depth of her cloak, Poppa pulled out her cross and clasped it. It always helped her calm down. A few deep breaths later, she looked Gisela in the eye. "Fine. You still have not answered my question. What do you want from me?"

"To leave Rouf alone! Tell him to return to his hall with me, and never see you again. Oh, and I want you to renounce your children."

Taken aback, Poppa recoiled. "What do my children have to do with it?"

The woman hesitated for a moment, then she said, "God has not granted me children, Poppa. Rouf has chosen William as his heir—"

"Of course my son is his father's heir!"

"But he is not of *my* flesh and blood. Nor is Adela." The ice in Gisela's eyes chilled Poppa. The woman was mad! "Rouf is getting on in years, and as William takes over more and more duties on his behalf, everyone knows he is not his legitimate son."

What was the woman implying?

"William is as much Hrólf's son as Adela is his daughter. We were wed—"

"By some old ritual our Church does not accept. I hear Rouf forced the poor priest to oversee the ceremony against his will. Ha, some wedding!"

"Perhaps the ritual is ancient, but we are still married."

"Not in the eyes of God." Gisela took a step towards her, and Poppa shrank back. "It is not legitimate. Nor are your children. Unless I am known as their mother, they will always remain bastards, and any claims will be challenged."

"This is ridiculous, Gisela. My children have a mother – me. Even Adela was born before your father's agreement with Hrólfr."

"In the eyes of the Holy Mother Church, I am his wife. And as such, I have a right to raise Adela – as my own."

"Never!" Poppa hissed. "I think we are finished here. I'm going back. And trust me, Gisela, Hrólfr shall hear of this."

She turned towards the path and took a few steps before a cry made her whirl around.

"I am cursed!" Gisela was on her knees, hands raised to the sky, wailing. What was the woman up to now?

Then she noticed Gisela was crying. Tears flowed as she continued to wail. "No one wants me…"

With a sigh, Poppa approached her. She reached out a hand and touched the woman's shoulder. "Gisela? Don't upset yourself. Come with me. We'll find a way."

"That's easy for you to say," Gisela whispered between sniffs, her voice hoarse. "You have it all – a husband who loves you, children – whereas I…I have nothing."

You have beauty. But even as Poppa thought it, she knew it was no substitute for a man's love and your own offspring.

"Come," she repeated. She bent forward to help Gisela on her feet.

The woman stumbled and fell into Poppa who tried to retain her foothold. Then strong hands grabbed her wrists, pulling her towards the cliffs.

"Gisela?" Poppa fought to free herself from the grasp, but the princess was quick, and strong. "What are you doing?"

Together, they stumbled over their gowns until they reached the edge of the cliff. Was Gisela trying to kill her?

Had her crying been a ruse?

Hrólfr was right. She should never have allowed the woman to catch her unawares. Digging her boots into the muddy ground, Poppa shifted her weight away from the steep drop.

"Let me go!"

"No!" Gisela's eyes were blazing as she twisted Poppa's arm, forcing her forward. "You must pay for my husband's sin."

"Murder is a sin too."

Harsh laughter rang close to her ear. "Yes, but this is God's will. Die, harlot!"

Poppa thought briefly what this macabre dance at the top of the cliffs must look to the guards on the boat. She prayed they'd seen their fight, but deep down she admitted to herself that no help would arrive on time. With her last gasp, she heaved herself away from the abyss.

"Gisela!" A shout rang out.

Hrólfr! He'd come for her.

As relief flooded through Poppa, Gisela moved in close behind her. Arms entangled in her own cloak, Poppa could not fight her off.

"Gisela, don't!" Hooves reverberated on the ground, but would he be on time to stop the raging woman?

"You're too late, Rouf!"

With a piercing scream, Gisela grabbed Poppa's cross pendant from behind, then pulled the leather thong tight around Poppa's throat.

Did she want to strangle her now? The airflow dwindled, and Poppa's eyelids fluttered. Her consciousness began to fade.

With a last attempt before the darkness threatened to overcome her, Poppa managed to free a hand caught in the folds of her cloak. She pulled at the leather thong. Her fingers fiddled with the knot, and the strap suddenly came loose.

A scream behind her reached her, then faded. Poppa gasped for air, trying to sit up, rubbing her eyes, but all she could see were black spots in front of her eyes.

Where was Gisela?

Before she knew it, Hrólfr was by her side, holding her in a tight embrace.

"Let...me...breathe!"

He immediately let go, then shouted orders to the men who had arrived with him.

Safe in his arm, Poppa blinked. After several deep breaths, she looked around. Men were rushing down the path to the beach. She turned her head. A sense of dread surged through her. "Hrólfr, where is Gisela?"

He looked at her and brushed a stray strand of hair from her eyes. "She's gone."

She straightened, as panic surged through her. "What do you mean, gone?"

"She lost her balance and fell backwards."

"Fell...?" Poppa's heart froze. What had she done? Her hand went to her throat, devoid of its leather thong, her skin raw. Where was the pendant? She searched the ground nearby but found no trace. Gisela must have held on to it as she— "I have killed her." Tears stung in her eyes.

"No, you have not, my love." Hrólfr pulled her into a close embrace and gently kissed her brow. "It was an accident."

"If I hadn't untied the cord—"

"It would be your death I'd be facing now, not hers."

"But—"

"No buts, Poppa. Please." He wiped her tears away with his thumb. "We were close enough to see what she was doing, but I don't think I'd have been in time to save you. So I, for one, am glad you freed yourself." His voice was barely above a whisper. "I...I could not have coped if you'd died."

Whilst she understood him, his relief, something inside her had gone over the cliffs with Gisela.

Whatever the future brought, her life would never be the same again.

PART FOUR

~~~

DESTINY

Chapter Eighteen

Summer, AD 924
Rouen, Earldom of the Normans

Why am I so tired all the time?

Hrólfr leaned back into the chair and stretched his legs. His knees clicked as he placed one leg over the other, and not even the plump cushions could not stop the wooden back dig into his ribs. By the Gods – or God, whichever – he hated old age! At two-and-sixty winters, he'd been told repeatedly to take things more slowly.

Already, he coordinated everything from his hall in Rouen. Rarely did he venture out on horseback these days. The aches the jarring movement caused him were getting too much. Even old wounds, long healed, had begun to irritate him.

Ageing was bad for a warrior. He'd always loved to be out there, with his men, ensuring the peace was kept across his land, and on the borders. But fortunately, things had calmed. Attacks from Danes along the coast had slowly subsided. Their focus was now on the fertile lands in Anglia and Northumbria. And the Franks squabbled amongst themselves after King Charles' death, leaving him alone.

"Here, let me help you out of your morose humour, Hrólfr." Sigurd, sitting beside him, leaned forward and poured each a cup of mead.

Hrólfr stared at the vessel as he cradled it in his hand. Had he misplaced his drinking horn again? He looked around but could not see it. Was it in his bedchamber? But why?

His lost memory be damned!

With a swift move, he brought the cup to his lips and emptied it in large gulps, then, with an anguished cry, he threw it into the fire pit. At least, that had been his intention.

Instead, the vessel cracked against the side of the hearth and smashed into little shards.

Sigurd sent him a sideways glance. "What ails you?" He pulled his chair closer. "Talk to me, Hrólfr!"

Hrólfr let out a long sigh. Closing his eyes, he rubbed them with swollen fingers. Tears threatened to well up, but he'd be damned if he cried like a babe in front of his friend. Eventually, his breathing calmed, and he swallowed hard. Then he blinked, momentarily blinded by the flickering light of the fire.

"I don't know." He leaned on his elbows, folding his hands. "Don't grow old, is all I can say." He gave a wry smile, but it failed to fool Sigurd.

"Too late already. I'm fast following in your footsteps."

"'Tis not worth it. You'll grow fat and lazy; your bones begin to creak; and your reaction with a sword is like a snail's – painfully slow. I couldn't even defend myself in battle these days."

"Of course you could. Your body may be getting older, but your mind is as sharp as always."

"That's where you're wrong, my friend." Hrólfr grimaced. "My mind cannot even remember what I did with my drinking horn."

Sigurd cocked his head. "Perhaps not, but nor can I! Those things are not important. You can still hold your own in the practice yard."

Hrólfr scoffed. "Aye, when they tell me their next move in advance. No, Sigurd, my fighting days are done. I have made a decision."

"What decision?"

"I shall share it tonight, when all the men are assembled. William is due to arrive from Bayeux before nightfall, and Poppa has prepared a feast for him."

"Ah." Sigurd grinned. "That's why there is a clamour in the kitchen as if a swarm of bees had descended on it."

Hrólfr nodded, a smile tugging at the corners of his lips. "It gives Poppa pleasure to host guests. William will be accompanied by a lord from Burgundy, someone whose name

214

she mentioned, but I've forgotten – see! That's what age does to you." He shook his head. "And after everyone has drunk and eaten, I shall share my tidings."

Sigurd grew sombre. "Please don't do anything in haste. You have many years ahead of you yet." He leaned back and picked up his cup, sipping slowly.

Hrólfr's eyes were drawn back to the fire. It was lit all day for his health, he knew. He'd overheard Poppa issue instructions to Pepin. The flickering light drew him in, and he let his mind wander. His decision stood. It was for the best.

The sound of chatter and laughter reverberated through the room. Beside him, Poppa sat, a contented smile on her lips. With her back straight and her gaze roaming the room, there was no mistaking who was in charge in the hall.

He did not begrudge her a little happiness. She'd made Rouen her home soon after Gisela's death. On leaving Bayeux, she'd sworn never to return. It still saddened him. The town had been hers all her life. Now, William used the hall whenever it took him there.

The stretch around Bayeux did not yet form part of their earldom, at least not officially, but Hrólfr was keen to change that. His ships patrolled the coast, and the peninsula, up to the border of Brittany, where more Danes had settled since he kept them off his lands. It was his wife's inheritance, even though her father's earldom expired on his death.

Now, William had the thankless task of convincing the local landowners of the advantage of joining forces. Negotiations were slow, often dragging on for many moons – or months as the Franks called it. Even after ten-and-three years of having converted to Christianity, Hrólfr still found much of the Frankish words baffling.

Poppa insisted it made sense, and William and Adela were wholly assimilated. The only one still not used to it was he.

A tinge of sadness hit him at the brief memory of his own upbringing. It had been harsh, a constant fight for survival. That had been the reason he left for new shores as soon as he was able to.

His children had it much better, and he thanked the Gods…God – whichever – for it. And for Poppa. She was a hard but fair mother.

Unlike Gisela, who would have merely seen children as a way to further her own ambitions.

Regarding his wife, he wondered why Poppa had not wished for them to repeat their vows in Church, now that Gisela was gone, and there was no obstacle in their way. The act would legitimise their children, making it easier for William to be more widely accepted amongst the Franks.

But the only time he'd suggested such a wedding to her, she'd turned on him, insisting they were already wed. If it was good enough for her, Bérengar, and the Norse Gods, it certainly was good enough for the Christian God. And with that, the matter was closed.

Hrólfr smiled at the recollection. The feisty young girl he'd conquered in Bayeux all those winters ago had grown into a woman who knew her mind and spoke it, and who was not too shy to share her opinion. His heart burst with pride.

Yet beneath the confidence she exuded lay a shadow he could not extinguish. Gisela's death continued to play on her mind, and Poppa spent hours, alone, in their newly built chapel. He'd assumed she went to pray, but when he came upon her once, he'd found her talking to a statue of the Virgin Mary. Not wishing to disturb her, he'd watched from the shadows at the back as an intense exchange seemed to develop.

Poppa was of sound mind – more so than he, Hrólfr suspected – so he'd quietly left her to herself, but from that moment onwards, he made sure she remained undisturbed whenever she escaped to the chapel. They could not risk rumours of her losing her mind…

A peal of laughter brought him out of his reverie. People had finished eating, and thralls were already removing empty plates and leftover meat and bread.

Ale and mead flowed freely tonight for everyone except his table, which enjoyed a deep red wine their guest from Burgundy had brought with him.

William, sitting to his right, was in deep conversation with Sigurd on his other side. Poppa listened to the Burgundian lord beside her sharing a tale. Her occasional 'ah' and 'oh', always accompanied by a suitable facial reaction, showed him she was attentive, but he could tell she was bored. Yet the Lady of Bayeux would never insult a guest.

Perhaps now would be a good time, before folk began to leave to return to their homes. He stood, and moments later, the hall fell silent. All eyes were on him, some wary, others curious. It had been many moons since he'd last made a speech.

"My friends, please listen." He cleared his throat but ignored the goblet Poppa held out to him. It was enough that he appeared visibly weaker than he used to. "Our little corner of land has been safe for many years, with much gratitude to our allies in Burgundy," he pointed at their guest, "and in Francia. Danes and Franks have settled here, and live peacefully side by side." He paused, finally taking a few sips of the offered drink.

William looked up at him. "What is this about, Father?"

Poppa gave a slight shake of her head, and their son leaned back, sending her a long glance. She, of course, knew Hrólfr's heart. He kept no secrets from her.

"I have spent a long time fighting to gain this peace, and even longer to maintain it. But now I'm old, I feel it is time to pass the remaining duties that come with the earldom to my son."

Gasps echoed around the chamber. William shot from his chair, nearly knocking over his goblet. "What are you saying, Father? Are you not well?"

Hrólfr shot him a sharp glance. "No, there is nothing wrong with me, if that's what you're implying. At two-and-twenty, you are old enough to take on the responsibility. You know everything about the land, the villages and towns, and the agreements with our allies. And I'm still here, to keep an eye on you." He gave a wry grin, then turned to Poppa. "But I now want to spend more time with your mother. She has supported me ever since we met, and she deserves recognition for that." His gaze swept the room. "Friends, I shall remain your jarl, or earl, but from the morrow, you will be following William's lead."

His son stretched to his full height, equal to his own, even though he did not have the same breadth of shoulder and chest, and beamed with the confidence of youth. Difficult times would lie ahead, mostly filled with challenges from those who did not accept William as his legitimate heir – high-born Frankish, Burgundian, and Breton lords with an eye on their new earldom in such a strategic position.

In recent summers, he and William begun to expand their territory, and the young man would have his hands full.

But watching William graciously accept the felicitations from their people, Hrólfr knew he'd made the right decision.

His son was ready for the challenge, and Hrólfr had more time to spend with Poppa…

Chapter Nineteen

December, AD 929
Rouen, Earldom of Normannia

"How much farther?"

Poppa linked her arm in Hrólfr's. "Not far at all. Enjoy the fresh air. It does you good."

"Ha! It'll more likely send me to an early grave, wife! You and your walks."

She took a deep breath. Of late, Hrólfr had begun to lose his temper more quickly. Truth was, his bones hurt him, especially in the colder seasons, but sitting by the hearth all through winter did nothing for his health. And recently, he'd started put on more weight, which did his joints no good at all.

So Poppa decided he should join her on her daily walks. Wrapped up as if he was still in the northern realms, he grunted and grumbled as they strolled outside the gates, towards the riverbed. The Seine flowed high after the heavy rains of the past few weeks, but it was still safe if you stayed on the muddy tracks that ran alongside the swirling waters.

Getting out into the open spaces had been her main joy of living in Rouen. Not for her, crouching over needlework by the poor light of the candles all day. No. Those women developed coughs and grew fat from lack of movement. They also grew miserable, and Poppa had no intention of becoming one of them.

Her deepest thoughts were miserable enough, although she did not share them with anyone, except Hrólfr.

Since William had taken over her husband's duties, her son was forced to quench several short-lived rebellions against his rule.

From a distance, Hrólfr had exerted his influence, but William knew by now well enough how to handle these traitors.

First, you negotiate, and if that did not work, you threatened them with consequences.

Despite these small uprisings, William held the support from many Frankish lords. Now, it was mostly the Burgundians who caused trouble, and Hrólfr had been spending many long nights discussing a suitable strategy with William and Sigurd, who acted as her son's right-hand man. Sigurd's knowledge of the earldom was only matched by Hrólfr, and she was content that William trusted their friend.

"Look, even the swans have had enough of this frost!" Hrólfr pointed at several of the animals huddled together in the reeds.

Poppa laughed. Why was it that the older men became, the more they turned into children? All that remained was for Hrólfr to stamp his foot.

"Of course. They have to keep warm."

"Exactly." He stopped. "And the best place to warm yourself up is the hearth."

She sighed, casting a longing glance over the glistening surface where the water was frozen in places. The atmosphere of the winter's calm soothed her. Not so her husband, it seemed.

"You are right. I've dragged you far enough for today."

"For the week, I dare say." But the corners of his lips quivered, and he did not bear a grudge. "Come. Let's return home for a cup of warm, spiced ale." He turned around, then tucked her arm in his.

Together, they walked back slowly in comfortable silence.

A fortnight later

"Thank you, Pepin. I would be lost without you."

"That's why I'm here, Lady Poppa. Leave it with me." The *majordomus* grinned. New wrinkles played around his eyes.

Then he left the hall through the side door that led to the

kitchen building. He had much to discuss with the cook in preparation for the feast of Christ's birth.

One issue less to worry about, the food. Poppa gave a sigh of relief. Another was the hall, but that had also been taken care of. She glanced around the room, proud of her daughter. Together with several of her friends, Adela had swept the floors and replaced the rushes, wiped all the candelabras, and decorated the walls with boughs of fir adorned with red and green ribbons.

Picking up a cup, Poppa poured herself some ale, then she sat and snuggled into the comfortable cushions of her high-backed chair which Pepin had moved closer to the hearth, so the warmth of the flames would warm her. The chair was Hrólfr's most recent project, together with a new one he'd made for himself. With solid arm rests and a curved back that allowed you to lean back without making your spine ache, the seats also had separate small footstools that fitted neatly beneath. When he'd presented them to her a few days earlier, it had come as a surprise. A very pleasant surprise, one that filled him with pride. It was what he needed, these days, something useful to keep him occupied.

She sipped the ale that had cooled off a little. Her head was full of plans for the feast days ahead. What did she have to prepare next? The guest cottages were ready for anyone who might arrive unexpectedly. As during every visit to Rouen, Sigurd would stay in his hut near the newly erected palisade. William had his own hall now, grander and of better built than theirs, and an important step in his claim to the earldom. She smiled at the shift in title.

Following his agreement with King Charles all those years ago, Hrólfr had been named Jarl of the Northmen. Some years later, their Frankish allies had begun to refer to him as Earl of the Normans. Now, everyone called William an earl, clearly to emphasise his Frankish origins.

Men were so narrow-minded at times. She rolled her eyes.

A shout outside made her straighten up. Another followed. Then the door burst open, and one of the stable lads rushed in.

"Lady Poppa, riders! Where is Lord Hrólfr?"

"I'm here," came her husband's voice from the top of the wooden stairs. "What is it?"

Poppa bristled. Every afternoon, he withdrew to their bedchamber to rest and should not be disturbed. But he'd obviously heard the clamour outside.

The boy gave her a brief bow, his gaze apologetic. "Strangers are arriving, lord. Four of them. Three men and one woman."

"And they've come to see us? Or are they merely visiting Rouen?" Hrólfr slowly descended the wooden stairs, adjusting his tunic as he went.

"They're asking for you. And for Lady Poppa."

She rose. "So it must be someone we know."

The boy shook his head. "Definitely not Franks. They are…different."

Hrólfr frowned, then took his sword belt from the back of his chair. Poppa helped him with it. "In what way, different?"

"They dress not like us, but…Norse."

A small group of Norse would visit them? Poppa wracked her brain. It had been years since they welcomed Northmen guests to their home. And never before women…

Hrólfr chuckled. "Lead the way, boy! Let's have a look at those strangers."

They left the hall just as the small group arrived. Poppa's eyes widened when she saw a woman, roughly of her own age, sit astride a grey mare. No, she was clearly not Frankish. Nor did her clothing mark her as such. Long leggings clad in fur-lined boots peaked from beneath a coarse cloak. Reddish curls escaped the confines of a hood. The woman had an open face, with a straight nose, high cheekbones, and a wide, full mouth. Something about that face seemed familiar, but Poppa could not think of a reason. She'd never met her before, yet…

Confused, her gaze wandered to the males in the group, all dressed in clothing made for the colder season, but very unlike their own Frankish style. Then her breath hitched, and her hands flew to her mouth.

"Ranulf," Poppa muttered. She took several steps forward until she stood close to a tall man, his shoulders broad, who had dismounted.

He turned, handing the reins to one of his companions, and familiar green eyes met hers. "Poppa!" He grinned, that crooked grin she so loved in her youth. "How you've grown!"

"Oh Ranulf, you're alive!" A sense of exhilaration surged through her. Ignoring the stares of those around her, she closed the distance and pulled him into a firm embrace. "I'm so glad to see you."

Gently, he extricated himself from her arms and took her hands. "I never thought I'd see you again, but when we heard you and…Hrólfr…are based in Rouen, we had to come. You see," he took a step back, releasing her, "I wanted to show Kathlin Bayeux where folk told us you were still alive."

The woman had dismounted and was sauntering towards them. The chill in her eyes made Poppa halt. "Of course," she glanced from one to the other, "welcome to Rouen."

"Why don't you come within," Hrólfr's voice reached them, and she swung round to face him. In her moment of joy, she'd forgotten about her husband. He stood outside the entrance, arms folded, glancing at them warily.

"Yes, come to the fire, you, Ranulf, and your friends. I want to hear all about your years away from home."

"His home is in Orkneyjar." The woman spoke for the first time, and the low tone sent shivers down Poppa's spine. She'd approached him as a friend, so there was no need for jealousy, although her impetuous embrace could be misunderstood.

"That's so far away. We once considered travelling up there but ended up in East Anglia instead." Poppa knew she was prattling. Why did they make her so nervous? She joined Hrólfr and ushered the couple inside. Their two companions took the horses away.

Once they were settled around the hearth, Poppa raised her cup of hot spiced wine that she'd ordered from the kitchen.

A pitcher rested on a hot stone beside the blazing fire.

"To returned friends." She beamed at Ranulf and his... wife?

As they drank, she looked at them more closely, as was Hrólfr who sat to her right. His brow was furrowed, and he seemed unable to take his eyes off Kathlin. Had he forgotten his manners? Then she realised the woman was returning his stare. What was going on?

"I have so many questions about...what happened to you, Ranulf, but first I want you to know about Landina."

His face fell, and he bit his lip. "I've heard already. We visited her grave. There was a child?"

Tears pricked Poppa's eyes. "Yes. A daughter, Emma. The girl died of a fever. Landina – she found the burden hard to bear. She'd longed for more children, but God never listened to her prayers."

"My sister was wed to a Northman, we were told. Are you acquainted with him?"

"Sigurd, yes. He loved Landina dearly and waited years for her to become his wife." After a quick glance at Hrólfr, who stayed unusually quiet, she added, "We are expecting him for the feast of Christ's birth. He lives on the coast, now, near the mouth of the Seine."

"I assume he has remarried."

"No." She shook her head. "For him, there was always only Landina. You would like him. He is a good friend. I... we would love for you to remain for the feast, too."

With a sigh, Ranulf lowered his gaze to the cup he cradled in his hand. "Thank you, but that depends, Poppa..."

"On what?" She stared at him.

"It depends whether we are allowed to stay or thrown out," Kathlin said, her voice harsh.

"Of course we are delighted if you stayed. Why ever not?" At a loss, Poppa looked from one to the other, then she followed the woman's gaze to Hrólfr.

Her husband grunted. "As Poppa said, you are welcome."

"Well, you asked about my life, Poppa." Ranulf abruptly changed the subject, and Poppa was even more baffled. "In

224

short, Leif took us to Orkneyjar. I worked for him, and for the old jarl." He took a sip before leaning back. "Life is harsh in the north; the winters long, cold, and the nights long. The summers are short and wet. Yet, working the land made me appreciate its rough beauty."

"It was not as romantic as you make it out to be Ranulf," Kathlin interjected. "And whilst Leif was kinder than others, you were still kept with the other thralls."

He sent her a grateful smile, and Poppa saw a deep love in their eyes.

"'Tis true. Our clothes were too threadbare against the fierce winds, and some of us did not survive. But at least he saved us from a life spent at the oars. And I met you…" His hand reached out to hers, and their fingers entwined.

Poppa felt a sense of discomfort. It was rare that she and Hrólfr showed off their love like that.

After several long moments, Ranulf looked towards the flames. "Yes, it was tough, but worth it."

"So how did you two get together?" Curiosity won Poppa over.

"Ranulf saved my life." Kathlin's cool blue gaze rested on her.

Again, a sense of recognition hit Poppa, yet she did not know why. Those eyes, so familiar.

"Well, if you hadn't gone off trying to catch a puffin on the cliff's, I'd still be working hard for someone else, probably the new jarl."

She laughed, and her face changed. Warmth emanated from her, and Poppa understood what had drawn her childhood friend to this woman. She had a presence that could not be ignored.

Yet another similarity of…what? Unable to solve the riddle, she shook her head.

"I wanted it as a pet. I still do. One day, I'll have one."

"What is a puffin?" Poppa asked, intrigued. "And why is it so difficult to catch?"

"It's a beautiful sea bird, about his high," Ranulf held his hand at knee level. "With a sharp red beak and beautiful

225

plumage. But they nest in the rockface. It keeps them safe from predators – and us."

Poppa smiled. "They sound delightful."

Ranulf's eyes shone. "Oh, they are. Very naughty too."

"I remember puffins," Hrólfr said quietly.

"You do?" Poppa turned towards him, but she could tell his mind was somewhere in the distant past.

"Yes. They are the most peculiar birds." He smiled into the fire.

Poppa stared at him, his eyes a deep blue in the flickering light. Then realisation hit her. She met Kathlin's open gaze.

Sweet Mary, could it be?

"Ah, you guess correctly, Poppa," the woman said, nodding.

"She guessed what?" Hrólfr's voice was surprisingly hoarse. He put his cup on the table with a thud.

Kathlin sent him a wry smile. "I'm your daughter, Hrólfr."

Chapter Twenty

Hrólfr awoke with a start. It was night, still. His bedchamber lay in darkness, and outside, all was quiet. Beside him, Poppa breathed deeply.

With a sigh, he propped his hands under his head, staring into nothing. It had taken him hours to fall asleep, as it happened every night since Kathlin's arrival. The two of them spent many hours talking, crying, and eventually, laughing. Her early recriminations wounded him. He'd truly not known that Åsa had been pregnant when he left the Orkneyjar Isles all those winters ago.

Leif never mentioned it, nor did the old jarl, her father. Apparently, Åsa had sworn them to secrecy. Raising a child on her own was no shame in their community, and she did not want him to return out of pity.

Pity? Ha! Of course he'd have gone back. But had he truly loved her? To this day, he was not certain. The feelings he'd held for Kathlin's mother had not run as deep as his love for Poppa. For him and – he was certain – for Åsa, it had been youthful lust. Yet he was sad to hear the woman never wed, never considered sharing her life with a man, instead retaining her own household. Was that his fault?

Kathlin had inherited some of her mother's independent spirit. Whilst she was Ranulf's wife, as it turned out, she was also feisty, and did not hold back her opinions.

Not very unlike Poppa, in fact. Hrólfr grinned, remembering his wife's stubbornness and sense of adventure. She'd almost freed Ranulf and the other thralls that long-ago night on the beach.

He turned his head, barely making out her features in the sliver of moonlight that was streaming through gaps in their shutters. A sense of utter happiness surged through him. He'd done Poppa a grave injury when he married Gisela and lived with the princess as man and wife. Now, he bitterly regretted the decision. How much it must have hurt Poppa, yet she never spoke of it, even after Gisela's death.

But grooves of worry criss-crossed her beautiful, still youthful face, and he knew she still blamed herself. Nothing he ever said could convince her otherwise. The situation would have led either to her own death, or Gisela's. Poppa had saved herself, though she could not guess how the Fates had laid their traps for the vengeful Frankish princess.

Tired, he closed his eyes, but rest would not come. Today was the feast day of Saint Adela – after whom they had named their daughter at her baptism – and it was the eve of Christ's birth. Tonight, they would celebrate, with food, and wine, and storytelling. Then, as every winter, Poppa insisted on attending a mass at midnight in the nearby chapel.

A very long day, but one spent with family and friends. He was glad Kathlin and Ranulf were staying several weeks, and William was expected to arrive in the morning, as was Sigurd. His son had been warned of his older half-sister's presence, and Hrólfr dreaded his reaction, but William's response, relayed by a messenger, had been one of excitement. This pleased Hrólfr and Poppa greatly. Only Adela had at first regarded the woman, who was closer to her mother's age than her own, with a strong pinch of jealousy. But Kathlin tried hard to gain her little sister's trust, and Adela's doubts soon disappeared.

Hrólfr was grateful for a chance to get to know Kathlin, before he passed from this world.

The feast days should have been such a joyful time. But this winter, he would miss Knud's grumpy reluctance at being pulled to join them in church, something the Northman had only done to please Poppa.

But his oldest friend was gone, having died from an infected leg wound in the summer.

Even though, his shadow still stalked the hall, Hrólfr was convinced.

Soon it'll be my turn...

"I'm getting miserable in my old age," he muttered, then moved onto his right side, facing Poppa. Her breathing was still steady, and soon, he drifted off to sleep again too.

As the temperature dropped outside, a biting wind swept through the hall. "Shut the door behind you!" Hrólfr bellowed across the room.

William sent him an apologetic glance, then closed the door behind Adela and Kathlin, who'd been taking their time entering. Ridding themselves of their cloaks and furs, they hurried towards the fire.

"Sorry, Father." William grinned, ruffling his hair. He took a goblet from a tray a thrall held up, then handed one each to his sister and half-sister.

Hrólfr shrugged deeper into his fur coverlet. Despite the heat from the hearth, his body was racked with shivers. Bones were grating, and muscles aching. Oh, how he hated old age, especially in winter. He cradled a goblet of hot, spiced wine. It warmed his fingers.

"Are you chilled, my love?" Poppa leaned over and arranged the furs, so they were tucked in beneath his chin.

Embarrassed, he waved her away. "I'm fine. Don't fuss." But realising his tone was too abrupt, he took her hand and kissed it. "Thank you."

She tutted, then beamed at Kathlin. "I hope our two have not bored you to death with their many questions."

The last few weeks, it had not only been Hrólfr who spent much time with his eldest. Adela and William also sought her company, clearly wishing to know more of her past.

The beautiful woman, whose features resembled Hrólfr's much more than Poppa's children did, returned her smile. "Oh, I love it. I always felt alone, and Mother never wanted another child." She cast a quick glance at her father, then returned her attention to Poppa. "So having found a brother and a sister is truly a gift from the Gods."

Hrólfr suppressed a cough. He pushed away the guilt that began to creep into his head again. It often resided there, alongside the pride he felt at having such a wonderful family. Did he deserve them?

Only after Åsa's death in the spring had Kathlin broached her intention to Ranulf – that she wanted to meet her father, whose reputation had spread northwards to Orkneyjar. Hrólfr's only regret was that he was too old now. He would not live to meet his two grandsons, who were being looked after by Leif's son's family.

There was so much he wanted to learn; so many things he needed to tell her. Yet time went by too fast.

He grunted, huddling deeper into his furs.

Adela, sharing a bench with Kathlin, took her sister's hand and held it in hers. "It's me who is grateful." She looked over to him and Poppa, her eyes full of love. "My family is together. That's all I can ask for."

"And at such a precipitous time of the year, too," Kathlin said, with a glance to the large log that lay in the fire. "It's good to see you maintain our traditions too."

He laughed. "I spent most of my life straddling two different ways of life, daughter. Maintaining our old Norse customs, and the new path, following the Franks…"

"You've successfully embraced parts of both in our home." Poppa nodded. "And taught me much about your ways along the way."

The door flew open again, and the howling wind chased through the hall. Hrólfr was prepared to glare at whoever dared to let the late afternoon chill in, but the sight that met him filled him with joy.

Sigurd entered, dragging the door shut behind him. Slowly, he took off his cloak and hung it on the hooks.

As his friend approached the hearth, Hrólfr noticed his hesitant walk. The face he knew so well was deeply lined; the long hair turned grey. How long had it been since their last gathering?

A year was a long time. Too long.

He stood and bid Sigurd welcome.

William brought a chair for their friend who was soon settled with a warming goblet of hot wine and a fur around his shoulders.

After the greetings, Hrólfr's gaze went to Ranulf, who had been quiet since Sigurd's arrival. Kathlin's husband was watching the old Northman carefully, assessing him.

"Sigurd, as you can see, we have guests. You may vaguely remember this fine man opposite you…from our Easter raid in Bayeux all those winters ago. He is the boy Poppa was trying to save that night Leif caught her on the beach."

Sigurd frowned, studying Ranulf's face for recognition. Then his eyes widened. "Of course. You went with Leif, didn't you?"

"Not voluntarily," Ranulf snorted, "but yes, I did travel to Orkneyjar with Leif."

Sigurd sent Poppa a sideways glance. "You were a brave girl that night. Not many people are prepared to face a bunch of Northern warriors armed with a mere knife." He grinned.

Poppa laughed. "Oh, that was an adventure." Then she sobered. "Ranulf arrived a fortnight ago, with his wife, Kathlin."

"I'm pleased you have found a good woman, Ranulf, and I hope Leif did not treat you too badly."

Ranulf shook his head. "No. He was a good man, hard but fair. It wasn't easy at first. But everything changed when I…"

"When he saved my life," Kathlin finished. "Did you know the jarl whose name you share?"

Sigurd nodded. They'd all heard stories of old Jarl Sigurd's prowess. "Yes, although I only met him once."

"Kathlin's mother was Åsa, the late jarl's daughter."

"Åsa?" Sigurd cocked his head. He stared into the fire, as if delving into the past, and finding pieces missing.

Hrólfr exchanged a concerned look with Poppa.

"The woman I left behind when I first journeyed to Francia…"

Sigurd's eyes widened. "That Åsa?"

"Yes. Kathlin is my daughter…and Ranulf is Landina's older brother."

His friend shuddered, the goblet falling from his hand. "Landina…"

Concerned, Poppa surged forward, waving the thrall away, and picked up the vessel. "Get me some cloths to soak up the stain, quick," she ordered, and the thrall rushed away.

"Are you well?" Poppa placed her hand on his wrist. "This must come as a shock. We understand."

He shook his head and patted her hand. "I'm sorry, Poppa. Yes. I should have remembered it all."

"It was all a long time ago, Sigurd," Ranulf said, leaning forward. "And from what I've heard, I have to thank you for making my sister happy…while she lived."

Tears shone in Sigurd's eyes, reflected by the flickering fire. "I made her happy? I suppose. At least for a while, until…" His breath hitched.

"Why don't I take you to your chamber, Sigurd? You'll stay here with us, upstairs. Travelling in this awful weather is exhausting."

"And we should be retiring until the feast later." Kathlin stood and gestured Ranulf to follow suit. "It will be a late night."

As the couple left, and Poppa helped Sigurd up the stairs, Hrólfr could not fail to notice how sad his friend appeared. As if all his life juice had been sucked from his veins. Ranulf's appearance had brought up memories Sigurd always kept closely hidden. Now the gaping wound in his life was laid bare for all to see again.

Never one to relish the late mass on the eve of the feast of Christ's birth, Hrólfr's mood sank to a new low. Opposite him, across the hearth, William sat watching him.

What he would give to have his son's youth again!

***

"Hrólfr, wake up. 'Tis time." Poppa gently nudged her husband's shoulder.

His pallor concerned her. He'd slept through the late afternoon and into the evening.

Downstairs in the hall, the family had gathered, together with their closest retainers and their families. The sound of excited voices reverberated through the wooden floor, yet Hrólfr had not woken.

She grabbed his arm and shook it harder. "Hrólfr!"

"What? Where?" With a jolt, he leaned on his elbows, blinking.

She rose, resting her hand on his shoulder. "We're all gathered, my love. Only you are missing."

Hrólfr stared at her. "How long have I slept?"

"Well, the meal is on the table, but no one wanted to begin without you. Can I tell them you'll arrive forthwith? At least, then the food won't grow cold."

"Of course." He waved her away, still looking around as if trying to remember where he was. "I'll get dressed, then join you. After a piss…"

A half-apologetic smile told her he'd recovered his sense of humour.

"You do that. I'll ask William to start the meal. And Hrólfr?"

"Yes." He swung his legs out of the bed.

"If you're too tired later, you won't need to join us for midnight mass. Stay here, by the hearth."

"I'll see how it goes, wife. Now be off!"

"As you wish, my lord." Chuckling, she left him and closed the door behind her.

At the top of the stairs, Poppa paused for a moment, taking in the festive atmosphere.

The heat from the large fire spread across the room. Torches flickered in their sconces in the walls. The tables were adorned with candles, pinecones, branches of red winter berries, and small laurel wreaths made by Adela and Kathlin.

She searched for the girls and found them.

Girls? With Kathlin almost her own age, Poppa could not call her a girl. Yet the two were inseparable, and Kathlin was her stepdaughter.

Was that a good sign? Possibly.

But soon after the feast days, Ranulf and Kathlin would return to their home in Orkneyjar, to their own children.

And Adela would feel bereft. Perhaps it was unwise of the two half-sisters to form such a close bond. But seeing her daughter's bright laughter at something the Norse woman said made Poppa's thoughts unwarranted.

Could Adela join them in the north? No. As the daughter of an earl, she would wed to form an alliance. Hrólfr would choose a husband. Hopefully soon! It was something Poppa had nudged him for years, but all her suggestions of potential husbands had fallen on deaf ears.

Hrólfr was not ready to let go of Adela just yet. And he would never allow for her to take such a dangerous journey, to a land so far away.

No, Adela had to stay. The farewell from her sister, when it came, would be painful, and Poppa would be there for her daughter.

Along the large table on the dais, William sat, chatting to Sigurd and Ranulf. She was pleased the two men – Landina's brother and husband – were getting on well. And William's easy way brought them even closer together. T

he men laughed at something her son said, but Poppa could not swallow a sense of unease as she watched Sigurd. Her friend was too pale, too…weak. Did he suffer from an illness?

No! She straightened her shoulders. Sigurd was a warrior, like Hrólfr. He was not weak. Nor was he sick.

But he is getting old…

"I thought you'd gone downstairs to begin the meal. It looks like everyone's still waiting."

Poppa jumped as Hrólfr whispered in her ear.

Where she stood, in the shade of the rafters, she was shielded from view below. And over her musings she'd forgotten the most important thing: their feast!

Her head tilted, she sent him a light smile, but before she could descend, his arm encircled her.

"What concerns you? I was watching you for a little while. You seemed deep in thought."

"Oh, 'tis nothing. I was just admiring the decorations the girls had prepared."

He scanned the room, then leaned closer to her. "I can see that, but something occupies your mind. What is it, sweeting?"

"I… I'll tell you later, Hrólfr. Now we must ensure our friends eat. Come!"

Hand in hand, they slowly descended the steps.

Later that night

With relief, Poppa heard the final words of mass. Despite her fur-lined boots, her toes had turned into blocks of ice, and the chill was creeping through her body. She was relieved that Hrólfr had stayed at home, at her insistence. Of late, he caught a cold easily, and with so many guests coming and going, it was more important that he remained in relatively good health. Although she was concerned about his increased forgetfulness lately. But that often came with age, and her husband had led a long life of warfare, always in motion.

Perhaps the peaceful years made him susceptible to a sickness of the mind.

Not that Hrólfr had put up an argument to join her. She smiled. Even though he converted to Christianity many years ago, he would never become devout. It sufficed if he attended the occasional Easter mass.

William, on the other hand, was always by her side. His whole demeanour was far more Frankish than Norse, which made much sense. She cast a glance at him standing tall, every inch an earl. Trouble had been brewing ever since he'd taken over the reins, but so far, she'd been impressed with the way her son had handled each attempt at diminishing his power – with negotiation, or if that proved futile, with promises or threats.

Fortunately, his followers were loyal, and he was already expanding his father's territory. Poppa was a very proud mother.

Around them, people sighed and shuffled their feet.

It amused her that everyone else shared her relief at the end of mass. A warm hearth at home beckoned.

William took her arm and led her outside. A sharp blast of wind hit her, and she pulled her hood up and wrapped a thick scarf around her head and neck. But even the woollen mittens could not keep her fingers warm.

"Let's head home, shall we? I could devour a whole barrel of hot, spiced wine." William grinned, rubbing his bare hands.

Poppa nodded. "Yes. Is everyone here?" She glanced around.

Ranulf was behind her, with Kathlin who had come along as a favour to Adela. Poppa's daughter hovered by her half-sister's side. Around them gathered their hearth men with their wives and children.

Searching the group in vain for a familiar face, Poppa frowned. "Where is Sigurd?"

William shrugged. "I saw him talking to someone when we left. Perhaps he's still inside and will join us later."

"Ah. Quite likely."

They had walked several yards when a shout rose from behind, followed by a commotion.

Poppa and William turned to see the priest emerge from the chapel.

He waved at them. "Lord William, Lady Poppa, come quickly!"

"Head home with the others, Mother. I'll go."

"No, I'm coming, too. What could possibly be so urgent?"

They hurried back, careful not to slip on the icy path.

"Father, what is the reason for your agitation?" William took charge, and Poppa gladly let him. She did not like the look of panic on the priest's face.

"'Tis Sigurd the Northman, my lord. He has…" he gestured into the building, "…collapsed."

Poppa swallowed back a sharp retort. Sigurd was a devout Christian, settled here for a long time. There was no need to point out his heritage. But beneath her anger, concern for her friend rose.

William rushed inside, and she hurried to catch up with her son.

"There he is."

Sigurd lay crumpled on the stone floor. His head had rolled to the side, his jaw fallen open.

William knelt beside him and pressed a hand on Sigurd's heart. Then he leaned close to their friend's face.

"What is it, William? Is he breathing?"

Holding on to Ranulf's hand for balance, Poppa crouched. She stared into Sigurd's open, unmoving eyes and gasped. A shudder ran down her spine. He was looking right through her.

"No. He is gone, Mother. But…how?"

A man she did not know joined them on the other side of Sigurd's prone body. "I saw him clutch his chest moments before he staggered. I held on to him, but he dropped to the ground. I…I am so sorry, Lady Poppa."

Tears rolled from her eyes, and she sighed. "He is at peace now." She closed Sigurd's eyes, then nodded to Ranulf to help her up. Addressing the stranger, she asked, "Did he say anything?"

The man nodded. "Yes, lady. One word. It sounded like a woman's name, I think."

"Landina," Ranulf muttered, and the man's eyes widened.

"Yes, that's right. Is the lady his wife?" He glanced around.

"She was." Ranulf's voice broke.

William crossed himself. "Now they are together again."

"Father, where are you?" Poppa turned to find the priest. He was hovering behind her. "Have you given him the last rites?"

The priest's mouth dropped. He rushed forward and bent over the body.

"You may as well kneel," Poppa suggested. She raised an eyebrow, and he lowered himself to the ground, avoiding her gaze. Why did she have to remind him of his duties?

They stood in silence as the priest intoned the words that would grant Sigurd everlasting life.

With William's arm wrapped around her shoulders, Poppa let the tears fall. Sigurd had been a true friend, ever since the day he arrived in Bayeux. For many years, he'd patiently waited for Landina to acknowledge him, only for tragedy to strike. He'd seen his share of sorrow and sadness, and Poppa knew he'd never recovered from her best friend's death.

Now, he was finally reunited with his beloved wife and daughter.

Beside her, Ranulf sniffed. Poppa felt for him too. After all those years of not knowing, he'd discovered another man who had loved his sister, only to have him taken away so soon. She pressed his hand.

When the priest had finished his administrations, she breathed a sigh of relief and forced a smile. "Farewell, my friend. Until…we meet again."

"Father, please see to it that Sigurd's body be prepared for vigil. Give him all the honours any other Christian receives. I shall return later to stay the night."

"I will join you," Ranulf said, his voice hoarse. "I owe him a debt of gratitude."

William nodded.

A thought occurred to Poppa. "I think Sigurd should be buried alongside his family, in Bayeux."

"A sensible decision, Mother. I will make arrangements in the morning. For now, there's nothing else we can do here, so let's go home. We must tell Father."

Poppa winced. Hrólfr would be distraught. First Knud, earlier in the year, and now Sigurd. His closest friends. "I will do it. Come!"

She gathered Adela in her arms, and together they led the small group back to the hall.

A light layer of snow began to settle on the thatched roofs when Hrólfr, William and Ranulf, followed by many of their men, set off after they'd received word that Sigurd's body was laid out for the vigil.

Hrólfr had insisted on going, and neither Poppa nor William could stop him.

Not that she really wanted to, despite her fears for his health.

Sigurd had brought half a dozen warriors with him, and they also joined the vigil. The men now looked to William for reassurance.

Poppa stood outside the hall, watching as the men gathered. The air froze beneath her breath, and she was relieved her husband was wrapped up warm, in layers of woollen garments, fur-lined boots, and a thick cloak covering his body. A large wolf pelt wrapped over his shoulders and covering his neck and back provided extra warmth. But would it be enough, with hours spent kneeling on a cold stone floor?

With a shiver, she shut the door to the hall behind her. Tomorrow was the feast day of Christ's birth, but this year, it would be spent in mourning. People would still arrive for the meal, which would otherwise go to waste, but already the atmosphere in town was changing. Sigurd had been popular, a man both fair and brave. The chapel would be full tonight.

Stopping at the hearth, she held her hands towards the heat, relishing the feeling. Then she waved to a servant clearing up a table. "Brida, please see to it that stones are placed near the fire. We must make sure Lord Hrólfr's bed will be warm on his return."

As the girl scurried to fetch the smooth stones used for heating, Poppa lowered herself into her chair. Beside her, on a bench, sat Kathlin. Adela had gone to sleep not long ago.

The woman looked at her over the rim of a cup of warm, spiced wine. "Do you think it wise that Father joined the vigil?"

Poppa shook her head. "No. But Hrólfr is a man so stubborn, it's impossible to change his mind."

"You fret about him?"

"Yes, always. As you may have noticed, he has moments of…forgetfulness, and his knees are giving him trouble."

"So a vigil is the last thing he should be doing."

"It is. But we can't stop him. If we did, he may as well stop breathing."

Kathlin gave a dry laugh. "We are more alike than I thought, in that case."

Poppa watched her. The resemblance between father and daughter was strong, and not only in appearances.

"I'm so glad you are here, Kathlin." She reached out and squeezed the woman's hand. "I truly am."

"We will stay for as long as we're needed, Poppa."

"Thank you." But Poppa knew the day would soon come when Ranulf and Kathlin would have to leave – to return home, to their sons.

William would also be gone. His presence was already demanded in Chartres for yet more negotiations.

And she would be left alone with her worries.

Chapter Twenty-One

Late September, AD 930
Rouen, Earldom of Normannia

The air was still, and the night unseasonably warm. Poppa's skin felt damp, sticky. She pushed the thin cover off and placed her legs on top of it. A sliver of moonlight filtered through the open shutter, illuminating the bedchamber in a silvery glow.

Hrólfr grumbled in his sleep, then turned onto his back. Moments later, his snores pierced the silence.

Not again! Now, she would not be able to fall asleep. Over recent months, her nights had become more and more disrupted. When he was not snoring, it would be a coughing fit or a nightmare. Then he would sit up and stare around him with an aimless gaze. Each time, she reassured him that he was at home, with her, and safe. But in the last fortnight, his dreams had worsened, as had his coughs.

And his memory suffered more gaps.

Poppa sighed and rose. She stood by the open window, breathing in the humid air, gazing up at the sky illuminated by stars too many to count. The moon was nearly full, and so close, she could almost touch its surface.

What was it like up there? Did people live like they did here? Or was it deserted, a small light in the heavens that brightened up the nights? Áslaug would know.

Poppa blinked. She'd not thought about the old Norse wisewoman in Anglia for many years. The old crone was probably dead. But yes, she held ancient knowledge about the moon and the stars, and the mysteries of life.

"If only I'd listened to you more often…" Poppa whispered.

"Hrmph…" The bed creaked. She turned to see Hrólfr rubbing his eyes. "Who are you talking to? Is it morning already?" Frowning, stared at the moonlight.

"Not yet. Go back to sleep, my love." She returned to his side but stayed on top of the cover as he huddled back under it. "Are you cold?" He nodded then curled up on his side, facing her, and she tucked the blanket over his shoulders. "There you go."

"Will you stay with me, Poppa?" His eyes were falling shut.

"Yes, always. Now rest. I'm right here." She lay back, close to him, her hand in his, but sleep eluded her.

Soon, Hrólfr's breathing steadied, and Poppa let out a long sigh. The light of the moon illuminated his face: the still glowing hue of his skin at the end of a long, hot summer, the deep grooves at the corners of his eyes and mouth, his hair flopping into his face, and the blond beard streaked with grey that needed trimming again.

Her heart swelled with love for this man who'd changed her life forever.

But with each day, her worries about him grew. She sorely missed Kathlin. Her stepdaughter had helped her by being there, lending a hand, and by listening. When he grew agitated because he'd forgotten or mislaid something again, Kathlin had been the only one, apart from Poppa, who could calm him.

Poppa gently brushed a strand of hair back. He looked so peaceful.

Until he woke and found more memories gone…

In the morning, Poppa slid quietly from the bed, not wanting to wake her husband. She'd lain awake half the night, until the moon moved on and their chamber was plunged into darkness.

Now, she tried to rid herself of the tiredness that engulfed her still by stretching her limbs. Her shoulder clicked uncomfortably, and her neck felt stiff, but the movements helped.

She rinsed her face in cold water from a bowl on the small table, then dried her skin with a linen cloth. From outside, the sounds of daily life drifted into the chamber: horses neighing, men calling out, carts creaking. She walked to the window and looked out. Now, the view was very different. A low fog had descended, the humidity settling everywhere. Quietly, she pushed the shutter closed. Damp air was not healthy.

Hrólfr did not stir, so she put on her shift and tunic in the semi-darkness. Poppa picked up her belt and pouch and slid her feet into her shoes. Tiptoeing from the chamber, she left the door open. Hrólfr hated the feeling of being locked in, something she did not understand. The man was never once trapped in his life!

As she took the steps down into the hall, she fitted her belt around her waist, then plaited her hair loosely at the back. Once Adela was awake, she would ask her to wash her hair.

The ale in the pitcher on the high table had been replenished, as every morning, and she poured herself a cup and emptied it in long, deep draughts. A second cup revived her spirits, and she felt more awake.

Today, she would meet with the blacksmith. William had a new sword made, and she checked the progress in her son's absence. It would be a special weapon, to suit his height. A sword longer than his father's, and sturdier than those the Franks carried. Pride surged through her. William was ruling Normannia with a firm grip.

She frowned, as she set the cup down. Still, the dogs were snapping at his feet. Landowners and minor Frankish nobles who sought his fall. And then there were the Bretons, an altogether different tribe, full of men going back on their word. Their loyalty changed with the wind, which changed often on these shores.

Poppa sighed. With Hrólfr's health failing, William needed new allies, men who would fight for him and his rights.

William needed an heir. At nearly thirty years of age, it was time. But he'd been too busy suppressing rebellions.

Tonight, she would speak with Hrólfr. They must find a suitable bride for their son, and soon.

***

Mid-December, AD 930
Rouen, Earldom of Normannia

Hrólfr sat near the central hearth and pulled the furs closer around him. A thick woollen blanket was wrapped around his legs, and he could feel the heat of the fire on his face. But still, the cold would not leave his body.

Poppa leaned over and handed him a cup, and he cradled it, enjoying its warmth. The steam of the hot wine rose from it, but he could no longer smell the spices. He missed the scent of red grapes, of cinnamon, of burnt rosemary.

His senses deserted him, one by one. All food now tasted the same; of nothing. His eyesight had begun to fade, as had his hearing. The cacophony of voices in the hall was now mere noise to him. A low hum that constantly sounded in his ears made it worse.

He hated ageing. Having survived nearly seventy winters, he was fed up with himself, with his body, and especially with his head.

The occasions when Poppa mentioned a visit from a friend, or a mass in the chapel, or a feast. Often, he would wake up the next morning, and not know what had gone on the day before; what he'd eaten, or who he'd spoken to.

"Ranulf has sent word, my love," Poppa said as she wrapped herself into a large blanket. "He and Kathlin have arrived safely in Byrgisay."

Hrólfr drew his eyebrows together. He stared into the fire, not wanting her to see his confusion, before meeting her gaze. "Who? Arrived where?"

She sighed. "Ranulf. Landina's brother. Your daughter's husband."

"Adela has a husband? I thought... Didn't her betrothed die?" The recent past was a fog in his head, but something was there. Was there not?

"Not Adela, Hrólfr. Kathlin. Your eldest." She patted his arm. "She stayed with us until the summer, together with

Ranulf, her husband and my childhood friend. You liked her."

"Ah." He strained his mind, and the vague vision came back to him of a woman with thick red curls. Not Adela, but older. Not a Christian, but Norse.

Hell's teeth, now he could not even remember his own daughter! Tears pricked his eyes.

"'Tis all right, my love. Don't force it. Have your wine while it's hot."

Nodding, he raised the cup with shaky hands. He hated his head. Why were all those memories gone? And where to? Poppa remembered everything. Why could he not?

He gulped down the wine then put the cup on the floor. But he let it go too soon, and it broke on impact, bursting into small shards.

"Thor's balls!" He drew in a shuddering breath. What was wrong with him?

A smile played on Poppa's lips as she soothed him. "It's just a cup." She signalled to a thrall who swiftly removed the offending pieces. "Fetch a new one, please."

The girl disappeared, returning moments later with another cup.

"I don't want any more. I'm tired."

"Then why don't you lie down for a while? We'll eat after vespers. You may hear the church bells, but if not, I'll wake you when everything is ready."

"I'm not hungry," he said stubbornly. What was the point of eating if your body did not obey you? "I'll stay in bed. You have a nice meal with the others."

Hrólfr glanced around. Several of their followers sat in small groups together, chatting quietly. The heavy rains had arrived in the afternoon, putting an early end to any sword training they would normally undertake.

Poppa had told him.

Glaring at them, he racked his brain, but could not remember the last time he'd lifted a sword or axe.

William was earl now. There was no reason for Hrólfr to live.

Apart from Poppa.

He looked at her, taking in her long braid streaked with a few grey hairs, tucked under her wimple, her softly rounded curves beneath the dark blue tunic, the large light brown eyes, and the fine lines beside them that apparently meant she'd laughed a lot in her life.

Had she?

"Have I made you happy, Poppa?"

She sent him a sharp glance. "Of course. Why are you asking?"

He blinked, biting back more tears, and grabbed her hand, holding it tight between his. "Because I…I can't remember."

Poppa knelt at his feet and placed her free hand on his cheek. "Yes, my love. You have made me happy."

"But…were there days when you were unhappy?" He had to know. This wretched head!

Briefly, she averted her gaze, and he swallowed hard. So it was true.

Then she let out a long breath. When she looked at him again, her eyes glistened with moisture. "There have been moments, Hrólfr. But they are a long time in the past."

"I'm so sorry, Poppa." His breath hitched. He would be lost without her. "I never meant to hurt you. You are the only woman I have ever loved."

Around him, the room had fallen silent. Or was that just his damned hearing again?

Poppa smiled, for him only, as if they were alone in the room. "I love you too. I always will." Placing her hand on his knee, she pushed herself upright. "Come. It's time for you to rest."

Nodding, he rose too. "Yes…must rest…"

Several pairs of eyes followed their progress across the hall and up the steps. With much effort, he kept his back straight and his head high. He was still Hrólfr, Jarl of Normannia.

He let Poppa take him to their chamber, where she helped him, fully dressed, into the bed. She removed his belt and boots, and he slid beneath the cover with a sigh.

"To keep you warm." She smiled as she tucked the furs

over his shoulders. "Fortunately, the shutters are closed, so it's not as cold."

"It feels cold to me." His throat felt dry, probably from sitting too close to the fire since the morning. "Is there any ale?"

"No, but I'll get a cup for you." She sat on the wooden frame of their solid bed and trailed her fingers across his brow. Her touch was light, like a feather. He felt content.

"Why don't you close your eyes until I return? I'll leave the candle here, so it's not too dark. You won't need to worry." She leaned over him and kissed his forehead, then, after a final glance from the door, she left the chamber. The door remained open. She always remembered.

He did not.

Faintly, he heard her steps recede, then silence engulfed him.

Hrólfr shuddered, suddenly feeling very alone. He looked around the room, taking in the familiarity. This was his sanctuary. Here, he felt safe.

The flame flickered, as if a draft disturbed it. Mesmerised, he stared into its orange glow. A strange sense of warmth spread through his bones, into all the limbs. His skin tingled. It was pleasant after the cold air.

He closed his eyes to watch the summer sun set over the sea in a great big ball of fire. Waves crashed against the karve, and, breathing in deeply the scent of the sea, he felt each movement of the sleek ship in the water. Salty air settled on his tongue, and he licked his dry lips.

"Poppa?" he whispered, but she did not reply. Where was she? "Poppa…"

The waves grew larger, until, right in front of him, a giant wave rose, with a large hole gaping in its centre. Inside, a cave glowed blue and green; inviting. The karve slid into the cavity, and suddenly the stormy sea that had surrounded them subsided. In here, all was silent.

The colours shimmered as the ship slid through the gentle water. Through them, shafts of sunshine illuminated the watery cave.

As if urged forward by his mind, the vessel edged deeper and deeper into the shimmering, wondrous colours. Soon, he was surrounded by fish of all sizes. They floated around him as if in welcome.

Then he spotted it, and gasped. A light in the distance. It grew brighter as the ship approached. Heat suffused him, stretching down into his fingers and toes. Was this the entrance to Valhalla? No, it was too quiet for a warriors' hall. Or was this the Heaven the priests spoke of? But Heaven was up there, in the skies! This light led him down, on his karve, into the heart of the earth.

A tear fell from his eyes as his breathing slowed. Oh, what would Poppa say when he told her about it?

Where was she?

He gave a shuddering breath and his heart – filled with the calm beauty of the place he found – stilled.

Poppa...

Chapter Twenty-Two

The feast day of Saint Stephen, AD 930
Rouen, Earldom of Normannia

The large church, finally completed this summer, having been destroyed by the Danes years earlier, was illuminated by dozens of torches. The flames cast an eerie dance of shadow and light on the bare stone walls.

Poppa blinked back the tears as silence fell over the gathered crowd. It seemed that all of Rouen had arrived to watch their first earl being laid to rest. But many had travelled from beyond the town – from as far as Bayeux and even Burgundy.

But no one joined them from Paris. King Raoul had more pressing concerns. From the east, the Magyars were snapping at his heels, but it was his meddling in Aquitania which had seen him undertaking several hazardous journeys recently.

She scoffed. No, the King of the Franks was not interested in the death of the man his predecessor had created Earl of the Northmen nearly two decades earlier. If he wanted anything from them – which was frequent – he went straight to William.

Pride surged through her as she glanced at her son standing solemnly beside her, exuding power.

Between them, Hrólfr and Poppa had taught William well.

On her other side stood Adela, who let the tears run freely down her face. At three-and-twenty, she was still unwed, and her demeanour was that of a girl much younger than her years. The early death of her betrothed meant she still remained unwed. As did William.

The conversation Poppa had wanted to hold with Hrólfr about potential alliances through marriage came to nothing.

Her husband had been too frail, his mind too fractured. Poppa had lost count how often she'd told herself off for not having raised the issue earlier.

As Archbishop Gonthard intoned Hrólfr's burial mass, her thoughts returned to yet another subdued feast day of Christ's birth, for the second year in a row. None of them felt like hosting a meal, but they had a duty towards their people, so they shared their grief, their sadness, and their anecdotes with them.

The archbishop's voice changed tone to a higher pitch, and she startled. Hrólfr would have laughed at her wandering mind.

She stared at his once strong body wrapped in a linen shroud, lying on a wooden plank. His sword lay on top of him, the hilt placed between his folded hands. Even in death, Hrólfr exuded power and influence. Despite his age, he'd still been tall and broad of shoulder. Her fingers itched to touch him one last time, to hold his hand, to lean into his demanding kiss.

But the man she'd loved almost all her life was gone. Never again would she hear his voice, his laughter, or look into his eyes the colour of a frozen winter's lake.

Her breath hitched, and she straightened, not wishing to show any weakness, even in widowhood.

Finally, the monotonous droning stopped, and Archbishop Gonthard gave the signal to lower the body into the sarcophagus set deep in the ground in front of the altar. Soon, she lost sight of the shroud, and a gasp escaped her.

Tears welled up again, and this time, she let them flow.

Together with her children, her arms interlinked with theirs, she stepped in front of the hole and looked down. A final glance at the proud warrior who'd sacked her hometown, before marrying her in the Danish manner, before leaving her to grow up.

Yet he always referred to her as his wife, and later Countess of the Normans.

The memories of another woman invaded her sorrow, but she quickly brushed them aside.

A sense of guilt for Gisela's death, now such a long time ago, remained firmly locked in her heart, despite Hrólfr's continued insistence that it had been an accident. Today belonged to them – to Hrólfr and her, Poppa, and to their children. Not the usurper princess.

The past was just that, the past. Gone irrevocably.

Now, Hrólfr was part of it. Soon, he would be forgotten.

No! She unlinked her arms and wiped the tears from her face. She and William would make certain Hrólfr was remembered for a very long time. As a family, they would see that it was done; that their offspring would end up ruling vast lands; and that their lives would be spoken of for centuries to come.

She sent her son a wry smile.

But first, she must find a wife for William, or there would not be any offspring!

After a final glance at her husband inert figure, she nodded, and the lid was lowered onto the sarcophagus.

She waited for the archbishop to finish his prayers, then turned and strode through the crowd, her head held high. She would return when Hrólfr the church was empty.

Then she would say her final goodbye, just between him and her.

Chapter Twenty-Three

Late summer, AD 933
Bayeux, Earldom of Normannia

"Is the chamber prepared?"

"Yes, Lady Poppa. All is ready for our guests."

"Thank you, Claudia. They should arrive any moment."

The servant dismissed, Poppa paced the hall, her gaze roaming the room.

In the two years since her return home, much had changed, and all for the better. The old, leaky building had been replaced by strong walls, with solid oak beams propping up the newly thatched roof. A new hearth graced the centre of the large room.

Her father's hall existed no longer. The inside had been completely redone. Instead of the cramped private quarters at the back, with their rickety walls and flimsy doors, there was now an upper floor, reached by narrow wooden stairs from the main hall. The space contained not only her generous bedchamber, but also small room where she could withdraw to. On the opposite site of the narrow corridor were two guest chambers, one of which would soon be host Sprota and her toddler, Richard. She'd be accompanied by her adopted sister, Gwenn.

Richard. William and Sprota's son. A son no one knew of apart from their closest circle. Poppa would ensure it stayed that way, for the time being.

A few days earlier, William had sent a messenger from Rouen with an urgent request – to accommodate his handfasted wife and child. After a year spent at his new fortress in Fécamp, he deemed it no longer safe for his family.

Poppa sighed. Oh, how history repeated itself! Married in the Danish custom, just like she'd been, their marriage was not accepted by the Church, so William – as earl of Normannia – was still free to marry for political gain.

It had been William's compromise to Poppa's wishes: to wed Sprota *in more danico*. To her surprise, the young woman agreed without complaint. Having never met her, Poppa felt gratitude towards her. Unlike herself, a count's daughter, Sprota was the daughter of a minor lord; the woman had owned a tavern in the Breton countryside and apparently brewed the nicest apple wine in all of Brittany. Perhaps that was something they could start up in Bayeux too? Plenty of apple trees lined the fields.

William had rescued the women from Danish raiders during one of his journeys into Brittany to keep the peace. It appeared he'd arrived just in time, or Sprota and Gwenn's fate would have been sealed.

Poppa often wondered how Sprota felt about her status. Did she love William, like he obviously cared for her? And how did she handle the secrecy?

Few people outside their inner circle knew of their relationship. William preferred it that way. A wife and child made him vulnerable. And as his challengers snapped at his heels, he sought a safe place for her. That was the reason they joined Poppa. He relied on her discretion, and that of her household.

William rarely visited since she moved back, but she did not complain. Only recently, he'd sworn fealty for his lands to the Frankish king, Raoul. In return, the king had granted William islands off the coast and large tracts of Brittany, but the dispute over these lands continued.

Together with allies in Evreux, Count Alan of Brittany incited Breton rebellions from the safe distance at the court of the West Saxon king, Æthelstan. Yet the coward dared not show his face, nor did he care that the upheaval allowed Danish raiders to attack and destroy his people.

Her mouth set into a thin line, and she glared at the empty hearth.

As a lady married to a warrior, Poppa had no time for men who schemed and stabbed you in the back, but who did not dare face you in a fair fight.

Her thoughts were interrupted when Pepin entered. She'd been relieved when he offered to join her in Bayeux. He sought a quieter life than the busy hall in Rouen, and she was delighted to have someone she could rely on.

He held the door open. "They've arrived, lady."

"I'm coming." Poppa strode past him, hoping her nervousness did not show.

In the square outside the hall, several riders hovered around a litter. The men were armed well with swords and axes.

Poppa nodded her approval. Her son had learnt well from his father never to take chances. Inclining her head, she acknowledged the escort.

The curtain of the litter shifted, and a girl of perhaps ten-and-seven years peeked out.

"That can't be her," Poppa muttered under her breath.

The curtain was swept aside, and she was relieved to see a woman passing a child to the girl, then alighted with Pepin's help. She thanked him with a warm smile, a small gesture that made Poppa content. Acknowledging those who assist you was a duty for a lady, but many of her own status who she'd met did not have the same views.

The woman took the boy from the girl who also emerged. Both glanced around, uncertain.

Then their eyes met, and Poppa knew she liked her daughter-by-marriage. William's handfasted wife was beautiful, her green eyes shining in the sunlight as she took everything in. A long, black braid was loosely tucked beneath a wimple. She was tall for a woman, about half a head taller than Poppa herself.

"Welcome to Bayeux," Poppa said as she stepped forward, hands outstretched in greeting. "You must be Sprota."

"Thank you, Lady Poppa." Both women curtseyed, but she waved them to rise again.

"Call me Poppa, please. And who do we have here?"

Sprota juggled the child. "What's your name, sweeting? Tell the lady."

But he glared at Poppa, then burped.

Sprota's eyes widened, but Poppa burst out laughing. "May I take him? You must be weary from your journey."

"If you are certain, Lady…Poppa."

The bundle ended up in Poppa's arms, and she beamed. "You must be Richard, aren't you?"

The boy nodded, wide blue eyes staring at her. "Dog!" He pointed a chubby finger at one of Poppa's hearth dogs.

"His name is Wulf, like the wild animal that feasts on little boys."

To her delight, Richard giggled. "Noooo!"

He stretched his arm towards the beast, but Poppa kept him out of reach. Wulf was a gentle old soul, but you could never be certain how he'd react to being prodded by a curious toddler.

"Aren't you fortunate, then? But our Wulf does not have a habit of eating children. He prefers rabbits." Turning back to Sprota and her companion, she added, "Come within. Your chamber is ready."

"Thank you." Sprota took her signal and entered first, coming to a halt inside the door. "This is lovely, Poppa. You've made this hall so warm and welcoming."

"Well, William has had the whole house rebuilt. It took almost a year, with the new upper floor and roof, and our much nicer hearth."

"Ha! The same graces the hall in Fécamp." Sprota laughed.

"The castle he has built? Is it finished yet?" Poppa hefted the boy from her right onto her left hip. The chubby lad was heavy, and it had been a long time since she handled small children.

The girl reached out, and Poppa handed him over with relief. It had been too long since she handled a small child.

"What's your name?" she asked.

"I'm Gwenn, lady. I look after Lady Sprota, and now little Richard."

"Gwenn was taken in by my late parents after her own had died. I consider her my sister," Sprota said, her gaze wary. "She was with me when William saved us from the Danes."

Sisters in all but blood. That explained the closeness.

"Watch out."

They moved aside to let two men carry a large chest past them. "Upstairs, the first chamber on the left." Poppa waived in the direction of the stairs, and the men heaved the box up the wooden steps.

"I'm afraid that chest contains most of my household goods." Sprota hesitated. "There are two others, with our personal effects."

"Your household goods? That means William expects you to stay here for a while?"

The young woman stared at her toes, wringing her hands. "He's not certain for low long. I hope...we won't be an inconvenience to you."

"Fret not, Sprota. You and Richard will be safe here; it makes sense to stay until the danger has passed. But the chamber is not big enough for two women and a young child, I'm afraid."

"Oh, I'm happy with a pallet beside Sprota's bed," Gwenn said quickly.

"There is no need for that. We have plenty of space. Claudia?" Poppa called, and the woman arrived from the back of the room. "Please have the chamber beside Sprota's made ready for Gwenn."

"Of course." Claudia turned but Gwenn held her back.

"I can help." She smiled, and after handing Richard to Sprota, she followed Claudia upstairs.

"Come over and take a cup of chilled wine. In the meantime, Pepin will show Richard the animals."

A dry chuckle reached her ears as Pepin, father of two grown sons, bowed to Sprota. "It will be my pleasure. I'll look after him like my own, lady."

Grateful, Sprota handed the fidgeting boy over and followed Poppa to the dais. When she settled in a comfortable, cushioned chair, Sprota gave a deep sigh.

Grinning, Poppa filled two cups and handed one to her.

"To family."

"Thank you, Poppa. I'll happily drink to family."

"You will want for nothing here. William has left Bayeux well-defended. Will your escort stay, too?"

Sprota shook her head. "No. William needs every warrior there is to spare." She frowned.

So she was concerned for William. She cared for him, then. The thought made Poppa content.

"Very few people know of Richard, and you can rely on the members of my household to keep their mouths shut. And with our defences in place, Bayeux cannot easily be overrun."

The young woman took a few sips, then reclined, stretching her legs. "That's a great comfort to me, knowing my son is safe."

"My people will defend him with their lives. He is Hrólfr's grandson, and one day he will inherit a vast county. It makes William's constant struggles worthwhile, thinking that there is a little boy here in Bayeux, who will walk in his father's and grandfather's impressive footsteps." She blinked back the tears that threatened to well up. Oh, how Hrólfr would have loved to meet his grandson. "My husband would be very proud."

Sprota reached out and squeezed Poppa's hand. "That's what William says also." She withdrew her hand swiftly and brushed back a stray lock of black hair, as if embarrassed.

"I want this to be your home, Sprota. No, please let me finish." She sighed. "This hall was redone for me, so my son tells me, but I suspect it was rebuilt as a symbol to defend his lands, and his family. I don't know how many more years God will grant me on this earth, but I would like us to be friends. Through your marriage to my son, you are part of the family that Hrólfr and I created. My blood runs through little Richard's veins and it will do so for generations to come. This hall is now yours as much as mine."

A smile played on Sprota's wide mouth, and she blinked a few times. "Thank you. I had hoped for us to become friends, and I'm very grateful for your heartfelt welcome. If you wish – and I don't mean to intrude upon your role as lady of this household – I can help with the duties. But please do tell me if I overstep my mark."

Poppa laughed. She put the cup down on a small table between their chairs, then, brushing down her skirts, she straightened. "Oh, I would be relieved if you took some of the tasks off my hands. I must admit, I tire easily these days. And Adela, well, she will one day have her own hall, once she's wed…whenever that may be."

A shadow fell over Sprota's features. "I'm so sorry to hear what happened. William still feels guilty."

Poppa waved a hand in the air. "He doesn't need to. I told him numerous times, as did Adela. It was a skirmish, and these things happen. Men are killed. It could have been William, but fortunately for us, it was not."

"I heard that, Mother."

Poppa turned to look over her shoulder as Adela, who now had her own small home nearby, entered through the side door. "I did not hear you, Adela. You're late in welcoming our guest."

"I'm sorry." But her daughter's expression did not match her words. "I was busy."

Sprota's face fell, and she looked down at her hands.

Anger surged through Poppa. Ever since William's message, Adela had been in the foulest of moods. Poppa knew her children were close, so was her daughter jealous?

"You can catch up now. Have some Rhenish wine with us and you can tell us about your day."

"No time," she hissed and turned towards the door.

In a swift move that surprised herself, Poppa rose and grabbed her obstinate daughter's arm. "If I say you will join us, then you shall. Now I would like you to start again. Act like the adult you are. So, meet Sprota, your brother's wife and mother of his son, Richard."

"Yes, I saw Pepin with a boy. He's feeding the pigs. Like he belongs there—"

The slap from Poppa's hand echoed around the chamber.

"Mother!"

"I think I shall see if I can help upstairs." Sprota excused herself, and moments later, Poppa and Adela were alone in the hall.

"Sit down!"

Poppa's voice allowed no resistance, and her daughter perched on a bench. Holding her cheek, she glowered at Sprota's receding figure.

"What worries you?" Poppa sat, but still ready to pounce again if needed. The stubborn girl would not get away with such vile behaviour. Girl? Adela was a young woman. "You should know better than to insult a new member of our family."

"The harlot is not part of my family." Adela's lower lip wobbled, but still, she did not look at her.

Poppa raised her eyebrows. "Ah. I see. Your brother loves this woman. He wed her in the same manner your father and I did. Therefore, by your way of thinking, can I assume you consider me a harlot, too?"

Adela stared at her, mouth agape. Then she pulled herself together. "Umm, no, of course not, Mother."

"Your response took a little too long, daughter. What is your issue? Is it with the way they are married? Or the fact that your brother found happiness with a woman not of our circles?"

"Hmph."

"I'm beg your pardon, Adela?"

"He's been ignoring me ever since he met her. Never sends a message or visits."

"Your brother has a large county to defend, the size of which has recently increased. I rarely hear from him, and I would not call his wife a harlot or consider his son to be the equal of pigs." Her fury surged to the surface again.

There had been times in the past when Adela dropped hints that she was not happy with the way her parents were married.

Like a stain on her own worth as the daughter of a Norse jarl.

259

"Is this about yourself? That your own betrothed was killed, and your brother has no time for negotiations? Do you wish to be a wife?"

Adela's face turned a dark shade of red, and Poppa knew she'd hit her mark. Tears glistened in her daughter's eyes, and she bit her lip.

So that was it. The girl was six-and-twenty years old. By rights, she should have a family and a large hall of her own. Poppa shook her head. Both Hrólfr and William had been remiss in their responsibilities towards Adela. And she'd not pressed them hard enough…

Poppa rose and went to sit on the bench beside her daughter. Taking her hand, she held it tightly between hers. "Sweet Adela. You shall have a husband, and children."

"But I'm too old now…" Adela's voice shook.

"No, you are not, my sweeting. I know that your brother is considering a few options, but we both want the best for you."

"But what if the best is never enough… What if there is no *best*?"

"Oh, but there will be, my love. There will be. Come here!" She wrapped her arm around her and pulled her close.

Adela's tears flowed, and she wiped her nose with the back of her hand. Poppa kept rocking her gently. Like Sprota, she'd been young when she was wed to Hrólfr, here in Bayeux. Yet it had taken them years to have children, with her young age, his constant raids, and then their frantic escape to East Anglia.

"I…I really want a babe of my own, Mother. I fear my body is getting too old. Every woman of my age has a child. Every single one!"

"Hush now, dearest. And you shall, too, one day. I have no doubt."

"But I do…"

"Oh Adela." With a deep sigh, she cradled her crying daughter. Perhaps they could start again. "But until then, why don't you offer to look after your nephew? I'm sure Sprota won't mind. Then, when it's your turn to have a child, you will know exactly what to do…"

She let the thought hang in the air, not wishing to push Adela any further. The next step would have to come from her.

Eventually, Adela's breathing slowed, and her sniffs grew rarer, as the two of them sat undisturbed, in companionable silence, ignoring the noises that drifted into the hall from outside.

This was their moment. Mother and daughter. How rare these times were!

Poppa closed her eyes.

Please, God, let my family hold fast together; all of them.

Chapter Twenty-Four

August, AD 935
The ancient palace of the Counts of Poitou, Poitiers

"You are such a beautiful bride, Adela. Guillaume won't keep his gaze off you."

Tears pricked Poppa's eyes, and she swiftly wiped them away. For today was a day of celebration, not sadness. Walking on tiptoes around her daughter, she adjusted the delicate veil over Adela's dark tresses, until it floated low down her back. It was likely the last time she'd had a chance to brush her daughter's luscious hair. With a wistful smile, she sent a little prayer of gratitude heavenwards. She had been fortunate to enjoy her company for much longer than most mothers.

Much longer than her own, whose memory faded a long time ago.

Reluctantly, Poppa let go of the gossamer veil made of beautiful light green silk. Adela had chosen the colour from the rolls of fabrics they admired. To her, green signified nature – and fertility.

Poppa had merely raised an eyebrow but complied with Adela's wishes. The young woman had waited long enough.

Now, she stared in wonder at her beautiful daughter. A gown of the same green hue as the veil hugged Adela's slim frame, its cut emphasising long legs and the light curve of her hips where a belt sat tied loosely. It was adorned with precious stones. Red and dark green garnets interspersed with oval cuts of deep amber shimmered in the light flooding in through the open windows of the chamber.

William wondered if the choice of dress colour was appropriate for a church wedding, but Poppa had brushed off his concerns. It was not the archbishop's duty to advise a bride of her gown, whatever the Bible may suggest.

"Do you think he likes me?"

"What a silly question! Of course he does. Did he not pay you attention last night at the banquet?"

A frown marred Adela's fine brow. "I don't know, Mother. It felt…forced."

Poppa shrugged. "'Tis probably because you have only recently met. It will come."

"He's so young. He seemed almost like a spoilt child."

"Hmm." Poppa sighed. She agreed with her daughter's view. Adela's betrothed, a man chosen by William to consolidate his power, was six years younger than the bride. At two-and-twenty, he was boisterous and rough; like all young men.

"And he was drunk!" Adela pouted. "If that happens on the night before the wedding, what will he do tonight?"

Poppa laid her hands on her daughter's shoulder, staring at her in the looking glass. "Well, he'll probably fall asleep…"

"Mother!"

She laughed. "Don't fret, sweeting. Guillaume is going to behave himself. A husband has responsibilities, after all."

Adela's cheeks turned a becoming shade of rose. "Not only husbands." She swallowed hard.

Poppa gave her daughter's shoulder a gentle squeeze. "There is nothing to worry about. He will do right by you. Now we must not tarry any longer. The church will be full, I've heard. After all, the wedding of the new count of Poitou is of high significance. With his father dead barely six months, the young man will have to prove his worth."

"By marrying me." Adela raised an eyebrow. "According to the Church, I'm not even legitimately born."

"Nor was Guillaume's father, God may rest his soul. You will do well together. I know it."

"'Tis highly likely I won't do anything of importance. You've met his counsellors."

"Ah," Poppa waved her hand in the air, "old men! You have been present at several historic moments, and you have witnessed first-hand how your father and I reigned our lands. Your husband is going to look to you for your guidance, have no doubt."

"If you say so…"

"I do. Now smile, child. This is meant to be the happiest day of your life – a moment you have waited for a long time. Show them the power of the House of Normannia!"

A sigh, then Adela nodded, the corners of her lips turned up.

"That's better. Make us proud, Adela!"

Darkness had long descended when the end of the wedding day drew near. And what a feast it had been!

The Church of Our Lady had been decorated with summer flowers, and the vivid white, yellow and red petals had brightened up the otherwise severe, dark building. Sadly, any scent of summer meadows was soon overpowered by the acrid stench of frankincense. As far as Poppa remembered, she'd always hated that smell.

The priest was officious; far too arrogant for Poppa's liking, and as he went on and on, her mind wandered back to her own handfasting ceremony on the steps of the old little church in Bayeux. She still remembered the words.

'I promise to care for you,
And to keep you from harm.
From the first bloom of spring
To the darkest winter's night,
I shall be by your side.'

It seemed so long ago.

But her daughter's marriage was not celebrated in the Danish custom. Hers was a true blessing by the Church. Adela would not bear an illegitimate child. Poppa was relieved for her. Adela would not be called names. Her virtue was intact, something the priest seemed to be very interested in, as he continued to praise the Virgin whilst pointedly staring at Adela and her green gown. It made Poppa smirk.

She watched with pride when Adela repeated the vows without a hint of hesitation or shyness. The young woman was a worthy Countess of Poitou, and Poppa was pleased to see approval in the faces of those present.

Now, in the great hall of the palace, Poppa was impressed with the food her new son-by-marriage had provided. Pheasant infused with juniper berries and rosemary, game steeped in a thick red wine sauce, wild boar with a blackberry compote, all accompanied by loaves of freshly baked bread and bowls steaming with carrots and cabbage.

The count had not spared any cost. Vats of strong wines from Aquitania were being emptied at terrifying speed as all revellers took advantage. Tonight, not even the lowliest guest was offered ale.

Having eaten her fill, she wished she did not have to walk all the way to her quarters. She laid her hands on her full belly and breathed in. The seams of her gown felt stretched to their limits, and Poppa straightened in her chair.

"It has been a memorable day, Lady Poppa, has it not? I hope Adela will think of it for years to come."

Poppa nodded to Guillaume, her daughter's husband, then glanced past him. On his right sat Adela, her face lit by a mischievous smile, deep in conversation with her brother.

Adela's cheeks had turned a becoming shade of crimson following several goblets of wine, and Poppa was pleased her daughter seemed to delight in the festivities.

"I'm sure she will. I shall, for certain. I've not eaten this well for a long time."

He grinned, and his blue eyes sparkled in the light of the candles. His was an open, friendly face; piercing eyes, a strong, straight nose, and a wide mouth, all framed by wavy blond hair cut just below the shoulders. The count already had shown himself adept in power. He knew how to attract followers to his side and a reputation as a strong but honourable leader preceded him.

Just as Hrólfr had been...

Poppa liked the young man; she was relieved Adela had found such good fortune. Hrólfr would have approved.

"Then you must visit us again soon."

"I may." She let her gaze roam the spacious hall of the old king's palace. "Tell me, was this palace truly built for Charlemagne's heir?"

Guillaume nodded. "Yes, for King Louis, may God rest his soul. The palace is often cold and draughty, especially in winter." When she frowned, he was quick to add, "But our private quarters are warm and dry, as you've hopefully discovered. Much work has gone into making the chambers more comfortable to our needs."

"Ah, I see." She'd already admired the large wall hangings that adorned the rooms she'd been given, and the thickly woven rugs. The bed almost disappeared beneath layers of furs, most of which had landed on top of a chest. The summer was unusually hot, even within the thick walls of the palace.

Poppa only prayed Adela would be safe here, but from what she'd seen of the place, it was solid, seemingly impregnable, well-defended.

"There is much space, so you would be very welcome to live here too." He inclined his head.

Poppa breathed in sharply. "Thank you, Guillaume. That is a very kind offer."

Was she prepared to leave Bayeux? The new hall was her home, and she would miss its warmth. And she was certain that Sprota and little Richard would not be allowed to join them, however well her son and his brother-by-marriage were getting on.

Not as long as William was married to Luitgarde.

Her gaze went to the woman sitting on her son's far side.

His Frankish wife was the daughter of the powerful Count of Vermandois. Right now, she leaned forward, stony-faced, her small mouth set in a thin line. There was a bitterness about the young woman, who had barely passed her twentieth year, which reminded Poppa of Gisela. Was Luitgarde jealous of Sprota, just as Gisela had been of her?

Guillaume turned to speak to Adela, and Poppa was relieved to be left to her thoughts.

Her son's women were his own concern, but she knew from experience how badly the situation could become. And she wanted neither woman to suffer.

Yet whenever he could, William spent time in Bayeux with Sprota and his son, but rarely visited his wife who remained in Rouen. On the other hand, he tried to beget a legitimate heir, which brought great unhappiness to Sprota. Meanwhile, poor Luitgarde must feel like a breeding horse, humped once every so often to fulfil her wifely duties, but otherwise ignored.

It was a dilemma beyond Poppa's influence, but it was the main reason she could never leave Bayeux. Sprota and Richard needed her.

And I need them.

No, she could not possibly move to Poitiers, to this massive building with its draughty corridors and large rooms. Life in a palace was not for her. That was Adela's path.

Just as Bayeux had always been hers. Even though it would be much quieter there without her daughter. After all, they'd shared each other's lives for almost thirty years. It was bound to be hard.

But then, there was a new generation to care for. Richard, her beloved grandson. The boy was William's heir, unless Luitgarde gave birth to a son who, in the eyes of the Church and the Frankish king, would take precedence.

Yes, Richard had to be protected. And if Poppa was good at one thing, it was to protect her family, at any cost.

'You killed me…'

Cold, grey eyes stared at her, but she brushed away the vision of Gisela's ghost that haunted her dreams more and more often as she grew older.

She lifted her goblet with a shaky hand and took deep draughts of the potent wine. Then she straightened up and looked to the storyteller who had travelled from Aquitania. They called him a *troubadour*. Would he be like a skáld?

The room fell silent as the young man began to intone a melody unbeknown to her. Then he sang in a soft lilt of what she assumed was Occitan.

The meaning of his words escaped her, but their strong tone gave her strength.

Tonight, she would not feel any guilt.

Family always comes first.

Chapter Twenty-Five

Late November, AD 936
Bayeux, Earldom of Normannia

Not again!

Poppa winced in pain as yet another dry cough tore through her body. Her lungs burned, and with each cough, she found it harder to breathe.

"I have to sit straight," she mumbled, and allowed Sprota to help her into an upright position, her back comfortably cushioned against the hard wood-panelled wall. Her daughter-by-marriage arranged the covers and furs over Poppa's thin body.

Had she lost so much weight, or was the wind colder this year?

With her throat so sore, she found it hard to swallow food. Sprota – may God keep her well – had been trying to feed her broth. But even the chunks of meat had to be cut into tiniest morsels.

Tears welled in her eyes, and she angrily wiped them away. "I hate this," she wailed, gesticulating at her prone figure.

Then another cough overcame her, the pain like a hard punch to her chest.

"I'll bring you some infused water."

"I hate infused water. Bring me wine."

She challenged Sprota with a glare, and the young woman sighed.

"If that's what you wish for, then you shall have it." Sprota tucked the blanket tight around her again, then left her alone.

But when she reappeared moments later, the tray bore not only a cup, but also a bowl of something steaming.

Poppa groaned. Not more boiled water!

"I brought you apple wine." Sprota set the tray down on a small table, then handed Poppa a clay cup.

She breathed in the heady scent of ripe apples. Sprota had not lost her touch. The young Breton's apple wine was renowned across all Normannia. Closing her eyes, she took a small sip. It was all she dared. A larger draught would make her cough again, and she only wanted to relish this tasty liquid.

When she looked up again, Sprota stood beside the bed, smiling. "It's a treat, isn't it?"

Poppa nodded slowly. "It's wonderful. It reminds me of the many evenings of celebrations Hrólfr and I enjoyed here," she bit her lip, "and in Rouen." A shadow fell over her face despite the cheerful words.

Rouen.

Despite all the years she spent in Hrólfr's growing town, it had never been her home. Not like Bayeux was.

Rouen had been Gisela's domain.

"Gisela…" she whispered.

Sprota sighed. "She's long gone, Poppa."

"But what if she's waiting for me? On the other side?" Her hand shook, and Sprota quickly took the cup from her, then set it down on the tray. With it went the warm scent of summer fruit.

Now, the room smelled dank. Of sickness and fear.

Oh yes, she was afraid.

"That's nonsense, and you know it. Her soul is at rest; has been for decades."

"How can you be so sure, Sprota?"

"God knows. He can see into your soul, and what he finds there is a courageous and caring woman, not someone who plots murder."

"But I wanted her dead, so desperately. She…she'd taken my husband…"

Sprota sat and clutched Poppa's hand. Warmth spread through the skin, and Poppa's breathing calmed. It was good to have her around.

They were sisters of the soul, both wed in the same manner. Both deeply in love with their husbands.

They shared the same fate.

"Shhh, calm yourself. Hrólfr's heart never belonged to that woman. It was always yours."

Tears pricked Poppa's eyes again, but this time she let them roll down her cheeks. "But that was our...misfortune. Lovers divided."

"You know I understand you best of all. Fear not, I've shared similar dark thoughts about Luitgarde. But in the end, we have to accept God's will

"Or the Frankish king's will. These kings have caused us nothing but woe."

"But King Charles conveyed the lands to Hrólfr as part of the agreement. Never forget that without his marriage to Gisela, there would not have been this beautiful county William has inherited, and which will be my son's one day."

"Oh, Richard, my sweet little boy. Yes, you're right, of course. I have to think of my grandson." She looked sheepishly at Sprota. "Luitgarde will never have children. God has told me. Richard is safe."

While Sprota stared at her for a long moment, Poppa blinked. It was true.

"Well, an angel told me in a dream last night."

"Did he now?"

Was Sprota holding her breath? She seemed unhealthily still. Poppa silently tutted. "Yes. You should feel reassured."

"And you should rest now, Poppa." Sprota stood and brought over the bowl of steaming hot water. It smelled of camomile.

Poppa pulled a face, then turned away. "No, I don't want it."

"Then I shall leave it right here, on this little table beside your bed. Then you can take a sip when you need it."

Poppa opened her mouth, then closed it quickly. No, she would not have it. The taste was vile.

Sprota caressed her cheek with her warm fingers. "Slip beneath the covers, Poppa, or you'll make your chill worse."

271

She did as told, and let the young woman tuck the covers around her. Although even the layer of furs did nothing to remove the cold from her bones. But to humour her daughter-by-marriage, she did as she bid.

"I'll pop in later again, to see how you are." Sprota stood by the door, hand on the latch, smiling. "And drink your camomile water whilst it's still hot!"

Poppa woke, to be greeted by silence. Her chamber was dark, the shutter closed. The hall was quiet. She blinked. Was it the middle of the night, or did her sight desert her? She turned over, and another coughing fit racked her body.

God's teeth, the candle that was always lit must have gone out.

"Christ in Heaven, when will this pain stop?"

Her voice was deep, hoarse. Where was the water?

She swore under her breath as her fingers carefully felt the surface of the little table beside her bed until they found the bowl. Of course it was stone cold. Her hand shaking, she guided it to her mouth and drank in small sips.

The burning in her throat weakened a little as she swallowed the tepid water. The camomile even worked when less hot.

Slowly, Poppa emptied the bowl, then put it back down and lay back. Snuggling beneath the covers, she hoped her chilled bones would soon warm.

An owl tooted outside, and moments later another responded.

Poppa smiled as she closed her eyes. Nature was at peace, at least in Bayeux. But when would she find hers?

Gisela's face appeared before her, and Poppa quickly blinked, banishing the vision. "Leave. Me. Alone!" she intoned into the empty room.

I know you can hear me, Gisela. I never meant you any harm. It was you who wanted to kill me. Your death was an accident.

The air turned cold, and a shudder ran through Poppa's body. She clutched the covers closer over her.

"No!" she whimpered. "Go away!"

Moments later, a light appeared under her door, then Sprota rushed in.

"Poppa?" she called out. "Are you dreaming again?"

The young woman sat on the edge of the bed, and the air in the chamber warmed again.

Poppa heaved a sigh of relief. "No, it felt real. I'm so glad you're here."

Sprota placed a comforting hand on her frozen cheek and stroked it gently. Soon, Poppa's breathing slowed.

"The chamber is empty, Poppa. There is no one else but us."

"But she was here, I swear." Her heart still beat too fast, and she forced herself to submit to Sprota's calm.

"I see."

"Mother? What has happened?" William stood in the door in his shift.

"Oh no! Now I've woken the whole hall. I didn't mean to…" Tears pricked her eyes.

Sprota half-turned. "She had visions of Gisela."

"Ah."

Did her son not believe her? "Yes, William. *Ah*!" Poppa rolled her eyes. "The woman is haunting me."

He stepped inside and closed the door. Then he pulled up a stool beside her bed and sat.

"Gisela's death was an accident, Mother. Everyone who saw it said the same."

"She took my lovely cross with her."

"And Father gave you a new one after they couldn't find it on the beach below. Look, you're wearing it now."

"Yes, yes…" Absent-mindedly, Poppa patted the small pendant made of beaten silver and decorated with precious stones. It had been kind of Hrólfr, but it would never replace his wedding gift to her, the beautiful double-sided cross with the Norse swirls on the back.

"Such a shame," Sprota said. "It must have been unique."

"It was." Poppa smiled, then she squeezed Sprota's hand. "You shall have this one when I'm gone. If you'll have a daughter, I'd love her to inherit it after you."

Sprota blushed. "You're very kind, Poppa, but you shall need it for a while yet. When the time comes, I'll be honoured to wear it in your memory."

"Good." A sense of happiness surged through her. "And you shall have this hall."

Sprota's eyes widened. "I—"

Poppa faced her son. "William, please have a charter drawn up in my name. The hall of Bayeux, and everything that belongs to it – the fields, the mill, the customs duties – shall be Sprota's, and hers alone. She will need it when the time comes."

His smile broke into a wide grin. "It will be done, Mother. Trust me."

"I can't possibly…and it's too early to speak of this, anyway. You're still the lady of Bayeux."

"No. You are from this moment forward, my lovely daughter. I am but a guest now. You have been working hard these past few years, making your wonderful apple wine and building up a trade. You deserve the hall. It is yours."

Tears rolled down Sprota's face. She kissed Poppa's cheek, the teardrops lingering.

Poppa did not mind. "Be happy, Sprota. And remind this young man often who his only love is."

William chuckled. "I don't need reminding, Mother."

"Oh, but you do. The Church and that new Frankish king, Louis, will try to tear you from your true family. Do not let them!"

"Fear not. Father kept priests and kings at arm's length, and I intend to do the same."

"I am concerned for you, my son. Even more so than for your sister."

"Adela is safe in Poitiers."

Poppa nodded. "Yes. Her first child should be born soon. 'Tis a pity you can't travel to be with her at such an important time, Sprota. I wish I could."

"Luitgarde would complain to the king. You know the response Adela received the last time she suggested I visited her. Fear not; she has a whole palace to look after her. And you need me here, anyway."

Poppa acknowledged Sprota was correct. "Yes, but not for much longer."

"Oh Mother, please stop saying that." William sighed. "When the cough subsides—"

"But it will not. I'm certain, deep down." She touched her heart. "Have you made the arrangements I asked of you?"

He paled. "Regarding your funeral? Yes, I have. You will be resting beside Father. The archbishop was…amenable to my suggestion." His mouth twitched, but his eyes were full of sadness.

"He got enough money for it, I suppose." She snorted. Churchmen were as greedy as any Danish raider. But it was no longer her concern.

A sense of contentment washed through her. She'd said all she needed to say.

Despite his crestfallen look, William chuckled. "It helped."

"I never thought I'd be glad Gisela was buried in Paris. It would have been awkward for the poor archbishop had there been two wives to inter alongside Hrólfr…" Poppa sighed, content in the knowledge she'd soon be reunited with the man she loved.

Then man she missed more than anything.

"So, Poppa." Sprota rose, patting the furs into place. "Now you need rest. It will be dawn soon. The birdsong is getting louder." She smiled, then kissed Poppa's cheek a final time. "They will accompany you in your dreams."

"I like that idea." For a long moment, their eyes met, and Poppa knew that Sprota understood. She swallowed back the tears and suppressed a cough.

"Sleep well, Mother." William's lips brushed her forehead. "I shall have your charter drawn up in the morning."

Poppa smiled as they withdrew into the dark corridor and closed the door behind them, leaving a candle behind.

Shadows danced on the walls, reminding Poppa of when she was young.

Oh, how she used to love to dance across the fields, to run, to cause trouble. Landina's laughter, child-like, echoed in her ears. They'd had such fun! Soon, they would be together again.

Can you cause mischief in Heaven?

'Yes, you can.' Landina's voice sounded close. Was her friend looking for her?

"I'm here, my friend…" Poppa whispered.

As the singing of the birds grew louder, Poppa closed her eyes and took a shuddery breath. Suppressing a cough, she folded her arms over her chest to keep warm. Exhausted from her disrupted night, sleep soon claimed her.

It hovered before her, in all its glory, against a backdrop of a large fire across the horizon. Her cross pendant. The garnets gleamed in the flickering flames. It turned over, as if by God's hand, revealing the Norse lines on the back. Odin's horns. The swirls became real, interweaving, growing. Now, the fire was fading, replaced by crashing waves.

The swirls were close enough to touch.

Poppa reached out and felt the beloved pendant hot in her palm. It reassured her. Finally, after all these years, she was whole again.

Her breathing grew shallow, but she did not notice. A joy never felt before surged through her.

Then, from the whirling water, Hrólfr emerged, his light blue eyes boring into her. With a broad smile full of love, he waved her over.

Clutching the cross pendant to her heart, she moved into his warm embrace.

The sea rushed around them in swirling hues of blue and green, but it did not threaten her. She felt safe, protected.

'I have you back,' he mouthed.

Content, Poppa leaned into him and let out a long, slow breath.

I'm home…

Epilogue

Mid-December, AD 936
Bayeux, Earldom of Normannia

"I miss her." William's words were barely above a whisper, but Sprota knew what he meant.

A fortnight earlier, they'd buried Poppa. They had honoured her last wish, and her mortal remains now rested beside Hrólfr's in Rouen.

Reunited in death.

"So do I." Sprota laid a hand on William's shoulder, then lowered herself in the seat beside him – Poppa's seat. Sitting in it, she still felt her presence. "Every day."

The hall was deserted apart from a few men quietly chatting in a corner. The hour was too early for the evening meal, and many of William's retainers were still training in the yard.

Moments before, she had put Richard to bed. At over four years, he was beginning to take his chances, but she'd have none of his tantrums. Some warm goat's milk, and a story about faeries, and his eyes had begun to close.

Gwenn was sitting with him, until she was certain he was sleeping deeply.

Sprota breathed a sigh of relief. The girl treated him like a little brother.

Still, she was reluctant to let Richard out of her sight. He was still his father's heir.

Unless Luitgarde is with child...

Sprota sighed. Such morose musings did not help her, nor William. "Poppa casts a long shadow over our home, but she's looking out for us from wherever she is."

Taking his hand between hers, she squeezed it.

William sent her a lopsided smile. "I'm convinced of it. Mother could never let a matter go easily."

"It was that strength that kept her going when your father wed Gisela."

He furrowed his brow, then lowered his gaze. "I suppose so."

"Don't fret, William. I've said this so many times, I've lost count. It does not matter."

"But it does to me." He drew in a deep breath.

"As it did to Hrólfr. But whilst neither of you had a choice, Poppa and I did. We often spoke of the time she spent here in Bayeux, alone, while he was with Gisela in Rouen. And now, your path follows his. I would never be accepted as a countess by the Frankish king, even though my father's Breton bloodline is ancient. He was merely a minor lord, not an important noble with influence at court. You know that."

"I do, but it doesn't make it easier. I don't want to spend time with the woman, never mind…"

…bedding her…

He did not need to say it out loud.

Sprota leaned over and kissed him on the cheek. Here, in Poppa's hall – now her home – they were husband and wife, married in the same custom as his mother had been to Hrólfr.

Here, William was hers, and hers alone. But his visits were rare, and she treasured each moment.

Her mouth twitched, then she whispered in his ear, "There is still time before the evening meal, and Richard is sleeping in Gwen's chamber…"

Their eyes met, and he nodded, grinning. "There is indeed. Come, my love."

He rose and pulled her up with him. No one paid them any heed as they skipped up the steps to the bedchamber.

~

Thank you for reading **Ascent**, Poppa's story. I hope you've enjoyed your journey into early medieval 'Normannia'.

The *House of Normandy* series continues with Sprota the Breton's story. **Treachery** is due to be released later in 2022.

Sprota the Breton was handfasted *in more danico* to William, Poppa and Hrólfr's son. Her true background is uncertain. Some sources claim she is of Breton nobility; other records call her a captured slave girl.

I made Sprota the daughter of a minor Breton lord. It would have been almost impossible for Richard, her son by William, to claim the earldom had his mother been a mere slave.

Like his father, William was married in the Catholic manner, to Luitgarde, daughter and heiress of the Count of Vermandois. There is no record of any children.

Sprota and William's son, Richard, becomes heir to the growing earldom of Normannia. But William has many challenges to face, and when he is cruelly betrayed, Sprota must seek safety, for herself and for her son.

The vultures are circling, ready to rip apart the new earldom of Normannia.

How far will they go to succeed? And what must Sprota do to keep Richard safe?

Acknowledgments

My first 'thank you' goes to my long-suffering husband, Laurence. By now, he is used to sharing me with men from other times, be they knights, spies, warriors, or, as in Ascent, Vikings. Oh, and he also creates the most beautiful book covers!

I must thank my fellow authors at Ocelot Press for their continued support and suggestions. We 'Ocelots' are a small group of writers of historical fiction, women's fiction, and contemporary fiction with historical and paranormal hints. Please check out the novels of my wonderful author friends.

My special thanks goes to my lovely critique partner, Paula Lofting, who also writes brilliant historical fiction and non-fiction, and who always keeps my head firmly rooted in the distant past.

Author's Note

Ever since I first visited Normandy in 2007, I've been fascinated by the dramatic history of this beautiful, windswept county.

But whilst everyone knows about its most famous residents – William the Conqueror, the Empress Matilda, Eleanor of Aquitaine, and Rollo (Hrólfr) the Viking – very little is known about the early women of the House of Normandy: Poppa, Sprota, and Gunnora.

They were the *more danico* wives of Hrólfr, his son, William Longsword, and his grandson, Richard. Poppa and Sprota shared their husbands with 'legitimate' wives. Only Gunnora was fortunate enough in that Richard later married her in the eyes of God, to make his heir legitimate as perceptions of inheritance changed.

There is a statue in Bayeux commemorating Poppa, but we don't really know who she was. Historians argue about the identity of her father, who was either Count of Bayeux or Count of Rennes (or both). I gave him the title, Count of Bayeux, as it was the closest and made more sense, given their base was in the small town. And although Poppa is recorded as the mother of Hrólfr's two children, a son and a daughter, we don't find many more details about her. Yet it appears that she outlived her husband.

Poppa is supposed to have shared Hrólfr with Gisela, illegitimate daughter of King Charles of the West Franks. There exists no official record of Gisela, however, so why was she mentioned at all? Was it to add a level of legitimacy to Hrólfr – a Christian wife for a converted heathen? Was poor Poppa cast aside for the power of the Frankish court, and a fertile county to rule over?

I do feel sorry for Poppa. Handfasted to a stranger at a delicately young age (too young for our modern western laws!), but whose children were only born years later. Her life at Hrólfr's side must have been quite the adventure, although I can only hope she enjoyed the challenges it brought. They held Bayeux after her father's death, but her children were said to have been born 'abroad', most likely in East Anglia. Were they chased out of town by Franks? It appears so.

Equally recorded is their return to Neustria with their children, as are his on-off raids along the River Seine, and deeper into the borderlands between Neustria and the Duchy of Burgundy.

Hrólfr's ascent to great power, well preserved in the Treaty of Saint-Clair-sur-Epte between King Charles and Hrólfr from AD 911 changed the course of Poppa's life. Was her happiness the price for peace in Neustria?

If he married Gisela, did he cast Poppa aside? And when it turned out that his new wife was barren, did he reclaim his son, William, as his heir? Both children were baptised around the same time as he was, in 911. This implies they were not set aside at all.

Records are sketchy if Hrólfr was indeed the first Duke of Normandy. I personally have my doubts. King Charles would not have appointed a Northman to one of the highest titles in the land, one usually granted to younger sons of kings, not ordinary men. Hrólfr's power was great, but not on a par with the Duke of Burgundy. I'd rather think he'd have called himself a *jarl* – or earl, as the Franks would have said. So that's what he became in **Ascent**.

According to Icelandic sagas, Hrólfr fathered a daughter, Kathlin (or Kaðlin), in the Orkney Isles, but if there was any truth in it, she would possibly have been born after he became Jarl of the Normans. As there are hints that he was in the north prior to his successes in Neustria (not after), I've decided to make Kathlin his eldest child, and to be happily married to (fictional) Ranulf.

But ultimately, this is Poppa's story.

In **Ascent**, I have focused less on Hrólfr, but rather on her – fictionalised – life. I gave the young Poppa hopes and dreams, and the adult woman, happiness, loss, and fortitude. And ultimately, as the matriarch of the emerging House of Normandy, victory. I would like to think she looked down on her descendants from wherever she went after her death. And she would have been mightily proud.

I have tried to stay as close to known events, but this is a work of fiction, therefore any errors and embellishments are my own.

Cathie Dunn
Carcassonne, France
April 2022

Thank you for reading this Ocelot Press book.

If you enjoyed it, we would greatly
appreciate it if you could take a moment
to write a short review.

You might also like to try books by fellow
Ocelot Press authors. We cover a small range of
genres, with a focus on historical fiction (including mystery
and paranormal), romance, and fantasy.

Find Ocelot Press at:
Website: **www.ocelot-press.com**
Facebook: **www.facebook.com/OcelotPress**
Twitter: **www.twitter.com/OcelotPress**

Printed in Great Britain
by Amazon

22795989R00169